BULLETPROOF

A JOHN MILTON THRILLER

MARK DAWSON

PROLOGUE

It was raining when they put her in the ground.

The coffin was suspended between ropes at the front and back, and the four men slowly lowered it into the hole that had been dug. Rufus Lewsey felt nothing. The emotion had all been boiled out of him, the disbelief and fury and sadness and bone-aching grief scoured away until all that was left was emptiness. He had forgotten to bring an umbrella, and now he stood there, the rain washing down his head and plastering his hair against his scalp. It soaked into his suit and ran into his eyes. The only thought in his head was that the coffin was small—obscenely small—but then Roxy had been small, too, even as she left her teens. It was a reminder, as if one was needed, that her life had been taken from her too soon. Twenty-one years old. The future had been stolen from her, and it had been stolen from him, too; he wouldn't have the chance to walk her down the aisle, or hold a grandchild in his arms.

There were forty or fifty people gathered around the open grave. Roxy had been a popular girl, and although she had withdrawn into herself in the weeks before her death, plenty of them had come. His wife, Hazel, was with her parents, standing on the other side of the grave. He hadn't seen her for a week, not after she had told him to leave, and he had noticed that she had removed her wedding ring. He had known that they were finished, that what had happened to their daughter had been the final cut that severed their union, but seeing her finger without the ring gave it a certainty that perhaps hadn't been there before.

Lewsey was too deep in the pit to think that there might have been an easy way back, but perhaps there had once been a flicker of optimism that things might change.

That flame was extinguished now.

There was no hope, not that it mattered; Lewsey knew now, as the vicar started to speak, that he would follow his daughter. His days were numbered. He wasn't frightened; he welcomed the prospect of the end.

There was just one thing left to do.

He was going to take the bastard who'd murdered his daughter with him.

PART I

WEDNESDAY

1

John Milton stood and paced the cell. It was small, with just enough space for three strides from one side to the other. He had been imprisoned here since Control and Thorsson had visited him, and, since there were no windows and no other way for him to gauge the passage of time, he couldn't say how long ago that had been. He knew that it must have been days. He had occupied himself by working out, hammering out sets of three hundred push-ups on the floor and then putting the backs of his legs on the bed that was cut into the wall and using the angle to isolate his abdominal muscles in ten sets of twenty crunches. Each time, he was slick with sweat and aching once he was done, but after pacing the cell to get his breath back, he did it all again.

His training in the Regiment years ago had drilled into him the only way to address the issue of captivity: he would occupy himself as best he could and continue to resist by all means necessary. He would not cooperate, and he would make every effort to escape. The routine had served Milton well during his SAS selection and some of the more extreme resistance to interrogation training he had taken part in as a soldier, but the situation he found himself in now was very different.

He had been captured by the Group, reeled in after years of operating below the surface of things, in the margins and grey spaces where he could blend in and vanish from the world. He had never been fooled by his success in evading them; he knew it was just postponing the inevitable, that they would never stop looking and that, eventually, they would find him. He was an expert at disappearing, but even the very best had to surface from time to time; and that, when ranged against the bottomless budget and facilities of the Group and the Firm within which it was accommodated, would be the time that they found him.

It was exactly what had happened. He had gambled by coming to Scotland, and, like Icarus, flying too close to danger had been his undoing. Björn Thorsson had captured him and flown him to London.

He shook out the aches and pains in his arms and shoulders and dropped to his hands and knees again. He stretched out, bearing his weight on his toes and fingers, and dipped down to begin another set.

∽

THORSSON CAME to collect him later. Milton was sitting on the bed, his back against the wall, his eyes closed as he worked on his breathing. He heard the rattle of the lock and opened his eyes as the door was pulled back. The big Icelander filled the doorway from top to bottom and side to side. He wasn't armed, but Milton wasn't particularly surprised by that. He was younger than Milton and certainly bigger and stronger. Milton might have been able to fight his way free, but even if he did, where would he go? He didn't know where he was being held, and he was quite sure that Thorsson would not be the extent of the staff here to guard him.

There was nothing else for it: Control had him, and, unless she made a mistake, he had no choice but to accept that fact and behave accordingly.

"Up," Thorsson said.

Milton stood. "Where are we going?"

"She wants to talk to you."

"How long have I been in here?"

"We flew down on Saturday night."

"I know that. What day is it now?"

"Wednesday," he said. "Come on—move it. She doesn't like to be kept waiting."

2

Lewsey had been here so many times before that the sessions had all blurred into one. He saw Waller once a week for therapy and his psychiatrist, Dr. South, once a month to make sure that the drugs he was taking were having the desired effect. He had been optimistic when the treatment plan had started, but that was a long time ago; any hopefulness had long since been scoured away by the numbing lack of progress. He had been honest at the start, telling both his therapist and psychiatrist exactly how he was feeling, but in recent weeks, he had just gone through the motions. He made the appointments, told South what he needed to hear to get more pills, told Waller that he valued their sessions, then left them both until the next time. It was a grind, with no prospect of anything ever being different. He had reached the decision that he was a lost cause, that his mental illness was beyond repair, and that there was no reason to draw out the agony. He flushed the pills down the toilet and made up his mind: he would do something else about the cause of his problem, something that he should have done weeks ago.

Months ago.

He looked up at the light above the door, saw it change from red to green, and got to his feet.

Yes, he told himself as he reached for the door handle. *This will be the last hour that I waste here.*

"Hello, Rufus," Waller said from behind his desk. "Please—take a seat."

Lewsey sat down. The room was just the same as it always was: the same couch, the same vase of fake plastic flowers, the same box of tissues within easy reach. Lewsey had cried in the early sessions with Waller and had been glad of the box. The thought of it made him cringe now. Waller had told him that it would be good to cry, to let it all out, but that, like everything else Waller had told him, had simply been more of the same trite nonsense.

He saw it now. He saw it for what it was.

Waller smiled at him in that sympathetic way that had recently put him in mind of a well-meaning, elderly vicar. "How are you feeling?"

"Honestly?"

"That's always best."

"I feel like this has been a huge waste of time."

Waller cocked his head to one side. "Why would you say that?"

"Because I feel the same now as I did when we started."

"That's not what you said before."

"Yeah, well—I've said a lot of things that weren't true in here. That's one of them."

"You're still angry?"

"What do you think?"

"It's not what I think that matters."

"Yes, I'm angry. Angrier, actually. All this—" He waved

his hands around the room. "It's all just hot air. I talk, you listen. Nothing changes."

"Do you really think that?"

"No, that's unfair," he corrected himself with a bitter laugh. "One thing has changed—I don't have as much money as when we started."

"I'm sorry you feel that way."

Lewsey leaned back in the chair and shrugged. "*C'est la vie.*"

"What about Roxanne? You said you were dreaming about her last time."

"I think about her all the time. It doesn't matter if I'm awake or asleep. She's always there."

"The medication isn't helping? The pills?"

"I stopped taking them."

"Do you think that's a good idea?"

"I do, actually. They were just making me feel numb, and that's no way to live. I want to remember her. It makes it easier to accept what I have to do."

Waller frowned, and Lewsey clenched his fists in annoyance; he'd told himself he wouldn't say that, that he'd keep everything that he was thinking—the decisions that he had made—to himself.

"I'm sorry—you've lost me. What do you have to do?"

"It's nothing. Just... it's just that I know now I need to keep her memory alive, and the pills were making it hard for me to remember. I don't want that. The memories are all I have left."

Waller smiled beatifically. "Of course. Neither I nor Dr. South want you to forget her. The treatment we agreed on is just intended to make it easier for you to manage the anger about what happened. Stopping the treatment unilaterally isn't going to help with that. When are you seeing Dr. South again?"

"Next week," he lied. There was an appointment in the diary, but Lewsey had no intention of keeping it.

"Will you speak to him about the medication?"

"I will," he said. He didn't know why he had bothered to come today. The whole thing was a farce, and he was annoyed with himself for letting it distract him from the things that he should have been doing. His preparations. No more, though. No more distraction. No more delay.

Waller looked at his watch. "We still have forty-five minutes."

"It's all right," Lewsey said. "I've had enough. We can leave it there."

He swung his legs around and stood, making his way to the door before Waller could say anything else. He went out into the anteroom; there was usually another sad loser waiting to go in, to piss away a hundred quid with nothing to show for it, but he was so early today that the next patient was still to arrive. Lewsey zipped up his bomber jacket and checked his phone. It was still early enough to get back home and work on the list of things that he needed to do.

3

Thorsson took Milton along a corridor and then up a flight of stairs. The corridor into which they emerged looked much the same as the one that they had just left. It was austere and painted in the same dull beige that was familiar from the institutional offices that Milton had visited all over the world. The lighting was from harsh bulbs set within wire cages along the ceiling. A man wearing a drab brown suit and scuffed brogues wandered past them, his attention on the tablet that he held in his hand.

Thorsson followed behind Milton. "Second on the left," he said.

Milton opened the door. The room beyond was windowless, just like his cell, but instead of a bed and a toilet and nothing else, this one was furnished with a table and chairs, and there was a monitor fixed to the wall. There were six chairs around the table: a man Milton had not seen before was sitting in one of them, and, facing him with elbows on the table and her fingers laced, was Control.

"Mr. Milton," she said.

"Control."

"I'm sorry we've had to keep you waiting. There were some details we needed to iron out before we could have this meeting, and I doubt you would have stayed if we'd let you out."

Milton shrugged. "It gave me some time to think about things."

"It did?"

"I told you before that I don't work for you anymore. I meant it."

"Yes," she said. "You've made that very clear. My predecessor sent an agent after you in London, and you sent him back with a bullet in his leg. You managed to evade a team in Mexico, and then there was that rather bloody incident in Russia."

"I told him to leave me alone," Milton said. "I was clear about what would happen if he didn't."

"Indeed. You said you'd send his agents back in body bags. I've read the file."

Milton looked from face to face, trying to work out why he had been brought here instead of being made to kneel and face a wall while Thorsson put a bullet in the back of his head.

"And then," Control said, "bringing us almost up to date, there's the mess you made in Colombia." She shook her head and chuckled. "You have no idea how much work that affected. MI6 had been working on developing La Bruja as an asset for months, and you tore it all up. Millions of pounds spent, thousands of hours invested—up in smoke, just like that."

"She was a drug-dealing mass murderer, and she made the mistake of murdering my friend. She got what was coming to her. I gave up caring about the consequences a long time ago."

"Evidently. There are plenty of important people in Whitehall and the River House who would be very happy if we followed that behaviour to its logical end."

"You'll do what you have to do," Milton said.

"I said Whitehall and the River House. We have a different view here."

"I'm not going to work for you again."

She disengaged her fingers and leaned back in the chair. "I think perhaps we got off on the wrong foot. I know you wouldn't accept a file from me. I know all about your crisis of conscience." The sentence dripped with sarcasm, but she dismissed it with a flick of her fingers. "But your being here now isn't what you think it is. I told you before—it's a babysitting job." She gestured to the chair opposite her. "Please—sit down. At least do me the courtesy of listening to what I have to say."

Milton angled a look back at Thorsson, exhaled impatiently and went to sit. "Fine."

She nodded her satisfaction. "Thank you." She pointed to the third man in the room. "This is Weaver. He's my XO. He'll tell you about the job we'd like you to consider."

Weaver had a tablet on the table in front of him. He tapped a finger to wake it and waited for the screen on the wall to mirror what he was looking at. Milton turned and looked. Weaver had selected a paparazzi shot of two men: the man on the right was a well-known government minister, while the one on the left was familiar to Milton from years ago. He had a long, equine face, thick dark hair and an air of insouciant confidence that was impossible to miss. He looked relaxed and unselfconscious, and, of the two, it was the politician—his arm around the younger man's shoulders—who was seemingly the one looking for approval.

Weaver gestured to the photograph. "Do you remember him?"

"Tristan Huxley," Milton said. "I looked after him for a month or so just after I transferred to the Group."

"In Moscow."

"That's right. He was working on a deal, and intelligence suggested that a rival was unhappy about it. I remember."

"He remembers you, too," Control said. "It would appear that you made an impression. He's found himself in a situation where he's going to need similar protection."

"What kind of situation?"

"Huxley was a millionaire when you met him. That was then—he's a billionaire now. The source of his wealth is not completely clear, not even to the analysts who worked on his file for us. It would appear that he is a masterful networker, and he's used his contacts to become a fixer par excellence—a middleman who introduces parties to one another and puts deals together."

Weaver took over. "Just in the last year he was instrumental in the acquisition of two companies for one of his billionaire friends, and we're hearing rumours that he's so close to the dictators in Eritrea, Djibouti and Somalia that he is in *de facto* control of the deep-water ports in the Horn of Africa. Particularly relevant to this meeting is an especially large weapons procurement contract between the Russians and the Indians that he has been instrumental in driving forward. The Indian government is ready to pay five billion dollars for the Russian S-400 surface-to-air defence system. Of course, the Pakistanis are very unhappy about the prospect of the root-and-branch compromise of their air force, and MI6 has heard that they're planning something before the deal can be closed."

"Which is when?"

"Next week," Weaver said. "Both parties are flying to London. Huxley's been oiling the wheels for weeks."

"So the ISI is involved?"

"That's what we're hearing."

"Do we know what they're planning?"

"MI6 isn't sure," Control said.

"What does Huxley think?"

"He's adamant that he won't change anything."

"He doesn't believe the intelligence?"

"No," Weaver said. "He does. But you might remember how wilful he is. How difficult it is to have him act on advice."

"I remember him being stubborn. But I also remember him being paranoid about his personal safety."

"He's a lot wealthier now than he was then. His view is that he can just throw money at a problem and make it go away. In this case, it means he's beefed up his personal security, he only travels in an armoured car and he only flies in his own private 767."

"He has a 767?"

"Bought it last year from the Sultan of Brunei," Weaver said. "Two hundred million."

Milton remembered how attached Huxley was to the symbols of his wealth and imagined that he would be particularly happy with a purchase of that scale.

"What does he stand to gain from the deal?"

"Five percent."

Milton tried to work out how much that was.

"Two hundred and fifty million," Weaver supplied.

Milton looked at the picture of Huxley again. That

confidence and assuredness came from money; Milton had worked with rich men and women before, and he knew that if you had the funds, it was possible to insulate yourself from the vicissitudes of daily life. If you had enough money, you could create a bubble within which you could go about your life without care or concern. That kind of facility bred complacency, however, and a cocksureness that could easily trip over into arrogance. Huxley had the kind of personality where that could certainly have been possible.

Milton leaned back. "Fine. How do I fit into all of this?"

"We told Huxley that we didn't think his security was up to the job. He has soldiers—good ones—and they're led by a very capable man who used to serve in the South African Recces. That's all well and good, but if we're right and the Pakistanis come after him, it won't be straight on. Huxley's men won't even see them coming. We told him this, of course, but he made it very clear there was no prospect of him allowing us to run security for him. So we suggested a compromise—we'd embed two of ours in his team until the deal is done. We suggested Number One and Number Two, but he still said no."

"I can see where this is going," Milton said.

Control smiled, her lips tight against her teeth. "I'm sure you can."

"How long do I have to do it for?"

"A week," she said. "Two at the outside."

"And after that?"

"Your slate will be wiped clean, and you'll be sent on your way. You've been too much of a nuisance to go with my best wishes, but you'll have my word that your file will be rescinded. You won't have to look over your shoulder any longer—at least, not for us."

"Your word?" Milton shook his head. "I don't know you. That doesn't mean anything to me."

"I'm afraid it's the best that I can do." She smiled again and spread her hands. "So there we have it—you have two choices: you either work with Huxley again and then take me at my word, or you don't."

Milton knew, of course, that there was really no choice at all. He was sure that Thorsson would have killed him in Scotland if it were not for the request from Huxley. Milton hadn't seen Huxley for over a decade, yet it appeared that he had saved his life, even if unwittingly. And the job sounded simple enough.

"When do I start?"

"Tomorrow," Control said. "Huxley is expecting you tomorrow."

4

They kept Milton in the cell for another hour. He sat with his back against the wall and tried to work out the implications of the meeting and what he had agreed to do. He had considered the idea of ever working for the Group again to be out of the question before Control had made her offer. But he was not being asked to commit murder for his government and, with that in mind, things changed. The benefits of having his record expunged were significant. He was tired of running, and perhaps this would afford him the opportunity of being able to stay in one place for more than a few weeks. He had long since abandoned any hope of enjoying a normal life, but maybe he would be able to put down roots in a place and stay there. The arrangement did require him to invest his trust in Control, and, given that he didn't know her at all, that was a step that he would not take lightly. She had inherited his file and might otherwise not have borne him any personal animus. But Milton knew that he had caused her professional difficulties; she had said as much. She would have been dragged over the coals by the spooks in the River

House for the failures in South America and the Outer Hebrides, and he was the reason for her discomfiture in both instances.

There was Thorsson, too. Control had sent the big man after Milton in Kansas City, and Milton had returned him to London with his tail between his legs; he was Number One, like Milton had been, and operators who reached that pinnacle were prideful. He wouldn't take well to being humiliated.

And Milton was going to have to trust both of them.

He heard the sound of footsteps approaching along the corridor outside. Milton got off the bed and stood as the cell door was unlocked and opened.

Thorsson was outside. "Time to go," he said.

"Where to?"

Thorsson shrugged. "That's up to you."

"She's letting me out?"

"You're working with us now—right?"

"Apparently."

"So you're not a prisoner. She's prepared to trust you. I'm not sure I would've reached the same conclusion, but I'm not in charge." He looked at him. "And, anyway, we've already found you twice—we'll be able to find you again."

Thorsson stepped away from the door so that Milton could pass through it. He led him up the stairs again, but this time, they climbed two floors.

Thorsson reached into his pocket, took out a cellphone and handed it to Milton. "Keep it switched on," he said.

"Group One are tracking it?"

"Of course they are. I'll be in touch when it's time to come in."

Milton pocketed the phone.

"And this," Thorsson said, handing over an envelope.

Milton opened it and saw that it was full of banknotes.

"You'll need somewhere to stay," Thorsson said by way of explanation.

"I don't even know where we are."

Thorsson opened the door for him and stepped aside. Milton blinked the sunlight out of his eyes as the door slammed shut behind him. He climbed a set of steps to a pavement along which joggers ran and a pair of mothers pushed children in their prams. The pavement and the buildings next to it overlooked the Thames, the foreshore visible with the tide out. Milton looked across the water to the northern bank and recognised Churchill Gardens and, beyond that, Pimlico. He turned back to look at the austere red-brick building behind him. It was the headquarters of Global Logistics, the cover company under whose auspices Group Fifteen operated. He saw the company logo stencilled in the dusty windows.

He felt odd. The last time he had been here was when he had told Control's predecessor that he wanted to quit. He had been all around the world since then—from the Australian outback to the forests of Michigan's Upper Peninsula, from the Russian steppes to the chaos of the Brazilian favelas—and he had been sure that he would never have reason to cross this threshold again.

Yet, here it was; and here *he* was, ready to do their bidding once more.

5

Milton followed the path by the Thames until he reached Vauxhall Bridge. He climbed up to it, pausing by the rail to look down at the River House, the fortress-like headquarters of the Secret Intelligence Service. It was as if he had been transported back to when he had been recruited by the Group, a captain in the SAS, yet nowhere near ready for what the government would ask him to do.

A decade had passed since then. He had stood here, on the same spot, and had looked down at the building they called Babylon-on-Thames and wondered what his future might hold. Control had dealt in euphemisms when explaining the Group's work, but Milton had found out soon enough what he meant: he was to be a killer, an assassin who would put more than a hundred murders on his conscience. Looking back on it all now, with the benefit of what he knew, he would have advised his younger self to clamber over the rail and throw himself into the waters below. His sobriety had been spent desperately trying to repair the damage that he had caused, but most of the wreckage could not be fixed. Most of the people whose files Milton had been given were dead. Atonement was impossible.

Milton felt the approach of a maudlin mood and shook his head to clear the thoughts away. It was right to acknowledge the past, but dwelling on it would only lead him to the nearest pub and a whiskey. He set off, crossing over to the north bank, and followed Belgrave Road to the Holiday Inn. Milton did not own a property. His life in the Group had been peripatetic, and, as such, it had seemed pointless for him to bear the expense of somewhere permanent. He had used this hotel before, returning more than once due to its anonymity and central location.

He went inside and approached the desk.

"Good evening, sir. Do you have a reservation?"

"I'm afraid not," Milton said. "Do you have any rooms?"

"How many nights are you looking to stay with us?"

Milton paused. He couldn't really answer that. "Maybe a week?"

The receptionist said that would be fine and took his details. The invoice was for five hundred pounds; Milton took the wad of notes from his pocket and counted out enough to cover the charge. He had been running a little low on funds. His policy had been to work in whichever place he found himself, preferably taking payment in cash so as to avoid having to go into a bank. He had an account with Coutts that held several hundred thousand pounds from his inheritance and the sale of the place in Chelsea that he had inherited, but he had no bank card. He would have to be John Milton to access it; that might be possible if Control was as good as her word. John Smith and then Eric Blair had been essential in staying off the radar, but perhaps he would have no further need for them. It was such a radical thought after so many years of being careful that it felt alien.

"Here you are, sir."

Milton snapped back into focus and saw that the smiling receptionist was holding out a paper wallet. He took it, withdrew one of the two keycards from inside, and thanked her. He crossed the lobby to the lifts and rode the first one up to the third floor.

~

MILTON STAYED in his room until night fell. He showered, freshening himself up after the days spent locked in the cell, and dressed again in the same clothes because he had nothing else to change into. He went to the window and looked down into the street outside the entrance, sure that there would be agents from Group Three keeping watch in the event that he tried to leave.

He took the phone that Thorsson had given him out of his pocket. He had no desire to be tracked, so he left it on the bedside table and went to the door. He looked through the fisheye lens and saw that the corridor was empty. He opened the door and stepped outside, made his way to the lobby and, rather than take an elevator down to the first floor, opened the door to the emergency stairs and took them instead. He reached the ground floor and slipped through a door marked with a sign that restricted it to staff. He continued into the guts of the hotel, passing the door to the kitchens and offices. He went into the staffroom, closed the door behind him and opened the unlocked locker doors until he found contents that suited his purposes. He took out the leather jacket and Miami Dolphins baseball cap that were hanging inside and put them on, pulling down the brim of the cap so that it covered as much of his face as possible.

Milton went back out into the corridor, walked to the door at the end of it and went outside, emerging into an alleyway that accommodated the bins for the kitchen. He joined the road at the rear of the hotel. He ambled to the front of the building and immediately made the two agents who had evidently been sent to observe him: the woman sitting at a bus shelter, who ignored two buses that stopped, and the man in a car who was speaking into a hidden microphone. Two, for sure, but probably more.

He reversed course and cut through the side streets, doubling back twice to identify possible tails before taking the long way to return to Vauxhall Bridge. He diverted to Vauxhall Park and, hoping that his drop site had lain undisturbed since he had last visited, found the bench next to the tennis courts and went around to the oak tree behind it. There was a cavity just above head height, and Milton reached his hand inside, his fingers brushing through damp moss until he felt the sharp edge of the key that he had left there years ago. He retrieved the key and continued to Big Yellow Self Storage in Kennington.

The clerk was distracted by another customer, and Milton was able to pass through the reception and into the main body of the building without having to show identification. He followed the corridor to the small storage unit that he had hired over a decade earlier. Each month's bill had been met by a direct debit, so there was no reason to think that his things would not be there. He put the key in the lock and turned it, opening the door and stepping inside. The unit was around the same size as a large walk-in wardrobe: five by four by eight. It was empty save for the bag that Milton had left on the floor and the clothes bag that hung from a hook on the wall.

Milton switched on the light, closed the door and unzipped the clothes bag. One of his old suits was inside: a black Tom Ford O'Connor woollen three-piece, with a faint check design, notched lapels and a vented hem. There was a blue shirt with French cuffs, a black tie from Thomas Pink and a pair of black Crockett & Jones shoes. He zipped the carrier up again and knelt down, opening the go-bag and taking out the contents. He laid it all out: a thousand pounds in cash; an emergency blanket; a small first aid kit; snacks with high calorific content; a multi-tool; three passports, including one in his own name that had since expired; a charger for electronic items, now out of date; a Nokia flip-phone that had become a curiosity in the years since he had left it here; a Glock 17 with a full magazine and spare ammunition. He took the suit carrier, the cash, his own passport, the cellphone, the handgun and the ammunition. He put the remainder back into the bag, zipped it up and secured the locker.

He arranged the Glock so that he could carry it comfortably and left the lock-up. He made his way back to the tree, returned the key to its hiding place, and continued back to the hotel. He took his time, enjoying being back in London for the first time in years without being fearful that he would be arrested on sight if he was found. He made his way to the river and walked along it, looking from the south bank to the north and the lights of the buildings that reflected against the slow-moving water. An old Dixie steamer, converted into a floating party venue, churned up waves as it passed, music and laughter reaching Milton on the bank. A late-night jogger pounded the pavement, and the beacons of passenger jets blinked overhead as they stacked for their approach into Heathrow. There was a man roasting chestnuts on a brazier, and Milton bought a bag. He ate them with his elbows resting on the concrete balustrade, watching the world go by. He waited for a moment when he was alone and tossed the expired passport into the river.

He returned to the hotel, went in through the same door at the back, left the jacket and cap where he had found them and went back to his room.

The phone was blinking with a message. He listened to it and then went down to the front desk.

"I had a message that something was left for me. John Milton, room 312."

"Yes, Mr. Milton. Hold on just a moment."

The man went into the office behind the desk and returned with a padded envelope. Milton took it and went back to his room.

6

Milton opened the safe in the hotel room, stowed the Glock and the ammunition inside, then closed and locked it again. He took the padded envelope to the table and tore it open, tipping it so that the tablet inside could slide out into his lap. It looked like a standard retail device, but Milton knew that it would have been developed in the labs of Group Six so that it could offer encrypted communication between field agents and London. He laid his finger on the scanner, waited for his print to be recorded and compared to the print retained on his record, and then saw the screen wake. There was a single folder on the home screen and, when he tapped to open it, he was rewarded with a trove of files: documents, photographs and videos. The subject of each file was the same: Tristan Huxley.

Milton went over to the coffee machine, slipped a capsule into the top and put a mug beneath the nozzle. He pressed the button, and the machine bubbled and chugged as it prepared his drink. Milton opened the dossier that summarised Huxley's career and read.

Huxley's background was much less auspicious than might have been expected if one were to judge him by the lifestyle he led today. He was born in Manchester in 1964 and grew up in a normal, nondescript family. His father was an engineer and his mother worked in sales. He was an only child and, from all accounts, had been unpopular at school thanks to a combination of aloofness, arrogance and a vast difference in intellectual ability between him and his peers. He had shown early evidence of his entrepreneurial spirit by writing several simplistic board games that sold well. He had told his father that he didn't see the point of university and that he wanted to go straight into business, but had been overruled. He went to Cambridge to read mathematics at the age of sixteen, achieving a first class degree that he went on to consolidate with a master's. After graduation, he had travelled the world for a year before taking a position with a small firm of stockbrokers in the city of London.

Milton took the mug from the machine and sat down with it at the desk. He scrolled down as he sipped the coffee and continued to read.

Huxley's career in London had been stratospheric. It was quickly obvious that he was far beyond the other junior traders who had joined the firm with him and, thanks to the work he did on complex financial instruments—described as brilliant by the firm's management committee—he'd made partner within three years. His investment work attracted the business of wealthy individuals, and the report suggested that there might have been early professional contact with arms dealers who were profiting from the rearming of Iraq following their retreat from Kuwait in 1991. His relationship with a prominent Lebanese gunrunner had brought him to the attention of MI6 and led to his recruitment as an intelligence asset.

Huxley was a millionaire by the age of twenty-three. He had used his wealth to set up his own hedge funds and started to recruit well-heeled clients who were prepared to take calculated gambles on the stock market in search of outsized returns. His aggressive attitude to investing grew with the size of his fund, and, in no time at all, he had built holdings in the privatised utilities, newspapers, and, most presciently of all, nascent internet start-ups. He bought thousands of Amazon shares when the company went public in 1997 and sold them for an outsized profit twenty years later. Similar far-sighted acquisitions in Google, Facebook, Groupon and businesses involved in the production of semiconductors helped him to amass an enormous fortune, and, as he turned forty, the *Sunday Times* Rich List announced him as a self-made billionaire, one of the youngest ever to hold that distinction.

Milton sipped at the coffee as he scrolled down to a summary of Huxley's lifestyle. He was said to be extravagant with his money, regularly making showpiece acquisitions that were then trumpeted in the press. The purchase of his own private 767 was confirmed, and he had built a mansion in Surrey that was said to have cost fifty million. His most profligate purchase, though, had been an island off the coast of Sri Lanka. He travelled to it regularly and was said to enjoy the company of the similarly rich and famous away from prying eyes. The parties on the island were said to be legendary, attracting luminaries from the worlds of finance, politics and show business.

The report was thorough, with pictures of all the lavish baubles that Huxley had purchased to decorate his immoderate, prodigal lifestyle. Huxley was the constant through all of the images: his beaming smile, the understated clothes that Milton knew would have cost a small fortune, the gold and jewellery, the parties and events, the trophy women hanging from his arm. Milton remembered him as someone who liked to enjoy his wealth, and that was clearly a trend that had continued in the years since. Milton remembered him, too, as being a stubborn and obstinate man who had often had to be persuaded to follow the advice of his security detail. Milton hoped that the intervening years had imparted a little wisdom, but as he looked at a photograph of Huxley pouring a magnum of champagne into a flute atop a pyramid of similar glasses, he doubted whether things had changed very much at all.

Milton leaned back, put the tablet down and gazed out of the window. Protecting a man like that—wilful, bullheaded and full of the entitlement that came with great wealth—might prove challenging.

7

Control had been hoping to get home at a reasonable hour. Her daughters were cramming for their exams, and she had promised to help Flora with the quadratic equations that had given her fits all term. The twins were nervous, and she knew that they wouldn't eat properly unless she cooked for them. On top of that, her diabetes had been more difficult to control than usual this week, and she had promised that she would take a little more care of herself. Latimer, though, was one of those mandarins who paid no heed to the personal circumstances of those who reported to him. He insisted upon total dedication from his staff, and had instilled in all of them a fear of disappointing him that was so visceral that stories of juniors leaving their desk lamps on and their jackets on the backs of their chairs when they left the building—in the vain hope that he might think them still working—were well known in the intelligence community. It was no surprise to Control that he had requested a late-night debrief and that her attendance was obligatory. She had dismissed Weaver for the night and had walked across to the River House alone.

Latimer was waiting for her in his office. Just like hers, it looked down onto the river.

"Control," he said, "thanks for coming."

She was tempted to ask whether she had had any choice, but decided against it. "You wanted an update?"

"How did it go with Mr. Milton?"

"He agreed," she said.

"Under duress?"

"I think it would be fair to say that he wasn't thrilled at the prospect of working for us again, but, since the alternative was less appetising, he's decided to hold his nose."

"That's good. I spoke to Huxley today. There are some misgivings on the Russian side, and he says he's going to have to work hard to persuade them to go ahead."

"I thought it was a done deal?"

"That was our understanding. But you know what Huxley's like—he'd love us to think it was in the balance so that he can make it look like a miracle when he pulls it out of the bag. He's a prima donna."

"The file makes that very clear," she said.

"Indeed. He's talking about flying Timofeyevich out to his island this week. You'd better tell your man that he'll need to pack an overnight bag." He went over to a drinks cabinet and took out two large brandy balloons and a crystal decanter. "Can I tempt you?"

"No, thank you."

"So, Milton." He poured for himself and went back to his chair. "What did you offer him?"

"Just as we discussed—a clean slate."

Latimer smiled; it was a little patronising, as if she had said something particularly simple-minded. "You didn't really think I was serious about that, did you?" He sipped his drink. "Really, Control. It's out of the question. Milton can't be allowed to wander off again. The damage he's caused already can't be undone by this."

"So, what? He's put into custody?"

Latimer scoffed. "You know better than that. Wait until the ink's dry on the contract and Huxley doesn't need him to hold his hand anymore, and then tell one of your headhunters to do away with him." He leaned back and held his glass up. "Letting John Milton disappear was your predecessor's biggest mistake. This is how we put it right."

PART II

THURSDAY

8

The phone rang at five thirty the following morning. Milton had been fast asleep and fumbled for it on the bedstand where he had left it.

"Yes?"

"It's me," Thorsson said. "We're leaving at midday. Have you read the dossier?"

"I have."

"Good. We can't afford to have any passengers on this. Be outside at twelve—we'll pick you up."

∽

MILTON SPENT the rest of the morning relaxing. He went out and bought new underwear, together with four shirts. He bought T-shirts, a pair of shorts and a pair of running shoes and changed into them in his room before going back down to the lobby and out of the main door. He stretched on the road outside, amusing himself as he watched the new man who had been posted to watch him call in that he was on the move. He jogged down to Grosvenor Road, crossed the river on Chelsea Bridge and then ran three circuits around Battersea Park. He noticed a man on a bike at the children's playground and then again as he passed the boating lakes and gave him a wave to let him know that he had been made. The man studiously ignored him, but Milton noticed him raise his hand to his mouth as he made a terse report to whoever was supervising the surveillance.

Milton crossed the river again at Battersea Bridge and ran back to the hotel. He showered, dried himself off, changed into the suit he had picked up the previous evening and stood in front of the mirror. He had grown so used to wearing whatever was to hand—jeans and T-shirts, everything grimy with the dirt of the road—that he had to look twice. This was how he used to dress, and he felt a moment of unease at the memories triggered by his reflection. He toyed with taking the Glock with him, but decided against it. The quartermaster would ensure that they had everything they needed, and it was better to leave his own weapon where it was in the event that he might need it in the future. Control had promised that his slate would be wiped clean, but he had made the mistake of trusting the man who had held her position before, and he was not about to repeat his error. He would consider himself to be dispensable once the job was done, and act accordingly.

He went down to the front of the hotel. A Mercedes minivan with blacked-out windows pulled up, and the rear door swung open.

Milton slid inside.

Thorsson was in the back with a woman.

"You remember Number Six," Thorsson said, gesturing to the woman.

Milton did: she had been in the Colombian jungle with

Thorsson. She was hard-looking, tall and wiry, and although her athletic figure had a few curves, her loose shirt and trousers did nothing to show it off. Her hair was trimmed short, and her knuckles were dark with bruises. A small scar was visible on her cheek, and the socket of her right eye was stained with purples and blues from a contusion that was taking time to heal.

"I do," he said. "You were working with La Bruja."

"I was," she said, speaking in the broad Geordie accent he remembered. "You fucked up a lot of hard work. You'd better do a better job now than you did then."

Their first meeting had been awkward, to say the least. Six had interrogated Milton about the legend upon which he had been relying, and had almost shown it to be the tissue of lies that it was. Milton had been deep in the jungle and alone, and La Bruja would certainly have killed him if she had listened to Six's warning.

"Glass houses," he said. "Your record on keeping your patrons alive isn't what it could be."

Six stared at him with flinty eyes, then looked over at Thorsson. "This is a terrible idea."

"I couldn't agree more," Milton replied.

"Look at him," she said dismissively, ignoring Milton's remark. "How long is it since he was operational?" She turned back to Milton. "How old are you, anyway?"

"Not as young as I used to be," he admitted. "But still more than good enough to run rings around the two of you."

"Stop it," Thorsson said. "Both of you. Huxley wants him on the team, and Control said yes. It's done." He turned to Milton. "You aren't going to cause any trouble, are you, John?"

"I'm going to do the job I've been asked to do, and then

I'm going to disappear." He turned to Six. "What do I call you?"

"Anderson."

The driver drove them through Chelsea and then down to Battersea.

"How long is it?" Six asked.

"Fifty miles," the man said. "Satnav says two hours."

9

Lewsey pushed the trolley into the hair care aisle and found the shelves where the hair bleach was stocked. There was a wide selection of brands: Total Bleach, Jerome Russell, Garnier, Schwarzkopf. Lewsey took two of each, dropping them into the trolley. He had intended to be cautious so as not to attract too much unnecessary attention, but as he looked at the boxes that he had put into the trolley, he realised that no one bought more than a couple anyway, and, if he was going to attract attention, he would already have done that. *In for a penny*, he thought as he cleared the shelves and dropped the rest of the boxes into the trolley.

He pushed the trolley to the checkouts. He briefly considered using the self-checkout, but suspected that the purchases would need approval anyway, and it would look shifty if he avoided the cashiers. He wheeled the trolley to the checkout with the shortest queue, put the divider onto the conveyor belt behind the shopping of the woman ahead of him, and waited for his turn.

"Morning," the cashier said as he pushed the empty trolley to the end of the belt.

"Good morning."

The woman started to ring up the peroxide.

"I don't think I've ever seen anyone buy as much as that," she said. "You must've cleared us out."

Lewsey smiled. "I have, actually—I hope that's okay."

"Someone's got to buy it," she said. "I don't suppose it makes much difference if it's a few people buying one each or you buying the lot."

"Thank you," he said.

"Not my problem either way." She started to ring up the packets. "Why do you need so much?"

"It's my wife," Lewsey said. "She has a salon in town, and she's run out."

"She doesn't get it wholesale?"

"There's been a problem with the supplier. We've had to scramble around a bit."

The woman shrugged and continued to ring up the boxes. Lewsey took out his phone and pretended to read it, looking for an excuse to bring the conversation to an end. He had no interest in prolonging it; it looked as if the woman had accepted his explanation, and he knew that the more questions she asked, the more likely it would be that he would say something that might give himself away.

"There you go, love," she said once she had scanned the final box.

Lewsey gave his bank card to the woman and tapped in his PIN. The twenty boxes had cost just over a hundred and fifty pounds. He wasn't sure how much money he had left in his overdraft, and was relieved when the transaction was approved. He had a little cash at his flat, enough to finish his preparation, and then it wouldn't matter anymore.

He bagged the boxes, put the two bags into the trolley, and thanked the cashier.

"Which salon is it?" she asked him.

"Sorry?"

"Which one's her salon? I've been meaning to get a cut, and I could do with a change."

Lewsey almost panicked, before reminding himself that she wasn't trying to trick him, that this wasn't an interrogation; it was most likely an innocent question from a bored cashier who really was looking to get a haircut.

He grabbed for the first name that he could remember. "Hair She Goes," he said. "On the High Street."

"Excuse me," said the woman in the queue behind him. "I've only got ten minutes left on my parking."

"Sorry," the cashier said. She turned back to Lewsey as she started to ring up the woman's shopping. "Thanks. I'll make an appointment."

Lewsey took the opportunity to leave, pushing the trolley out of the store and into the car park. He went to his car, made sure that no one was nearby and then opened the boot. He had another three plastic carrier bags from pharmacies in the area: another branch of Tesco in Aldershot, the Waitrose in Haslemere and a Lloyds in Farnham. Each bag held several boxes of peroxide, and he had more back at the lock-up. Lewsey pushed the bags to the back of the boot so that he could get the two new bags inside and then closed the lid.

It had been a long day, and he had covered a lot of distance, but it had been successful.

He had enough now.

He could get started.

10

Tristan Huxley's mansion was a mile outside Chiddingfold, a quaint and pleasant village in the middle of the Surrey countryside. The village was arranged around a green, with period buildings, pubs and a church that dated back hundreds of years. The Mercedes passed through the village, eliciting the interest of the elderly couple who were sat at a table in the beer garden of the Swan Inn. They turned onto Mill Lane and continued into the countryside, driving for another five minutes until they reached a left-hand turn. The driver pulled up at a pair of grand iron gates, lowered the window and leaned out to press the button on the intercom. He announced that he was bringing guests to see Mr. Huxley and, after a moment when Milton could tell they were being examined by way of the camera atop a metal pole inside the property, the gates opened, and they drove ahead.

The drive swooped through open parkland with neatly trimmed grass and mature oaks standing sentinel on either side. There was a lake with a fountain that fired water high into the air and paddocks with horses that trotted alongside them as they passed. The house came into view, and Anderson swore under her breath. It was huge, a Palladian-style mansion with generous classical proportions, a colonnade entrance and a Georgian-style façade. From a distance, the house might have been able to pass muster as an authentic period property. It was only as they drew nearer that it became apparent that it was a much newer build. The buff sandstone looked as if it had only recently been quarried, not yet subjected to the patination that would come with years of exposure to the elements. The main house was gigantic, and the separate wing to the side looked to be even larger.

"Not very modest," Anderson said.

"Modesty was never his strong suit," Milton replied.

They drove along the winding drive and drew up in front of the main building. There were four other cars already parked: two other Mercedes, a Range Rover and a cherry-red Ferrari. Milton recognised the latter vehicle from the dossier that he had been sent. It was a LaFerrari Aperta, and the report was that Huxley had bought it at Sotheby's in 2017 for eight million pounds. It was, the dossier suggested, the most expensive car ever sold at auction.

The driver slotted their Mercedes into the space at the end of the line. Milton opened the door and stepped out. Thorsson and Anderson went around to the rear of the vehicle and opened the door to the cargo area. There were two large flight cases inside. They dragged them both out and set them down on the gravel.

"John?" a voice called out.

Milton turned and saw a man looking down from the steps beneath the colonnade.

"John! Bloody hell, it is you."

Milton shielded his eyes against the sun. The man was

middle-aged, but dressed in a fashion that would have befitted someone fifteen years younger: black turtleneck, fitted jeans, and biker boots. He jogged down the steps and crunched across the gravel to the cars.

"Mr. Huxley," he said.

Huxley stood in mock dismay. "'*Mr.* Huxley'? No need for formality. *Tristan.*"

"Tristan," Milton said.

"Can't tell you how pleased I am that you're here. The spooks think I've landed myself in hot water with the Pakistanis."

"So I understand," Milton said.

"I told them I could take care of my own security, but they insisted. I said I didn't need babysitting, but you know what they can be like. Stubborn. So I said I'd only go along with it if I could have you. They said you weren't working for them anymore."

"I left a long time ago. This is a one-time deal for me."

"Well, I'm flattered you came back. Flattered and relieved." He smiled, showing off his bright white teeth, then gestured over to where Thorsson and Anderson were standing. "Who are the others?"

"I'm Guðjohnsen," Thorsson said, using the legend that had been prepared for him.

"Sweden?"

"Iceland," he said.

"And your friend?"

"Anderson," Six said.

"And you work for the same unit as John used to?"

"We do," Thorsson said.

Huxley crossed over and shook their hands. "Thank you. I'm sure this is nothing, but they persuaded me better safe than sorry."

"I think that's wise," Thorsson said.

"Maybe." Huxley gestured to the two cases on the ground. "What's in there?"

"Equipment," Anderson said.

"I'll have them taken inside for you."

"It's fine. We'll do it."

"You'll want a room to set up in. I'll send someone down, and they'll find somewhere for you." He turned back to Milton. "They can do without you for a while, though?"

"We're fine," Anderson said.

"Great." He clapped Milton on the back. "Come on, then—let me show you around. We've got a lot to catch up on."

11

Milton followed Huxley up the steps and through the enormous front door. It opened into a huge reception hall with eight doors leading off it in all directions.

"Let's start in the study."

They went across the hall into a generously proportioned room that was notable for the bank of screens that had been fixed to one wall. Feeds from security cameras were displayed there, together with overlays that identified the rooms that were being shown: library, drawing room, kitchen, entertainment room. There was a man sitting at a desk, toggling a keyboard controlling the feeds that were displayed on the screens.

"I thought we'd start here so I could put your mind at ease," Huxley said.

"Looks comprehensive."

"And state of the art. There are cameras everywhere." He turned to the man at the desk. "Show him outdoors."

The man tapped the keyboard, and the feeds on the screen changed to show the exterior of the house and its grounds. One camera showed the iron gates that guarded the approach to the property, another was positioned midway along the drive, and a series were arranged to offer full coverage of the buildings themselves.

"There are motion detectors in the grounds, too," Huxley said. "And in the unlikely event that someone was able to get in here without being seen, there's a safe space in the basement. Bullet- and bomb-resistant doors, air-filtration system and a week's worth of supplies."

"Very thorough."

"I told London that, but they're still nervous."

"You've made some dangerous enemies."

"I know. But how are they going to get through all this? The security, too. We have dog patrols at night. I've got a team of six, all ex-military, and the man in charge is a hard bastard."

"I'm sure you're right," Milton said, "but I still think anything we can do to make you safer is a good thing."

"I know, I know. That's why I asked for you." He clapped Milton on the shoulder. "Come on—I'll show you the rest of the house."

They visited the library, the drawing room, the kitchen and the wine cellar, where Huxley ostentatiously pointed out a bottle of Chateau Margaux from 1787 and a Chateau Lafite from 1869; they had cost over $200,000 apiece at auction, he told him, and said that he'd open a bottle at dinner tonight; Milton didn't comment. He had suspected that Huxley would want him to drink. Milton had been different when they'd met before—it had been in the middle of his period of heavy boozing—and he knew that he would eventually have to tell Huxley that he was teetotal. It promised to be an awkward conversation, and Milton decided that it could wait.

They continued to the entertainment complex.

"The other two," he said. "Guðjohnsen and Anderson—what are they like?"

"Good," Milton said. "Anyone working in that unit is good."

"Those aren't their real names."

"I couldn't say."

Huxley grinned. "Whatever. You wouldn't believe how determined they were to send people here to look after me. I said no, I didn't need their help, but they kept on at me. I said if I was going to agree to something like that, then it had to be someone I knew. Hence I asked for you."

"That's very kind."

"No, it isn't. It's me being spoilt and selfish. I'm sure you had lots going on."

Milton shook his head. "My life is quiet these days."

"I don't believe that for a minute."

They made their way into the huge entertainment complex. There was a pool, a cinema and a full-size bowling alley. Huxley went over to a bar with a marble top and two large, well-stocked fridges. He opened one of the fridges and took out a bottle of beer. "Want one?"

"Not for me."

"Too early?"

"Something like that."

"But you are still the same reprobate as you were back then?"

"I don't know what you mean."

"Come on, John—don't be coy. You were the only one who could keep up with me." He popped the top off the bottle and took a long sip. "You remember when we went out to that club in Moscow? What was it called?"

Milton did remember. "Dyagilev."

"That's it—Dyagilev. You remember the women there? My God. Russian women..."

Huxley had an insatiable appetite for the finer things in life: fine dining and expensive champagne. He had an appetite for women, too, and wasn't shy about flaunting his wealth in order to get what he wanted.

"You remember Khamelon?" Huxley went on. "When the penny dropped that it was a gay club?"

Milton felt uncomfortable with the direction the conversation was taking. He had been irresponsible and unprofessional before. In Moscow, he had been charged with keeping Huxley safe, yet he had not demurred when Huxley had said that he wanted to go out drinking; Milton had wanted to do that too, and doing it on Huxley's shilling was more fun than doing it on his own. And Moscow had been *wild*. There had been clubs rammed with bandits and businessmen—they were interchangeable in Russia back then—and their women. He remembered Titanic, a club near Dinamo's stadium. He remembered Utopia, dedicated to a bohemian clique of expats and locals who could afford the sky-high prices. He could recall some of it, but much had been lost to the alcoholic blackouts that always afflicted him when he drank too much.

Milton decided that the conversation he would have liked to avoid couldn't wait. "There's something I need to tell you. I don't drink anymore."

"What? You're having a laugh." Huxley evidently thought that Milton was joking. He looked at him and saw that he was straight faced, then cocked an eyebrow and shook his head. "Are you serious?"

"I am."

"Why?"

"I was drinking too much. It got to be a problem."

Huxley leaned forward and grabbed Milton by the elbow; it was a tactile manoeuvre that Milton remembered well, an attempt at conviviality that was undercut by a knowing solipsism: *I'm rich and famous and good looking, and your personal space doesn't apply to me.* "Good for you. How long?"

"It's been years now."

"Are you going... you know, going to meetings?"

"Yes. Although probably not as often as I should."

Milton thought, for a moment, that Huxley was about to admit to his own drinking problem and to ask for help, but the moment passed just as quickly as it had arrived. Huxley raised the bottle in an awkwardly self-conscious salute, put it to his lips and drank. "Cheers, John. Well done. Bloody well done."

The atmosphere was a little strained after that, and Huxley was evidently pleased when a man Milton had not seen before approached them from the door to the main house. He was tall, perhaps an inch or two taller than Milton, and lean. His face was long, and his hair, receding a little at the temples, was swept back. His skin was tanned, and the lines suggested a life that had been spent outdoors.

"John," Huxley said, "this is Christiaan Cronje."

Milton extended his hand. "John Smith."

Cronje gripped Milton's hand firmly. The man's eyes were a pale blue, almost pellucid, with a blankness that Milton found disconcerting. He knew the effect that his own cold blue eyes could have on others, but it was unusual for the tables to be turned. Cronje's gaze suggested disdain and cruelty, and Milton found the effect unsettling.

"Christiaan is head of security."

"We'll be working closely together, then," Milton said.

Cronje kept Milton's hand. "Can't see the point of it,

personally. We've got things locked down nice and tight here. Can't help thinking you lot are going to be about as useful as a fart in a hurricane, but what do I know?"

The man spoke with a hard Afrikaans drawl. He kept Milton's hand in his, smiling a humourless smile that revealed a mouthful of crooked teeth.

"I hope you're right."

Milton maintained his own grip and held Cronje's eye until, after a moment that was beginning to stretch uncomfortably, the South African let go.

"The plane is ready for tomorrow," the South African reported to Huxley.

"And the island?"

"The team arrived this morning. It's been cleared. We're good to go."

"Well done."

Cronje dipped his head. "I'll see you in the morning."

He made his way back into the house.

"He looks like fun," Milton said.

"His bark's worse than his bite." Huxley gestured to the door, and they walked together. "You'll have dinner with me tonight?"

"Of course," Milton said.

"Bring the others. I'd better make an effort to get to know them if we're going to be working together for however long it takes to close this bloody deal." He took out his phone, distracted by an incoming call. "Need to take this. The staff will take you up to your rooms. Be downstairs at eight?"

12

A uniformed member of staff took Milton up to his room on the first floor of the mansion. He opened the door and saw that it was vast: double aspect, with four large windows along one wall and another two adjoining them; a bathroom within a glass cube, the walls made opaque at the touch of a button; a huge bed that was somehow rendered tiny by all the space around it. He put his bag down, unzipped it and unpacked his clothes. He went over to a chest of drawers and saw that a present had been left atop it. It was a bottle wrapped in brown paper and decorated with ribbons and a bow, with a small sealed envelope propped against it. Milton tore the paper away to reveal a bottle of Stoli Elit Himalayan vodka. He opened the envelope and took out a piece of card embossed in gold with the initials TH and inscribed with a note: *Still your favourite?* Milton knew that Stoli only made three hundred bottles of the vodka each year and that each cost around $3000.

Milton picked up the bottle and turned it in his hands, smiling ruefully. It was a thoughtful gesture, but now—after Milton had admitted that he didn't drink—it was only likely to be the source of more awkwardness. It would also be the source of temptation and, not willing to risk it, Milton opened the bottle and poured it into the sink.

He ran a bath and undressed, taking the tablet with him as he slipped into the hot water. He opened the dossier on Huxley and scrolled through the files until he found the report that had been put together on Christiaan Cronje.

He had been born in Durban forty-five years earlier to parents who were involved in the National Party. He had been sent to England for his schooling and had returned to South Africa to serve with the Recces, South Africa's principal special forces and counter-insurgency soldiers. After that, he started a business running safaris in Kwa-Zulu Natal. His file suggested that he had not been fulfilled in his work and had, instead, signed up as a soldier-for-hire for a man who ran a business supplying mercenaries to those who could afford them. Cronje had seen action in Angola and Sierra Leone and on Bougainville, an island belonging to Papua New Guinea. He was reported to have close ties with serving members of the South African Secret Service, and there was evidence to suggest that he had been involved in the failed coup d'état to topple the government in Equatorial Guinea. Twenty-four mercenaries had been arrested in Zimbabwe when their Boeing 747 was seized by local police and weapons and equipment were found to be on board. Cronje was alleged to have been in Harare before the plane was seized, but had fled the country before he, too, could be arrested.

The file suggested that Cronje had been introduced to Huxley by a mutual friend in South Africa and had been responsible for his personal security for the last five years. There had been allegations made against the South African in that time: a man protesting about Huxley's work in the arms business had been sent to hospital with a broken leg, and another protestor picketing a conference held by the government of Saudi Arabia had complained that Cronje had broken her nose when clearing her out of Huxley's way. Both claims had been settled with out-of-court payments.

Milton swiped through a series of photographs of Cronje, the most recent taken during the detailed reconnaissance undertaken by Group Three. There was a picture of him in a dark suit standing by a car as Huxley emerged. Another had him in jeans and a T-shirt, standing on a beach with another man. The cruelty in his face was impossible to mistake.

Milton put the tablet down. He didn't care if Cronje was cruel. Milton wasn't interested in making judgements beyond whether or not he would be helpful or an impediment to what he was there to do. Cronje was obviously experienced and competent, and that would be useful in the event that the threat against Huxley was more than just noise. Milton had worked against Pakistan's Inter-Services Intelligence agency before, and they would not have been his choice for an enemy against which to defend. Huxley could downplay the threat as much as he liked, but if the warnings were true, he would need all the protection that they could muster.

13

Dinner was set for eight o'clock, and Milton made his way downstairs with five minutes to spare. He heard the sound of conversation from the drawing room and crossed the hall to see Thorsson and Anderson in conversation with Huxley.

"Here he is," Huxley said.

Milton joined them.

"What did you think of Cronje? Bit of an acquired taste?"

"Is he good at his job?" Milton asked.

"He is."

"That's all I need to know."

"Amazing life story. Used to run safaris in Durban, and then he somehow turned himself into a soldier-for-hire."

"Military?" Thorsson asked.

"He served with the Recces," Huxley said, "then he set up a couple of mercenary groups and got into some rough-and-tumble in Africa before I hired him. You'll have to ask him to give you his life story—it's colourful. One for later. Can I get you a drink?"

Milton asked for a glass of water. Thorsson and Anderson asked for the same.

"Really?" Huxley said. "You're going to make me drink alone?"

"We're working," Thorsson said.

"You're all very tedious."

Huxley made himself a gin and tonic and raised his glass in an ironic toast. He took a sip and then turned to Milton. "Have you told the two of them what happened in Moscow?"

"I haven't."

"I've read the file," Thorsson said.

"I bet that doesn't even cover half of it," Huxley said with a grin. "Go on, John. Tell them."

"I think you might do a better job," Milton demurred, raising his hands.

"Fine." He took a sip of his drink. "So, this is more than ten years ago. I was working on a deal to bring liquefied natural gas from the arctic to the UK. The pipeline we used to bring it in from the North Sea was shut, and we needed to scramble to make up the shortfall. The seller was a Russian company—Siftek—owned by one of the oligarchs. You remember him?"

"Baranov," Milton said.

"Sergei Baranov. He's dead now—Putin got rid of him—but he was one of the big oil and gas tycoons back then. One of the others was a man called Bubka. He had his own gas that he wanted to sell us, and he wasn't happy that we chose Baranov over him. It was similar to what's happening this time—MI6 heard that Bubka wanted to get rid of me, and they sent John to keep an eye on things. Go on—tell them what happened."

Milton had no wish to recall past operations in front of the others, but Huxley was clearly intent on ploughing on regardless. "A man took a shot at him as he got out of his car."

Huxley was evidently angling for more detail and, seeing that Milton was not minded to provide it, took up the story again himself. "We were on Ulitsa Butlerova. I remember it like it was yesterday. This guy on a motorbike stopped alongside and pulled a machine pistol. John spotted him. He tackled me"—he clapped his hands—"put me behind the car, and then took a shot at him. Never had any doubt about it—if it weren't for John, I wouldn't be here. Bubka would've turned me into Swiss cheese."

Thorsson and Anderson were listening to the story with expressions that mixed feigned interest and enjoyment at Milton's very obvious discomfort.

"That's a very good reason for you to listen to us now," Milton said, hoping to salvage a little from his abashment.

"I didn't have Cronje then," Huxley said, but noting Milton's frown, he held up his hands in mock surrender. "Don't worry. I'm just messing with you. I'll be a good boy." Huxley looked over at the uniformed butler who had just appeared in the doorway. "Who's hungry?"

They went through into the dining room. Milton saw that the seating had been arranged so that Huxley was opposite him. To his relief, the awkwardness from earlier was gone, and Huxley had found his habitual gregariousness again. He was drinking freely, and Milton suspected that he was already a little drunk.

There was an uncomfortable pause as they all took their seats, but then Huxley defused it by clearing his throat and leaning forward slightly in his chair. "I probably don't look it, but I *am* grateful. I think we could have handled this in-house, but that doesn't mean I don't appreciate the three of you keeping an eye on me."

The butler returned with a colleague, similarly attired, and the starters were served.

"Alain," Huxley said, "what are we having?"

"This is Oscietra-Kaviari caviar from Paris," the man said, "served with Scottish langoustine, piel de sapo melon, samphire and ponzu."

Huxley thanked him and dismissed him with a wave of his hand.

Milton remembered that Huxley's favourite subject was himself, and decided to indulge him. "You were doing well for yourself before, but this?" He gestured to the opulent dining room. "This is something else entirely."

Huxley smiled self-indulgently, and Milton could see that he had read him accurately and that nothing had changed. "My fund has had a good run. It's either good luck or good business. My ex-wife would say it was the former, but better judges of character might tell you I know when to buy and when to sell." He shrugged. "*I'd* say it was probably somewhere in the middle. You can be brilliant, but there will always be obstacles you can't foresee—you need luck to make sure you can get around them in one piece. We always have a spread of assets. I try to match the speculative investments with the sure bets. For every biotech start-up, you need a Kraft Heinz. The steady holdings balance out the gambles. That way I can be sure that I'll always have a decent year, but it's when the gambles pay off that we really see returns. I was early into Amazon and Google and Facebook. They were gambles. Now..." He shrugged. "Well, you can see what happened when they took off."

The starters were cleared away.

"Have you heard anything else about the Pakistanis?" he asked them.

"Nothing that you haven't already been told," Thorsson said.

"You're confident in the intelligence?"

"We are. We believe the matter has been passed to Directorate S."

The main course—wagyu beef, oyster mushrooms, capers, tarragon and fermented pepper—was brought out, the plates set down before them. Milton sliced the beef and put a piece in his mouth. It was delicious, almost melting on his tongue.

"Good?" Huxley asked.

"Delicious."

"It's from the Highlands," Huxley said. "There's a business up there, near Dunblane. We bought it last year. It makes a healthy profit, but not enough for me to get particularly excited about." He laughed and shook his head. "I bought it so that I could always make sure we have the best beef in the world available in the kitchen. It's fresh, too. I won't let them freeze it. If it doesn't get eaten, we give it to the dogs." Huxley poured himself a glass of wine from the carafe on the table. "What did you say it was? Directorate…"

"S," Thorsson finished for him.

"And I should be frightened of that?"

"You should be careful."

"They've been responsible for assassinations both inside and outside Pakistan," Anderson said.

"But here?" Huxley said. "In this country?"

"They won't care about that," Thorsson said. "Not if you're important enough to take the risk. They'll just make sure that nothing can be traced back to them."

Huxley asked for more background on the Pakistanis and listened as Thorsson and Anderson outlined the threat that they posed. Milton had had dealings with the ISI and

Directorate S on several occasions. There had been a time, years earlier, when he had found himself in Afghanistan. An MI6 spy who had made his way to the heart of al-Qaeda leadership had been exposed by Directorate S and executed. The Pakistanis had denied burning the spy, but intercepts between their agents and Islamabad had revealed their lies. Milton had trekked to the eastern city of Jalalabad and then to the al-Qaeda training camp near the Darunta reservoir, several miles off the main road. Group Three had intercepted internet chatter suggesting that the Directorate S agent responsible for the death of the spy would be visiting the camp. Milton had lain in wait with an L96 sniper rifle and had taken out both the Directorate S agent and the terrorist responsible for the camp, the man who had murdered the spy. He had exfiltrated on foot, walking twenty miles until he was far enough away to be picked up by a helicopter flown in by a team from 658 Squadron Army Air Corps. The Pakistanis knew who had been responsible, but couldn't complain given what they had done to provoke the response.

They finished their main courses, and the butlers brought in four chocolate desserts.

"This is Mekonga chocolate," the man said. "From Vietnam. With coffee, coriander and vanilla."

Huxley picked up his spoon and twirled it between his fingers. "You know we're flying out to the island tomorrow?"

Milton had read that section of the dossier: Huxley owned a private island off the coast of Sri Lanka.

"I do," Thorsson said. "I'm not thrilled about it."

"Totally unavoidable. I can't always legislate for where I'm going to need to be, and, as it turns out, I need to travel."

"That doesn't mean I think it's a good idea."

"Was I supposed to ask for permission?"

"No," Thorsson said patiently. "All I'm saying is that it would be a lot safer to stay here."

"It's an *island*," Huxley said with exaggerated patience. "If you can't keep me safe on a bloody island, then I don't know why you're here at all."

"Who else will be there?"

"The Russians. They've got cold feet about the deal, and I'm going to have to work on them. I've always found it easier to do that face to face. Easier to distract someone that way, get them to take their eye off the ball. You do that and you find the margin you need to move things so that they favour you. That's how I've always worked."

"We're still leaving in the morning?"

"We are," he said. "Nine sharp. The cars will be ready outside." He finished his wine and reached for the carafe. "Now, come on—you're sure I can't tempt any of you with a glass?"

14

The meal finished at ten. Milton stood and said that he would have a look outside before turning in. Huxley warned him that Cronje's men would be patrolling with dogs and that he would be wise to be back inside before midnight, when the alarms would be switched on. Huxley bid them goodnight and made his way up to the first floor; Milton went outside and walked to the fountain set in the middle of the turning circle. It was crisp and fresh and, as he looked up, he saw stars spread across a cloudless sky. How much had they said the property was worth? Fifty million? What had Huxley done to make that kind of money? Whom had he trodden on? Of whom had he taken advantage?

A large figure stepped out of the house and crossed the yard toward him.

It was Thorsson. "What do you make of him?"

"He hasn't changed," Milton said.

"He thinks his money will keep him safe."

"I've worked with men like that before," Milton said.

"How did it go for them?"

"Not always how they'd like."

The two men looked into the darkness of the paddocks and grounds that surrounded the house.

"The Pakistanis are serious," Thorsson said. "The intelligence I've seen is crystal clear."

"Do you have any experience with them?"

"You know better than to ask that."

"I have," Milton said. "He'd be a lot less blasé if he knew how dangerous they are."

Thorsson exhaled. "You think we'd even see their cleaners if they were out there?"

"I doubt it. They're too good."

Huxley had spent a fortune on securing the house, and Cronje's men were probably competent, but keeping someone safe when they were in the sights of real professionals—and Directorate S was the best the ISI had—would be a challenge.

"You still up to this?" Thorsson asked.

"We'll see."

15

Brigadier Subhani Rashid turned off the highway and pulled up in front of the barrier. The campus was next to a hospital on one of the busier thoroughfares that circled Islamabad. The entrance would have been easy to miss: a single barrier barred the way through a tall wall that was topped with razor wire, bougainvillea spilling between the barbs. Rashid waited for the single officer in plain clothes to approach. It was dark, but the light from the gatehouse revealed the tell-tale bulge of a holstered pistol beneath his shoulder.

Rashid handed him his card.

The man checked it, then handed it back. "Good evening, sir."

The barrier lifted, and Rashid drove through. Soldiers in uniform emerged to check the car for bombs, waving him on after completing their inspection. A huge gate slid back, and Rashid drove through onto the campus proper, parking in front of a sleek space-age building that could easily have accommodated a tech company in Palo Alto.

He showed his credentials again and made his way

through the building to the conference suite where the briefing was due to take place. It was a wood-panelled room with soft armchairs, a table that was long enough to seat twenty and a wall-mounted screen. Servants dressed in uniforms that bore the ISI logo brought in trays of refreshments. Smoking was permitted, and the room was already heavy with the fug of cigars.

Lieutenant General Chaudhury Ali Khan was at the head of the table. He was the director general of the agency, a man as insidious as he was smug. Iskander Nazimuddin sat to Ali Khan's right and Irtiza Qamar to his left.

Nazimuddin was the head of the counter-intelligence wing and had made his reputation as being ethically flexible and utterly ruthless.

Qamar led the agency's Afghan bureau; she was urbane and charming, but behind her smiles lurked a nefarious operator who had protected the Taliban during the American invasion and who, it was rumoured, had leaked intelligence to them that had allowed their suicide bombers to successfully attack the *kuffar*. She had also been involved in the operation to imprison Osama bin Laden in the Abbottabad compound and keep him off the radar of the CIA until it had been determined that a sufficient *quid pro quo* would be delivered for giving him up.

"Take a seat, Brigadier," Ali Khan said, gesturing to the seat next to Qamar.

"Thank you, Director General."

He sat. Qamar was wearing her usual perfume, the vanilla scent mixing with the smoke from Ali Khan's cigar. Nazimuddin regarded Rashid through heavy-lidded eyes in a fashion that reminded Rashid of how a lion might observe a gazelle. The trio held the balance of power in the agency, and Rashid knew that his continued advancement depended on their patronage.

There was a humidor on the table. Ali Khan opened the lid and slid it over so that Rashid could choose a cigar. He wasn't a big smoker, but he wanted to maintain the goodwill that he had built up. The cigars would have been brought back from Cuba in a diplomatic bag; Rashid took out a *cuaba*, sliced off the end and allowed the director general to light it for him.

"Thank you, sir."

"We wanted to take the opportunity to confirm that everything is in place for the operation," Ali Khan said.

"Yes, sir," Rashid said. "I believe that it is."

"Your agents?"

"Abbas Kader has been in the country for several weeks. The quartermaster has equipped him, and the target's accommodation has been scouted."

"And Huxley?"

"Kader filed a report yesterday morning—he's due to leave the country to fly to Sri Lanka tomorrow. The flight plan has been filed, and the plane has been prepared."

"Timofeyevich has confirmed he will be there," Nazimuddin said. "He will be travelling with minimal security."

"Discretion will be important to him," Ali Khan said, his lip kinking upwards with distaste. "I'm sure he would prefer to travel alone were that possible. He won't want tongues to wag."

"He's always been very careful," Qamar said. "If Putin knew the truth, he'd be dropped in a gulag before the day was out."

"Let's hope he sees the good sense of keeping his perversions out of general circulation," Ali Khan said. He relit his cigar, puffing hard as he held the tip in the flame of his lighter. "What about the rest of your team?"

"They flew out earlier today."

"The British won't suspect them?"

Rashid shook his head. "They're cleanskins with pristine legends. They won't be stopped."

"Very good."

Qamar laid her hand on Rashid's wrist. "The Taliban are ready for you," she said. "The facility has been prepared, and the commander there knows not to ask questions."

"Thank you."

Rashid knew that a lot of work had been expended in order for the operation to be successful. Qamar had called in a very large favour from the mullahs, and Nazimuddin had taken a risk with a high-level asset in the Politburo in order to understand the scope of the deal that Huxley was trying to shepherd to completion. The operation had been given the green light, and now it was up to Rashid and his agents to bring it to a successful conclusion. There was glory to be had, but if it failed, there would be opprobrium enough to bring his career to an inglorious end.

"We shouldn't detain you," Ali Khan said. "I'm sure you have a lot to do."

Rashid thanked him and stood. The three of them wished him good luck and watched as he left the room. He closed the door behind him and took a moment to gather himself in the corridor. The stakes were high; Rashid had found sleep difficult for weeks and knew that there was no prospect of it again tonight.

PART III

FRIDAY

16

Heathrow Airport was busy, and the couple fitted right in with the rest of the passengers who disembarked from the flight from Prague. The names on their passports were Nawaz and Nadia Khan, and, if questioned, they would say that they were coming to the United Kingdom to study at the London School of Economics. Those were not their real surnames, though, and the places at LSE had been fabricated at the building in Islamabad where hundreds of hackers worked for Pakistani intelligence.

The couple were wearing fleece jackets and jeans, with trainers on their feet and carry-on suitcases trundling along behind them. Their real names were Nawaz Syed and Nadia Hussain, and they were both members of Directorate S, the ISI's secretive division responsible for deniable operations outside the borders of Pakistan. Nadia led the way along the airbridge to the terminal, following the slow-moving queue of people to the luggage hall. She picked a path between the carousels to the one that was advertised with the call sign of their flight. They waited patiently for their cases to be delivered. They were packed with the kinds of things that two mature students would need for a term in London, but they were purely for show. Even a barely competent immigration official would have been curious if they had arrived with only carry-on luggage.

The senior member of the team—Abbas Kader—had been in the country for weeks and had been responsible for liaising with the quartermaster. He should have collected the rest of their equipment at a dead drop two days ago. Their gear was to be hidden in the back of a Ford Mondeo that would then be left in the long-term parking at Hendon railway station, its key secured in a magnetic key box fixed to the inside of the rear-right wheel arch. It had been agreed that Nadia and Nawaz would meet Abbas at the safe house that evening. They would stay in character until they reached London, and then they would split up and conduct extensive and thorough dry-cleaning runs until they were sure that they were not being followed by hostile intelligence. There was nothing to suggest that they were, and both had been trained to avoid exciting any attention that might blow their legends, but it was impossible to be completely confident about the security of any operation, and they had planned accordingly. They had a saying at home: water overflows the river whose banks are weak. Careful and thorough preparation made accidents less likely.

They loaded their luggage onto a trolley and wheeled it to the immigration hall. There was a queue of passengers waiting to be processed, and they took their places at the back, waiting patiently as the line snaked between the fabric barriers. Neither spoke, although they were both anxious now that they faced the first real test of the operation. Both were green, their lack of exposure to foreign intelligence precisely why they had been selected; as cleanskins, there was practically no chance that they would be stopped and a greater certainty that they would be able to put the plan into operation. There were no files on them, no photographs on record, no risk of a biometric match that would ping an alarm to an analyst in the River House. Abbas was different. He was seasoned and better known, but the planners had concluded that the greater risk of his discovery was balanced by the expertise that he could bring. He had trained both Nawaz and Nadia, too, and the trust and familiarity between them was invaluable.

Nadia told herself that her nerves were normal and that she just needed to rely on her training. She had spent five years readying herself for exactly this kind of situation. She just had to trust in herself.

"Passport," the border guard said.

Nadia handed her passport to the man and stood back as he scanned it and then compared her to her photograph.

"What is your business in the United Kingdom?"

"Studying," she said.

"Where?"

"The London School of Economics."

"And where will you be staying?"

"Bankside House," she said. She recited the address of the hall of residence easily and confidently, remembering the details from the hours of preparation that she had undertaken while they waited for the green light to move.

The man checked the passport again and, satisfied, handed it back to her.

"Welcome to the United Kingdom," he said. He pointed to Nawaz. "Next."

Nadia waited for Nawaz on the other side of the counter. He handled the interaction with grace, attempting a friendly remark and smiling stoically when the guard rebuffed him. Nadia concentrated on maintaining her calm, well aware that there would be people watching even after new arrivals had been processed. The nerves boiled in her stomach, and she looked down to hide her relief as she heard the thud of the passport being stamped and the guard's dour welcome to the country.

"Easy," Nawaz muttered quietly as he joined her.

"Don't talk," she said through her forced smile as they set off for the arrivals lounge. "Act normal."

They walked together, passing through the sliding doors and then into the happy clamour of the large hall, where relatives waited behind the barriers with handmade signs, and taxi drivers with names scrawled on wipe-clean boards looked for their passengers. They had no one to meet them nor a car to drive them into the city. They would take the train, as befitted newly arrived students. Nadia exhaled; they were closer, but only when they had finished the dry-cleaning run and the door of the safe house was closed behind them would she feel able to truly relax.

That, too, would be temporary. They had a job to do, and it started tomorrow.

17

A small convoy of cars had gathered on the turning circle in front of the house. Milton assumed that the three Mercedes GLS SUVs were to be responsible for conveying members of Huxley's staff and security to the airport. Christiaan Cronje and several other men who looked as if they might be part of his team were conferring next to one of the SUVs. The Ferrari that Milton had seen yesterday evening had been prepared, too, and now Huxley and Thorsson were standing in front of it. Huxley was remonstrating with Thorsson; the Icelander had his massive arms folded across his chest. It was obvious from the body language of the two men that they were in disagreement about something. Milton crossed over to them both.

"*Finally,*" Huxley said. "Someone I can actually talk to."

"He wants to drive to the airport in that," Thorsson said, nodding down to the Ferrari.

Milton winced. "I'm not sure that's the best idea in the world."

"Come on," Huxley protested. "I hardly ever get the

chance to take her out. No one even knows we're going to the airport."

Thorsson shook his head. "No."

"I thought we cleared this up last night," Huxley said. "I don't take orders from you."

Milton raised his hands in a gesture of calm. "Look—I'll ride with him."

Thorsson looked as if he might complain about that, too, but in the end, he shrugged indifferently. "Fine," he said, and, as he walked away, he turned back and added, "Make sure he stays in the middle of the convoy."

"I will," Milton said.

Huxley scoffed.

"You heard him," Milton said.

"What?" Huxley said with mock innocence.

"He's trying to make sure you don't get shot."

"I know, and I'm terribly grateful. I'm not going to do anything stupid, but I'm not going to keep a car like that in second the whole way, am I?"

∼

Huxley kept the Ferrari in the middle of the convoy until they reached the village of Milford. The route to Farnborough Airport was off to the left, but, instead, Huxley pulled into the outside lane and flattened the pedal. The Ferrari's engine roared, and the car shot ahead, leaving the convoy behind, but not fast enough that Milton could not see the look of consternation on Thorsson's face.

"What are you doing?"

"I forgot," he said. "I need to make a stop first."

"Where?"

"Knightsbridge."

Milton groaned. "Come on, Tristan. You need to stay with the others."

"I'm going to the bank," he said.

"So put it on your itinerary and let Thorsson look after you."

"It's sensitive. I have something I need in one of my safe-deposit boxes. I trust you—I don't trust them. Call them and tell them we'll meet them at the airport in a couple of hours."

Milton's phone buzzed in his pocket. He took it out.

"Who is it?" Huxley said. "The big lump?"

Milton nodded and put the phone to his ear. "Hello?"

"You said you'd keep him under control," Thorsson said.

"He says he needs to make a stop first."

"Where?"

"Knightsbridge."

Thorsson cursed in Icelandic. "Did you know?"

"I didn't."

He swore again. "This is intolerable."

"I know."

"We can't work like this."

"I'll make sure he doesn't do anything stupid."

"Get it into his thick head that he can't just do what he wants."

"I'll do my best."

Thorsson ended the call.

"He's not happy," Milton reported.

Huxley glanced across the cabin. "Is he *ever*?"

The Ferrari turned off at Wisley and merged onto the M25.

"I'm sorry about last night," Huxley said.

"What for?"

"Giving you a hard time about the booze—it was completely unfair."

"There's no need to apologise."

Huxley continued as if he hadn't heard him. "I know what it is," he said. "Why I reacted like that. I knew the kind of people they'd send to babysit me. Humourless thugs—like your friend. Or frigid bitches, like the other one. The thought of being stuck with either of those two for more than a couple of hours..." He paused. "Frankly? I'd rather gnaw off my own arm."

"And you thought I'd be more fun."

"Don't you remember at all? We had a good time! Moscow was amazing. It was dangerous, everything on the edge. Doing deals in the daytime and then going out to the clubs at night." Huxley flicked the indicator stalk and pulled out into the fast lane, hammering down on the accelerator and roaring by the clutch of cars that were cruising at seventy. "That's why I asked for you. I thought if I was going to have to accept a government team, then it might as well have someone on it I knew. Someone who could be trusted to be discreet. You were the first person I thought of."

Milton wasn't sure why Huxley was interested in his discretion, but since the conversation was already uncomfortable enough, he let it pass. "It's very flattering. That kind of thing, though—that's not me now. It hasn't been for years. I'm afraid you're going to find me boring these days."

"Bullshit," he said, pressing down on the gas a little more. "We'll still have a laugh. You haven't seen the island yet."

∽

THE BANK WAS on Cheval Place, a narrow one-lane side street not far from Harrods. It was easy to miss, marked only by the corporate logo—two crossed keys—that was displayed on a sign that was fixed above the door. Huxley parked the Ferrari with two wheels on the pavement and opened the door.

"I'll be five minutes," he said.

He got out and went into the building. Milton watched from inside the car and wondered what could be in the safe-deposit box that was so sensitive that Huxley had needed to divert here so urgently, and had trusted only Milton with its location. It couldn't be money.

There was a knock on the window. Milton turned; a traffic warden was wagging a finger at him.

Milton opened the door. "Sorry."

"You can't park here. Double yellows. You'll need to move it."

Milton looked to the ignition and saw that Huxley had taken the keys. He was about to apologise again when Huxley reappeared beside the car.

"My fault," he said to the traffic warden. "Very sorry."

He got back into the driver's seat and started the engine.

"Did you get what you needed?" Milton asked as they pulled away.

"Got it," Huxley said. "Let's get to the airport. We need to be getting on our way."

18

Farnborough Airport was just an hour out of London and was a key hub for private passengers who were looking for comfort and discretion away from the hullabaloo of Heathrow and Gatwick. The Ferrari passed through the gate. Huxley's private jet was waiting for them on the taxiway, and he was able to drive right up to it. The SUVs were already there, Thorsson leaning against one with his arms crossed. Milton looked through the windscreen as the car drew nearer. The jet that was waiting for them was a Boeing 767-33A, a passenger plane that would have been more usually seen in commercial use.

"There she is," Huxley said. "Bought it a year ago and had it refitted. They seat two hundred when the airlines fly them, but we configured it so that everyone has a little more space. It's nice—you'll see."

Huxley brought the car to a halt and got out. He was greeted by a man in a pilot's uniform.

"Good morning, sir," the man said.

"This is Captain Maidment," Huxley said, introducing the man to Milton. "He'll be flying us out."

"Hello, sir," the man said with a warm smile.

"Are we ready?" Huxley asked him. "All checked?"

"I've just finished my walk-around. We're good to go."

"Excellent. Flight time?"

"Ten hours," he said. "We should have a following wind most of the way, and that'll shave some time off. We'll be there early evening."

Huxley thanked him, turned to make sure that the luggage was being unloaded and then transferred to the hold, and then excused himself and went to talk to a woman whom Milton had seen from the house.

Thorsson and Anderson walked over to him.

"You couldn't get him to follow a simple instruction?" Anderson said. "Stay in the convoy?"

"I asked him. He chose not to."

"Maybe remind him that we can't protect him if he doesn't do what he's told."

"I did," Milton said.

"Do whatever you can to make him see sense," Thorsson said. "You only get out of this with a clean slate if we get him through the next few days in one piece. Control won't accept failure."

Huxley came back to them. "Ready to go?"

Milton nodded. "I wouldn't mind a tour of the jet before wheels up, though."

Huxley beamed with pleasure, like a child asked to give a demonstration of his favourite toy. "Follow me."

Huxley climbed the air steps with Milton following behind. A uniformed flight attendant—young and impossibly glamorous—was waiting at the door. She beamed a perfect smile and leaned over so that Huxley could kiss her on the cheek.

"This is Genevieve," Huxley said. "She makes sure everyone is comfortable on board."

"Good morning, Mr. Smith," she said.

Milton was impressed: Huxley hadn't introduced him, yet she knew his name. The passenger manifest must have been sent in advance, most likely with their photographs.

"I'm just going to give John the tour," he told her.

She stepped aside, still smiling, and Huxley moved past her and turned left. It was difficult to remember that they were aboard a jet instead of one of Huxley's palatial properties. The floor of the 767 was furnished with a deep carpet that featured a monogram of Huxley's initials at regular intervals. The foyer divided the master bedroom from the rest of the aircraft and featured a staircase that led up to the distinctive hump of the jet.

"This way," Huxley said. "We'll start with my suite."

The interior had been partitioned, with a corridor that ran along the left-hand side offering access to each particular zone. They started with the stateroom in the nose of the jet. There was a private bathroom, an antique wooden desk with a large monitor and computer, and a seventy-inch TV fixed to the wall. There was a two-person loveseat, and the windows—three on each side—could be obscured by blinds that slid down at the press of a button. The bedroom was equipped with a king-size bed, and the sidewalls had been fitted with mahogany counters with drawers beneath. The bathroom included a shower with multiple jets and a heated floor. All the lights in the suite were controlled by touchscreens that had been fitted around the rooms.

They returned to the foyer and climbed the stairs to a living room featuring mahogany panelling, another vast TV and bookcases sealed behind glass doors to keep the contents in place in the event of turbulence. The seats were all taken. There were young men and women, all tall and pretty enough to be catwalk models, and three older men in suits who looked very satisfied with the seating arrangements.

"Who are they?" Milton said.

Huxley nodded and lowered his voice. "The man with the beard is David Walters—he's big in the music business. The man next to him with the glasses is Jimmy Baldwin—he's a fixer in Whitehall. The man with the shades is Michael Rose—he was the prime minister of Canada ten years ago."

"And the others?"

"Friends," he said, with a wink.

"Tristan—seriously, please."

"You know what I'm like. They're coming out for the party."

"You said it was a business meeting."

"I know, it is, but they'll want to let their hair down, too. All work and no play, John—that's not how I do things. There's not much point in having all this if you can't have a blowout every now and again, is there?"

Milton didn't push it any further, but he felt a shiver of trepidation. He knew that he was not cured of his addiction, that it was lurking, waiting for the moment when he was vulnerable enough for it to strike. He had been tempted in Tokyo, staring at a whisky for hours until a kindly bartender recognised his plight and gave him the talking-to that he had needed. He doubted that he would find such a friendly ally here; he would most likely be facing a trial and was going to have to fight his demons by himself.

A door from the lounge led to the cockpit. It was open, and Milton could see through to the banks of instrumentation and controls; the pilots had been provided with deep bucket chairs that lay ready before the windscreen.

"Is the flight deck secure?" Milton said.

"Completely," Huxley said. He tapped his fingers against the door. "Once we're up, this stays shut and locked, just like on a commercial flight. No one gets in unless the pilot wants them in."

Milton looked at the door. He knew how it would work: anyone who wanted to go inside would tap the code on the keypad next to the door; that would then sound a buzzer inside the cockpit, and the pilot could then check the identity of whoever wanted to gain access by way of the CCTV camera mounted above the door.

"Satisfied?" Huxley asked.

"I am."

Huxley led the way back down the stairs and led Milton into a salon with seating for twenty people. The back half of the salon was furnished with a polished table that could accommodate ten diners. The decor featured polished oak panels, leather upholstery, and fittings and accents that looked to have been crafted from gold. The room was busy with passengers; the seats were all taken by the same combination of men in suits and much younger women. Milton noticed the self-satisfied, smug look—almost a leer—on Huxley's face but made no comment.

Huxley took him through the room to the office that was behind that, and then to the aft of the fuselage, which held the galley and accommodation for the staff.

"That's it," Huxley said as he led the way back to the foyer. "What do you think?"

"It looks secure," he reported.

"It *is*," Huxley said impatiently. "They check it inch by inch before it flies. I meant the redesign. Like it?"

Milton knew that Huxley was fishing for compliments again, and had to fight the temptation to tell him that he wasn't impressed by baubles and trinkets, no matter how many millions of pounds they must have cost. But there was no point in irritating him; Huxley was gauche and arrogant and a show-off, but Milton hadn't been employed to point that out to him. He was here to keep him from being killed. He would pamper his ego if it made it easier to get him to do as he was told.

"It's spectacular."

"I know it's an extravagance, but it's practical, too. Eight thousand nautical miles of range—I can get practically anywhere on it."

Milton made the appropriate response, but before Huxley could say anything else, Thorsson came over to join them. The big Icelander was scowling.

"Problem?" Milton asked.

"The flight's full," Thorsson said.

"I know," Huxley said. "So?"

"You've only given us two places—for me and him." He jerked a thumb at Milton. "There's no seat for Anderson."

"Sorry," he said with a shrug. "Someone must've made a mistake."

"So free up a seat for her."

He shook his head. "And leave one of the guests behind? I'm sorry—I can't do that. Everyone on the flight is important. The two of you can manage."

"This is foolish."

"Come on," he said. "You and Cronje's men will be *more* than enough. We're flying on a private jet to a private island. It couldn't be safer. I'm sorry there's been an oversight, but there's nothing I can do about it now. Maybe we could get her a ticket to fly commercial?"

Thorsson seethed. "You seem determined to make it as difficult as possible for us to keep you safe."

"That's not how it is at all."

Thorsson bit down on his lip as Milton put an arm around his shoulder and guided him deeper into the salon. "We *can* manage," he said quietly.

"That's not the point."

"I know it's not."

"Was he this difficult before?"

"Challenging," Milton said tactfully.

"Impossible."

The PA crackled, and the pilot announced that they would be taking off in fifteen minutes and that anyone not on the flight should deplane now.

"Let's just get on with it," Milton said.

Thorsson exhaled. "I'll send Six back to the house. She can keep an eye on it while we're off doing whatever it is he wants to do."

"Seats, everyone," Huxley called out. "I've got half a dozen magnums of excellent champagne on ice. Glasses for everyone as soon as we're up."

Milton closed his eyes and reminded himself of the Steps.

"Like I said," Thorsson said. "Impossible."

19

Rufus Lewsey parked his car in the strip of open space that sat in front of the line of lock-up garages. He had rented the garage two weeks ago, once he had made up his mind that he was going to have to take matters into his own hands.

He unlocked the door, rolled it up, stepped in and switched on the single bulb. He rolled the door down again, leaving it open a little at the bottom for ventilation. He took out his phone and navigated to the video that he had recorded. His preparation had all been online. He had found the video on a jihadist website that offered instructions on how to put together the device. It was funny, he thought; a year ago, he would have been petrified that his search history would have flagged him as someone the security services should be taking an interest in. But he was a white man, middle-aged and middle class, and about a million miles from the profile of the kind of searcher who would trigger interest. He felt comfortable that he could act with impunity. He supposed it was possible that his online activity might prompt a visit from the authorities, but by then, it would be too late.

He approached the workbench and got ready to start. Lewsey had experience with homemade explosive devices, but that had usually been to defuse them. He had been an Ammunition Technical Officer in the Royal Logistic Corps and had served several tours as a high-threat IEDD operator. He had commanded the secretive Alpha Troop, which provided close IEDD support to UK Special Forces, and later had done a tour as a staff officer in HQ Director, Special Forces.

He had been round the houses and knew his stuff. During his time in DSF he had been part of a secret military delegation to Israel, where they visited Hamas factories where TATP was made in huge quantities, often with predictably catastrophic results. He had been shown enough evidence on TATP-based suicide bombs to know exactly what effects might be expected. He had attended a HME familiarisation course where, ironically, students whose role was to render IEDs safe prepared samples of various explosives and fabricated explosive devices to demonstrate their effects. That had been on a very small scale.

Nothing like he was preparing now.

The man in the video was dressed in a balaclava and had a holstered pistol on his hip. He offered praise to Mohammed before pulling on a pair of surgical gloves and beginning his instruction with the list of ingredients that would be needed. Lewsey had hair bleach for the peroxide and nail varnish remover for the acetone. He had driven all over the southeast, visiting pharmacies and supermarkets and stockpiling the things that he would need. The man in the video referred to the explosive as 'white ice.' It was triacetone triperoxide, otherwise known as TATP, otherwise known as Mother of Satan on account of its instability and the times when slapdash jihadists had blown themselves up while they prepared it. Lewsey knew that the chemical compound was sensitive to friction, heat and pressure, and that it needed to be handled with the utmost respect. He didn't need reminding; he had visited a workshop in Basra where a militant had blown himself to pieces because he did not respect the chemicals with which he was working. That would not happen to Lewsey. He had found his purpose and was not about to be thwarted because he was negligent.

He looked at the putty-like material that he had prepared, prodded it with his finger and nodded in satisfaction. It was just right, just like the example in the video, and just as he remembered from his service. He had put the TATP in a large Tupperware container that had then been adapted so that he could insert the detonator. He would put the container into a paint tin that he would then fill with screws and bolts. He had bought a seventy-litre rucksack to carry the device and the additional shrapnel that he would drop around it.

He went to the workbench. The detonator was contained within an empty Fanta can, with a wire leading from it to the dead man's switch that he had built for the trigger. It wasn't connected to the explosive yet. He pushed the button to switch it on and closed his hand around the trigger, feeling the pressure from the spring as it tried to force his hand open. He opened his hand; the trigger sprang open, and the circuit was closed. The electrometer recorded the charge; Lewsey confirmed that there was more than enough to trigger the primary blast. The TATP would follow, and that would be that. The switch would allow him to choose the moment of detonation, but would also ensure the bomb went off in the event that he was incapacitated.

He put the detonator into the container, put that into the rucksack and then poured in the bags of screws and bolts. He zipped the bag up and, making doubly sure that the detonator was not active, carefully set the bag down against the wall. He pulled up the roller doors, turned off the lights, stepped outside and pulled the door down again, locking it behind him.

He was ready.

He just had to find the right opportunity.

20

Milton and Thorsson sat opposite one another in the salon. Everything about the plane was luxurious, including their seats: they were made from a rich leather that still had the smell of newness, and featured individual screens and acres of legroom. Milton looked at the six-foot-four Icelander and doubted that he had ever been as comfortable on a plane; Milton knew that *he* certainly hadn't. One of the attendants circulated with a bottle of champagne. Milton anticipated more pressure to take a drink, but to his surprise, the woman asked whether she could make him a virgin cocktail instead. Huxley had apparently listened to him and was, for once, being considerate. Milton thanked the woman and then thanked her again when she returned with a Mango Mule served in a copper mug with a slice of lime floating atop the ice.

Cronje and his men were in the salon, too. There were five of them, and Huxley had suggested that there were another five on the island, sent as an advance party to ensure that everything was as it should be. They all looked to be ex-military: athletically built and with the economy of movement that Milton remembered from his own service. One of them caught Milton looking over at them and held his gaze for a long moment, his lip curled in a sneer of disdain. Milton could understand it: the presence of outsiders suggested that somebody didn't think that Huxley's men were up to the job. It was a professional slight, and men like these—all of them clearly competent operators—would not be pleased by that. Milton didn't spare it much thought. He had no time for bruised egos and, he reflected, perhaps they might use it as motivation to go above and beyond.

Milton opened the moving map and saw that the pilot had already angled them to the southeast and settled them into a flight path that would take them across Europe, then over Turkey and the Middle East. The distance to their destination was shown as five thousand four hundred miles, and their flight time was estimated at ten hours. Milton was about to comment to Thorsson when he heard the heavy thump of bass from the upstairs cabin. The music was loud, and Milton feared that it would be impossible to avoid.

Thorsson rolled his eyes. "You've *got* to be kidding me."

Some of the younger passengers undid their belts and took their drinks to the upper deck.

Thorsson reached into the cupboard at the side of his chair and took out the noise-cancelling headphones that had been left there.

"I'll go and have a look," Milton said.

Thorsson nodded sourly, put the headphones over his ears and closed his eyes.

Milton went to the stairs and climbed up to the lounge. Huxley was at the top, watching the first stirrings of the party that looked sure to develop. The passengers were helping themselves to drinks from an evidently well-stocked drinks cabinet and taking turns to select tunes from the laptop that was connected to the sound system.

"We call it the Party Express," Huxley said, leaning closer and raising his voice so that he could be heard over the music.

"I can't think why."

Huxley grinned. "Don't worry—I know it's not your scene. There are headphones at each chair. They'll take the edge off. The chef will be round in an hour to take your order for dinner. Watch a movie or something."

A woman who couldn't have been much older than twenty arrived at Huxley's side and said something to him that Milton couldn't hear. Huxley turned to him, gave him a stagey wink, and let the girl take him by the hand and lead him over to the drinks. Milton watched them for a while longer: some of the passengers had started to dance, and one of the women—also young—was gyrating between the spread legs of one of the men in suits. Milton had been to parties like this, but not for many years; he caught himself looking past the men and women to the inviting ranks of bottles, temptingly lit from behind, and removed himself before temptation could get the better of him. The flight had promised to be pleasant, but now he could see that it would, indeed, be a trial. There would be nowhere to go if it all got to be too much; they would be thirty thousand feet up before too long. He remembered there were books in the library downstairs. He would try to find one that he hadn't read, order a meal and tough it out.

21

Nadia crossed London from east to west and then back again as she made sure that she wasn't being followed. She went to Selfridges and spent an hour going from section to section, looking at products that were unrelated in an attempt to uncover anyone who might have been watching her. She rode the Central Line all the way out to Wanstead, then crossed the platforms and came back again, changing onto the Circle Line at Liverpool Street and then the Northern Line at Monument. She observed carefully, but saw no repeats in her fellow passengers. She was confident that she was clean, but was still cautious as she took a cab to the safe house. She walked along Gray's Inn Road to the junction with Guilford Street and the iron bollard that sat on the edge of the pavement outside Peregrine's Pianos. A wad of chewing gum had been pressed onto the side of the bollard. Nadia allowed herself a sigh of relief. The chewing gum was the signal from Abbas that the safe house was secure. She walked down Guilford Street and turned off the pavement as she passed an estate agent's For Sale sign, going to the simple black door and pressing the button for the flat on the top floor.

The lock buzzed open, and Nadia wheeled her suitcase inside.

There was a flight of stairs at the end of the dusty hallway. She hauled the suitcase up to the first-floor landing, took a moment to catch her breath, then climbed to the second floor. She rapped her knuckles against the panel and listened for the sound of footsteps from inside. The door opened, and Abbas Kader was there, smiling at her and beckoning her inside.

"How are you, *jaanam*?" he asked, using the term of endearment that he had given her at the academy.

"I'm good."

"You were careful?"

"Very. I was out for five hours." She propped the suitcase against the wall next to Nawaz's. "When did he get here?"

"An hour ago," Abbas said, smiling at her like a proud father. "But he's never been as thorough as you."

Abbas had been responsible for their training, and Nadia had drawn close to him during the three years that they had spent with him at the academy. He was in his late forties, although he could easily have passed for younger, and had the physique of a man who ran ten miles a day and practised taekwondo with the cadets in the gym. She knew that he had taken a paternal shine to her, and had been thrilled that he would be supervising her first assignment. She knew that he was still active. There had been weeks during their training when he had not been there, and he had returned to the front of the class with his arm in a sling after one absence.

Abbas had told them that he was known to other agencies; that said, the decision had been made that the target was important enough that Abbas's experience and expertise were necessary and worth the risk of detection. He had travelled into the country as a diplomat three weeks earlier and worked at the High Commission. MI5 had the building at Lowndes Square under surveillance, but Abbas was a master at going black, and Nadia had no doubt that he would have made sure he was clean before coming here.

Abbas showed her through to the living room. Nawaz was sitting at the dining table, eating from a can of baked beans.

"Hey," he said.

She dropped down onto the sofa, the fatigue of travel—the flight and then the long criss-crossing of the city—finally catching up with her.

"Coffee?" Abbas said, not waiting for her response before flicking on the kettle.

"Yes, please."

She looked around the room and saw the canvas bags that she guessed must contain their equipment. She nodded to them. "Is everything as it should be?"

"It is," he said. "The quartermaster has done a good job—we have everything we need."

He spooned instant coffee into a mug, poured water inside and handed the mug to Nadia.

"Nawaz says immigration was fine?"

"It was easy."

"Good."

She sipped the coffee. It was strong, just as she liked. "Are the instructions unchanged?"

"They are. They'll be on the island later today. ROOSTER tells us that they will stay for one day and then return on Sunday. We'll need to be ready in advance of that."

Nadia nodded. ROOSTER was the cryptonym that had been assigned to the source who was providing them with intelligence.

"When do we start?" Nawaz asked.

"Tonight," Abbas said. "I don't see any reason to wait."

Nadia felt the buzz of nerves in her gut. She had no reason to doubt the plan, nor the intelligence that underpinned it. She knew that Abbas was experienced and that he had been involved in operations that were magnitudes more complicated and dangerous than this one was likely to be. The stories of his work were common currency at the academy: he had taken out an Indian counterpart who was causing trouble in Kashmir; he had posed as a journalist to foment unrest in Kathmandu by seeding a story that the Indian army had tortured people in the valley; he had worked in the Hindu Kush with senior members of the Taliban. This operation—a simple in-and-out with very little to do in between—should be child's play by comparison. And Nadia knew that it was an excellent opportunity for her and Nawaz to make their mark and demonstrate that their tutelage had been successful.

The nerves were to be expected. Abbas had told them to anticipate them, to welcome them, to use them to keep themselves sharp. That was what she would do.

She got up, went to the window and parted the curtain. She looked down on the pedestrians going about their business on the street below and allowed herself a moment's exhilaration. She was on a mission, in a foreign state, and the authorities had no idea. She, Abbas and Nawaz were ghosts; they would do their work and disappear, leaving no trace of their ever having been here.

22

The party continued for the duration of the flight. Milton occupied himself with two movies and then connected his phone to the headphones and listened to the new Brian Jonestown Massacre album. Refugees from upstairs stumbled down to the lower deck every now and again and resumed their seats, quickly succumbing to drunken slumber. After a while, Milton went back up and saw that the mania that had characterised the earlier part of the flight had been replaced—most likely through drunkenness and fatigue—with a more louche atmosphere. The music was more trippy chill-out than the high-energy thumpers that had preceded it, and the passengers were either slumped in their seats or laid out on the floor, empty glasses and bottles removed by the staff. Milton saw a large silver platter that held a small amount of white powder and a rolled-up fifty, and noticed a pill that had been crushed into the carpet. He couldn't see Huxley and asked the flight attendant where he was; she smiled sweetly and said he had gone to his bedroom to relax. Milton couldn't see the woman who had been attached to Huxley as the party started and decided that, in this case, there was no need to enquire as to what he might be doing.

Cronje climbed the stairs and stood next to Milton.

"Can Mr. Huxley count on your discretion?"

Milton turned to him. "Excuse me?"

"Discretion," the South African said. "You know that'll be part of the job?"

"I'm not here to judge. I'm here to keep him safe."

"It's an overreaction."

"What is?"

"You being here. We don't need you."

"Let's hope not."

Cronje gave a little snort of disdain and picked up a bottle of beer from an ice bucket. Milton returned to his seat and looked out of the window as the pilot began the descent into Colombo.

Thorsson, who had been asleep for most of the flight, removed his eye mask. "Where are we?"

"Final approach."

"Have you checked on our friend?"

"A couple of times."

"And?"

"And I realise I feel old."

The jet dropped down through a band of cloud, and then Sri Lanka was visible beneath them. Ratmalana Airport was on the coast, with the Laccadive Sea to their right. Sri Lanka was one of the few countries in the world that he had never visited, and although he suspected that he was going to be busy for the duration of their short stay, he found that he was anticipating the opportunity to experience it. The pilot told the passengers and crew to prepare for landing; Milton clipped his belt around him and watched as the buildings of the city grew larger, swarms of vehicles buzzing between them. It was late in the day, yet the sun was still strong, and, as they dropped lower and lower, the fast-moving shadow of the jet was painted over the slums and shanties that surrounded the airport.

23

Milton made sure that he was first out of the door and descended the airstair. The heat was ferocious, and he regretted not bringing a pair of dark glasses to shield his eyes from the glare. The jet had taxied to a private part of the airfield, and a fleet of identical SUVs were waiting for them. The ground crew were already unloading the luggage that had been stowed in the hold, transferring it to a dusty flatbed truck. Milton looked for threats and, seeing none, turned back to signal to Thorsson that it was safe for the passengers to disembark. They did, some of them sluggishly, all of them blinking in the sudden brightness. Huxley emerged last of all, his eyes covered by a large pair of dark glasses; he was dressed in a clean white T-shirt and cargo pants and a pair of Converse high-tops. He saw Milton and diverted from the clutch of passengers gathered around the cars.

"You okay?"

"I'm good. How are you?"

"A little fragile," he said with a reedy chuckle.

He was a little unsteady on his feet, and Milton could see

flecks of red in his nostrils; it looked as if he might have had a nosebleed at some point during the flight. Milton thought of the powder that he had seen and didn't need to ask any more.

"Did you enjoy the flight?" Huxley asked.

"I watched a couple of movies."

"And the staff looked after you?"

"Very well."

He gestured to the SUV at the front of the line. "Want to ride with me?"

Milton said that he did. He told Thorsson—who said that he would take a place in a car at the end of the convoy—and went to join Huxley. There was a woman with him now, and the three of them got into the back of the car.

"This is Claudette," Huxley said as Milton sat down.

Milton assessed her quickly: young, blonde, perfect skin and teeth, her eyes a little out of focus and the smell of alcohol on her. "Hello," he said.

Before Milton could do anything to stop her, she had risen from her seat and deposited herself in his lap. "Hello," she said, her voice a little slurred.

Milton put his hand against the small of her back and gently pushed her to her feet. "Up you get."

She turned back, confusion and irritation on her face. "What?"

"Probably best if we have a seat each."

She crossed the cabin again and slumped back down into her seat. Milton noticed as she looked across at Huxley, perplexed. Huxley smiled back at her, turned to Milton and gave him a shrug and a wink. Milton was left with the impression that Huxley had told the girl to flirt with him and was tempted to tell him that he didn't appreciate it, but before he could find the right words, the SUV pulled away, and he let it go.

"The island's a hundred miles to the south," Huxley said as they rolled through the gate. "Traffic might be an issue on the way—it's Esala Perahera. Their biggest festival—something to do with Buddha's sacred tooth. It's mostly in Kandy, but they celebrate it everywhere. There are processions and street parties. Might add a bit to the drive."

Milton sat back. Claudette drew her knees up to her chest, rested her head against the window and closed her eyes; she was snoring lightly after five minutes. Huxley stared out of the window, apparently lost in thought. Milton watched, too, as they drove through the outskirts of the city. The streets had been decorated with paper streamers and posters of extravagantly costumed elephants and dancers bedecked with peacock feathers. They drove on. Huxley drifted off to sleep, too, but Milton stayed awake. He had expected the city to give way to the countryside, but it never happened. Colombo was larger than he had expected, a metropolitan area that had seemingly expanded and absorbed the towns that had once been in its orbit. The traffic was thick all the way, but they were never stationary for long and reached their destination after two and a half hours.

The cars pulled up one after another near to a small harbour. Huxley was awake and, leaving Claudette in the car, stepped outside and joined Milton as he gazed out to sea.

"How far is it?" Milton asked him.

"Twenty minutes," he said.

Fishermen lolled on the nearby rocks, smoking cigarettes and drinking beer as they watched others hauling their skiffs out and dragging them up the sand. Children gambolled in the surf, dashing into the waves and allowing themselves to be swept off their feet. A nearby stall, not much more than a dirty canvas stretched over a bamboo frame, offered freshly caught mahi-mahi.

A wooden jetty reached out into the surf, and, at the end, a tender had been tied up. "Come on," Huxley said, pointing to the tender. "That's us. It'll take three or four crossings to get everyone over. We'll get the first boat."

He walked onto the jetty and spoke to a man who hopped off the boat. He had a captain's cap on his head and was dressed in white, his uniform perfectly clean save for patches where sweat had leached through the cotton. Huxley finished his conversation, put his fingers to his lips and whistled. The passengers, all now disembarked from the SUVs, stopped talking to listen.

"We can take fifteen across at a time," he called out. "There's another tender on the way."

They formed into a rough and unruly line as Huxley and then Milton stepped across to the tender. It was a beautiful vessel, with a strip-planked yellow cedar hull, a varnished teak deck and chrome fittings that looked as if they might have been taken directly from the nineteen thirties. There was a bathroom and a galley with copper fittings. It had obviously been custom made and, again, Milton found himself wondering how much such a thing must cost.

The captain welcomed the others on board and, once they were full, he cast off. The twin engines purred into life as he angled them away from the coast and out to sea.

24

The island appeared on the horizon after ten minutes.

"That's Katchatheevu," Huxley said, pointing.

The island was rocky, with lush vegetation and a villa that was as white as ivory, the structure standing out in stark contrast to the browns and greens of the ebony and teak and the vegetation that thronged between them. The tender drew closer, and Milton saw more detail: the buildings, a wooden landing stage, a man in uniform waiting at the end of it with a tray of drinks set down on the small table beside him.

"The buildings were built by a Frenchman in the twenties," Huxley said. "He said he was an aristocrat, but most people thought he was a con artist. It's been passed around a lot since then—writers, movie people, anyone who wants a little bit of paradise. I bought it from a man who owns a rubber plantation inland. He was having money problems—I got it for a song."

They reached the jetty, and the captain tied up. A short gangplank was extended, and Huxley disembarked first with

Milton following behind. The member of staff bowed deeply before offering them both fluffy white face towels that were monogrammed with Huxley's initials. The towel was chilled and felt refreshing against the hot skin of his face.

"Good evening, sir," he said. "How was your trip?"

"Long," Huxley said.

Huxley and Milton followed the man along a path that led deeper into the interior of the island. Behind him, Milton could hear the rest of the passengers disembarking.

"Two hundred acres," Huxley said. "The big house is on the north side of the island, with the guest accommodation in the lagoon. You'll see."

The paths were lined on either side by deep clusters of frangipani and scattered with blossoms that had drifted down from the bushes and trees overhead. Gulls and crows wheeled above the top of the flame trees, their calls competing with the crashing waves. It was hot and humid, the air heavy with the smell of salt and fruit and blossom.

They reached an air-conditioned waiting area, where another uniformed member of staff appeared.

"Mr. Smith," he said, "welcome to Katchatheevu."

Milton saw the man's name—Avyukt—on an embossed badge that he wore on his lapel. Milton thanked him and then stepped out of the way so that the rest of the guests could be welcomed. A team of bellboys removed the luggage, loaded it into golden luggage cages and pushed it in the direction of the big house. Once the tender was empty, the skipper turned the boat around and raced back to the mainland.

Avyukt consulted quietly with Huxley, and then, a decision evidently made, he pressed his palms together and bowed again. "Please," he said to them. "You have had a long flight, and you must be thirsty. The staff will take your luggage to your rooms. You must come for a cold drink first, and then we will show you where you are staying. This way, please."

Milton fell into step as Avyukt led the way to a thatched building that was open to the air on all sides. Luxurious furniture was arranged beneath the roof, and a waitress, similarly attired in the white outfit that was clearly the uniform of those who worked on the island, offered flutes of champagne on a silver salver.

"This is a bottle of a rather nice Krug," Huxley said as he supervised the distribution of the flutes. "We have an extensive cellar on the island. I believe this was bought at auction last year."

The woman offered the tray to Milton, but he smiled and put up his hand to say no.

"Coconut juice," Huxley said to Avyukt. "Send one of the lads up the tree and get a fresh one down."

Avyukt nodded, excused himself and went over to a telephone that had been discreetly hidden next to one of the chairs. As he spoke into the device, Milton noticed a young woman in a bikini approaching from another path that led away from the welcome hut. She was tall and slender, and her tanned skin ran with rivulets of water from a pool or the sea. He was a dreadful judge of age, but he would have been surprised if she was older than twenty. She aimed directly for Huxley, and, without acknowledging Milton and Thorsson or any of the other guests, she put her arms around his neck and kissed him.

"This is Grace," Huxley said.

The woman turned to Milton and smiled. She was beautiful, with flawless skin and strawberry blonde hair that reached down to below her shoulders, but as she turned to smile at Thorsson, Milton noticed a glassy quality to her eyes. She was a little unsteady on her feet.

"What do you do out here?" Milton asked her.

She looked at him as if that was the stupidest question she had ever been asked. "Um—*party*?"

"Grace wants to work in conservation," Huxley explained when it was evident that she wasn't going to add anything else. "I have a foundation—we offer experience to young people who wouldn't be able to afford it otherwise. There's a group here for a bit of rest and relaxation before they go out to the jungle. The Sri Lankan wildlife here is incredible—leopards, elephants, pangolins and lorises, whales just out to sea. They're going out to the Madulkelle Tea Estate in the Highlands in the middle of the island. Trip of a lifetime."

Grace turned away from Thorsson and Milton and focussed her attention on Huxley again. "Come down to the pool?"

"I will," he said. "Just let me get settled in. We've just arrived."

Milton watched the interaction. There was no awkwardness on Huxley's part at this young woman, at least twenty years his junior, flirting with him so openly and with no apparent concern about what Milton or Thorsson or anyone else might think. He saw that Avyukt had scrupulously occupied himself with the other guests, but noticed that he glanced over at her with an inscrutable expression as she took her leave.

"We'll be here for a couple of days," Huxley said. "The Russians should be arriving tomorrow, and there'll be a party in their honour in the evening."

Milton looked at his watch. It was nine. "What about the rest of today?"

"I need to make some calls," Huxley said. "I'm not going anywhere, and the island is about as secure as it can be. Why don't the two of you take the rest of the day off? I'll be too busy to eat with you this evening, but you can call the chef, and he'll make whatever you want. He's good, too—I poached him from Hélène Darroze. Or Avyukt could arrange a boat to take you out into the ocean if you'd like to go down onto the reef and watch the sunset. Or the snorkelling just off the beach is pretty spectacular. Or you could just hang out by the pool and get drunk." He looked at Milton and theatrically rapped his own wrist. "Or not."

Milton stood. "I wouldn't mind a shower, and then I'd like to have a look around the island."

"Me too," Thorsson said.

Huxley shook his head. "Still not sure about how safe we are?"

"Better to be sure," Milton said.

Huxley was about to say something, but perhaps noticing Milton's resolution, he raised his hands in mock surrender. "Fine, fine. I can't force you to take it easy. Freshen up, have a look around the island and then relax."

25

A man in house uniform—the TH proudly stitched on his lapel—took Milton to a villa that had been built on stilts so that it sat over the ocean on the southern side of the island. It was reached by way of a horseshoe-shaped wooden pontoon that offered access to the trio of identical villas that were arranged at various points along the arc of the jetty. Each villa was constructed from rough-hewn timber and thatched with pandanus leaf.

"I'll be your butler, sir," the man said.

"I really don't need a butler."

The man ignored that. "My name is Kiyansh. If you need me, just call. There are phones inside. Just dial one and you'll be connected to me right away."

It seemed churlish to protest when the man so clearly took such pride in his job. "Thank you. I will."

"When you've had a chance to think about what you'd like for breakfast, just fill out the form and leave it outside the door. I'd recommend the fruit. I can set up a table on the terrace overlooking the lagoon. It's a lovely way to start the day."

Milton went inside and couldn't help but gape out of the wide picture window. The Indian Ocean reached all the way to the horizon, a cerulean blue that was almost unreal in its intensity. The sky was blue, too, and the colours matched so perfectly it was difficult to see where one ended and the other began. He looked down and saw that he was standing on a sheet of glass that offered a view to a technicolour maelstrom of fish: triggerfish, clownfish, parrotfish and a single baby green turtle. There was an infinity pool outside, a slide that curled down from the storey above, and a hammock. The room itself was furnished with pieces that looked to have been crafted from driftwood, the rustic charm only partially dispelled by one of the largest TVs that Milton had ever seen. Lofty wood-beam ceilings and exotic wooden panelling with fresh accents lent the villa an airy lightness. Milton climbed the stairs to the floor above and confirmed what he had suspected from outside: the place was large, perhaps twice as big as his old studio apartment back home in Chelsea. The hammered-copper bathroom was up here, with a sculpted tub that looked out over the lagoon. The balcony came with bamboo-offcut railings that had been twisted into skeletal patterns.

Milton undressed and went onto the deck and the outdoor shower. Privacy was maintained by way of screens of rattan and reed, together with the angle of the deck and the fact that the next villa was a fair distance along the pontoon. Milton opened the tap and stood under the cold water, scrubbing it into his hair and stubble and waiting beneath the flow until his skin tingled. The aspect off the terrace was open, and the shower offered a view out over the sea. Milton could see nothing else between him and the distant horizon.

He closed his eyes as the water ran off his head, down

his neck and shoulders and over the winged angel that was tattooed across his back. He realised that he had become a little too comfortable in the arrangement with Control, and was perturbed with how easy it had been to slip back into the business of the Group. Years had passed between his last official job in the French Alps and this unsatisfactory arrangement, but it felt as if no time had passed at all. The feeling of being sent out from London, with limited recourse to the resources of the other groups that comprised the Firm, was as familiar as putting on an old and comfortable pair of shoes. He knew he had to ward against becoming too at ease. It would be a simple thing to complete this job and then accept another. It would have been pushing things to say that he had found happiness during his wandering, but he might have been prepared to go so far as to say he was content. He had found a way to make up for the things that he had done; he would never be able to balance the ledger completely, but at least the path he had chosen allowed him to sleep at night, and helped him to stay away from the bottle. Working for the Group again—even if only in a limited capacity—was a sure and swift way back to the depths from which he had worked so hard to escape. He would return to being a nomad and hope that he might be forgotten.

He switched off the shower and walked out to the pool. He lowered himself into the water, warmed by the sun, and floated out to the edge. This, too, was private and not overlooked; it was just him and the baby black-tipped sharks that darted to and fro in the shallows of the lagoon. He thought of Thorsson, in the villa along from his, and reminded himself that the Icelander was not to be trusted. He was a Group man, not yet jaded enough to see the malignant truth that lurked behind the fine talk of queen and country and duty and national security and whatever convenient euphemisms Control used to help her agents justify the murder they did in her name. Thorsson had tried to kill him in Kansas City, and Milton knew that he would not hesitate to pull the trigger again the moment Control gave the order. She had been persuasive when she had told Milton that he could win a clean slate by keeping Huxley alive; it might have been enough to persuade someone less jaded than him, but he had the experience of listening to the lies of her predecessor and was in little doubt that she would prefer a full stop to his career over the prospect of him vanishing into the wind again.

He had had no choice but to say yes to her offer when she had him in a cell; now, though, he had to think of a way that would allow him to make his exit in one piece.

Milton climbed out of the pool and dried himself off. He went through the bedroom and opened the wardrobe. He was impressed to find that it was full of clothes that would fit him. There were pairs of neatly pressed shorts, loose shirts and several pairs of sandals and flip-flops. He dressed in cargo shorts and a light cotton shirt, put on a pair of sunglasses and went outside, walking across the hot wooden boards to the pontoon.

Thorsson was just emerging from his own villa.

"I'm going to walk the island," Milton said.

"I was about to do the same."

26

Milton and Thorsson walked around the island. A well-kept gravel path had been cut through the jungle that would otherwise have pushed right up to the beach, allowing them to keep the sea to their right as they walked counterclockwise from their villas. They saw another pontoon with a collection of villas that, if anything, were even grander than their own. The villa in the centre of the trio looked to be occupied, with two large men standing outside the front door.

"Security?" Thorsson said.

"That's what I would have thought," Milton replied.

"Huxley's? They weren't on the jet."

"He had an advance party," Milton said.

Thorsson shook his head. "They look different than the others."

They continued, passing the cottages where Cronje's men were accommodated and then the thatched welcome area. They followed the sound of music until they reached the big house at the centre of the island. The villa was large, with verandas instead of outer walls so that it was possible to look right inside. The wood was painted in the most pristine white, almost shocking against the green and blue backdrop of jungle and sea. The octagonal centre room, visible as they approached, featured a vaulted ceiling that must have been twenty-five feet tall in the centre, with various bedrooms and sitting rooms leading off it like the spokes of a wheel. There were a series of *palapas*—open, thatched structures that reminded Milton of the cabanas he had seen in Osaka—around the pool. The furniture was made from teak and bamboo, with other pieces made from leather, rattan, rosewood and mahogany. A swarm of jellyfish chandeliers swam overhead, repurposed woven fishing baskets served as lamps, and a flyaway octopus made from discarded fishing line was suspended above the bar. Before the house, though, was what must have been the island's main pool. It had been artfully carved from the native rock so that it blended in almost seamlessly. There were perhaps a dozen people gathered around the crystal clear water: Milton saw a collection of men and women, the latter all topless. There was a tiki bar that the guests seemed at liberty to use, and a slide twisted down from a raised platform and deposited a shrieking woman into the deep end.

"You see Huxley?" Thorsson asked.

"No."

They continued on, reaching the kitchen and staff accommodation. The facilities for the guests were found close to the beach, with the buildings and equipment needed to ensure the smooth running of the island found in the interior, where they wouldn't spoil the ambience. The island reminded Milton of a very well-run hotel. The guests could abandon themselves to hedonism while the staff made sure everything was as it should be, labouring discreetly out of sight.

"What do you think?" Thorsson said.

"The security looks acceptable," Milton said. "He's too close to the mainland to be completely comfortable, but I can't see anyone getting over here without someone raising the alarm."

They walked around to the jetty. Thorsson was quiet, but Milton got the impression that there was something that he wanted to say. They walked to the end of the wooden pier and stopped, looking out onto the gentle waves of the lagoon and the open ocean beyond.

Thorsson rested his elbows on the balustrade. "What's he like?"

"Huxley? You've read the file."

"But you know him."

"I *did*," Milton corrected. "A little. But that was a long time ago. Why?"

Thorsson paused, as if ready to say whatever it was that was on his mind, but then shook his head. "I don't know—there's something about him that rubs me the wrong way."

"He's a show-off," Milton said.

"It's not just that." He stopped again, but before he could go further, something on the horizon gave him a chance to change the subject. "Look."

A boat was cutting quickly across the gentle surf, the buzz of its engine deepening as it drew closer. They watched as the vessel aimed toward the jetty, close enough now that they could recognise it as the tender that had brought them to the island earlier that day. They retreated, leaving the jetty and taking up a position on the path where they could watch the new arrivals without being obtrusive. Huxley arrived on the jetty with Avyukt, the man who had greeted them when they had arrived, his voice loud enough that Milton could hear his terse instructions.

"Is it all ready?" he said.

"It is," Avyukt replied.

"*Everything* is ready? The villa?"

"Yes, sir. I checked myself."

The rest of the conversation was drowned out by the twin engines of the tender as it slowed down to approach the jetty. The skipper tossed over the line, Avyukt knotted it around a mooring post, and the tender bumped up against the fender. The new arrivals began to clamber up, and Milton could hear the sound of laughter as it drifted across the water. The two large men they had seen at the villa arrived on the jetty now, standing at a respectful distance yet close enough should they be needed. They shared a brief word and then stood quietly.

"Did you hear that?" Thorsson said.

"Russian?"

"Definitely."

Avyukt bowed deeply as the first guest put his feet on the wooden planks. The man was dressed in chino shorts and a blue cotton shirt. He carried tasselled loafers in his hands and wore dark glasses.

"You recognise him?" Milton said.

He could tell from Thorsson's expression that he did. "Nikolay Timofeyevich."

Huxley embraced the newcomer, each man clapping the other on the back.

"I'm a little out of the loop," Milton said. "Should I know him?"

"Probably," Thorsson said. "He's the Russian foreign minister."

27

Milton heard the music from his villa: a steady thump of bass, metronomic and loud enough to be audible all across the island. He had ordered *polos*—green jackfruit curry—at the recommendation of his butler, and now he laid his knife and fork on the plate and stood. He went to the door, opened it and went out onto the pontoon. Kiyansh appeared as if he had been waiting for him.

"Will you be going to the party, sir?"

"It's not really my scene," Milton said.

"I hope it's not too loud."

"I'm sure it'll be fine. Does Mr. Huxley have parties here a lot?"

Kiyansh paused, and Milton could see he was debating his answer. "Quite often, yes. He likes to entertain his guests."

"How often does he come out here?"

"Oh, very often. Once a month, perhaps."

"What happens on the island when he isn't here?"

"The staff look after everything for him. He likes everything to be just so." He smiled shyly, as if worried that he had said too much, and changed the subject. "How was your curry?"

"Delicious," Milton said. "Excellent recommendation."

"Can I get you anything else?"

"No, thanks," he said. "I'm going to go and have a look at the party. It's near the villa?"

"That's right. At the pool."

Milton thanked him and set off.

∼

THERE WERE ALREADY thirty or forty guests around the pool, and as Milton took a seat at a table where he could observe without drawing attention to himself, more arrived. There were more than had been brought over on Huxley's jet, young men and women who must have been offered accommodation in the interior of the island away from the glitzier villas that were seemingly reserved for more important guests. They looked to be in their late teens and early twenties, and they arrived in their bikinis and swim shorts, going to the bar and then taking bottles of wine and spirits to the loungers that were arranged around the water. The DJ ran through a playlist that was unfamiliar to Milton: bhangra and ambient, Latin and afro, baile funk and Balearic beats. The volume was gradually increased until Milton could see the vibrations in the glass of water that had been brought to him by a waiter.

Thorsson appeared on the other side of the pool, noticed Milton and acknowledged him with a nod. Other guests appeared: older, mostly male, dressed in shorts and shirts that were more sober than the clothes—or lack thereof—of those who had arrived first. The crowd grew more boisterous as the drink continued to flow, seemingly provided on a limitless basis. Milton saw drugs, too: pills passed around in plain sight, powders snorted from tables and platters without fear of consequence. He watched and felt the flickering of his appetite; the old compulsions were still there, dulled but not extinguished, ready to whisper into his ear that one drink wouldn't hurt, that he could have just the one to take the edge off, and then he could stop. He hadn't been to a meeting for weeks and regretted it; remembering the experiences of others would have provided him with the armour to blunt his cravings.

Huxley appeared from out of the large white villa, a younger woman on each arm. He paused at the steps down to the pool and surveyed the scene with a broad grin on his face. He said something to the women and stood back to watch as they peeled off their bikini tops and leapt into the water. Others whooped their encouragement and followed their example; in moments, the pool was busy with half-naked revellers, and Huxley was beaming his approval.

Huxley saw Milton and raised a hand in greeting. Milton returned the gesture awkwardly and, before Huxley could come over to him, decided that a moment away from the party would be wise. He caught Thorsson's eye and signalled that he was going to walk the island, then got up and strode away. He followed the path back to the overwater villas, intent on clearing his mind before he returned to keep an eye on the proceedings.

There was no escaping the music, but at least he was on his own and away from temptation. He went by his villa and kept going, making his way around the path in an anticlockwise direction. He reached the villa where he and Thorsson had seen the security and slowed his pace. The guards were gone—or at least more discreet than before—and the windows were obscured so that Milton could not see inside. He was about to walk on when he noticed two women approaching along the path from the direction Milton had just come. He recognised one of them as Claudette, the girl who had tried to sit in his lap in the car from the airport to the harbour. Milton stepped off the path and watched from behind the trunk of a palm tree as Claudette led the way to the door and knocked on it.

The girl whom Milton had not seen before looked anxious. Milton was close enough to hear her.

"What do we do?" she asked.

Claudette shrugged. "Whatever he wants."

The front door opened. The man Thorsson had identified as Timofeyevich stood inside the threshold, leered hungrily at the girls, and stepped to the side to let them in. They went through, and the Russian shut the door.

Milton stayed where he was for a moment and wondered about what he had just seen. The transaction—for that was what it clearly was—appeared obvious: Huxley had sent the girls to entertain his important guest. Claudette's behaviour in the back of the car made better sense to Milton now: she had assumed that, as Huxley's guest, she would be required to seduce him.

The arrangement was troublesome and made Milton uneasy. He waited in the gloom behind the tree for a moment longer, and, once it was obvious that Timofeyevich and the two women would not be coming out, he continued on his way, back to the pool and the din of the party.

28

Abbas drove them to the house and parked a little way down the road from it. It was on a quiet residential street in the kind of neighbourhood where interlopers would be noticed, especially when they had brown skin. They wouldn't be outside for long. The house was mock Tudor, with white render and black beams on the walls. It had a quaint porch with a decorative wooden design at the edge of the roof, and a maple tree spread out its boughs over the otherwise concreted-over front garden. Nadia had downloaded the brochure from the last time the house had changed hands, and had noted that the purchase price had been a little over one and a half million pounds. Thames Ditton was a prime location, close to London in one direction and the countryside in the other, and the amount of money it took to live here reflected that. They already knew the family was wealthy, and their house—together with the BMW parked on the driveway—confirmed it.

Nadia saw a light go on in one of the upstairs windows of the house across the street before the curtains were closed.

She looked at the numerals that glowed out from the clock in the dash: two thirty.

"Ready?" Abbas asked them.

"Ready," Nawaz said.

Nadia nodded. "And me."

"Good," Abbas said. "Let's go."

PART IV

SATURDAY

29

The plan was for them to be in the house all day, and they didn't want to risk an unfamiliar car drawing unwanted attention to them before they were ready to leave. Nadia reached into her jacket and took out the Glock 43 that she had specified in her kit bag; it was a slim, light handgun that fitted into her palm comfortably, and she had shown herself to be very good with it out on the range. She checked it now, ensuring that it was ready to fire in the unlikely event that proved to be necessary. The profile of the woman inside the property suggested that she would be compliant, but there was no way of ever being sure about how a person would react to an event like this, and they needed to cover all outcomes.

They were ten houses down the road from number twenty-eight, and Nadia saw lights in only two windows as they walked along the pavement. There was no traffic and no pedestrians, and the only other signs of activity were the blinking red and white lights of a passenger jet passing high overhead.

They reached the house, and Nadia checked up and

down the street once more. Satisfied that they had not attracted attention, she turned off the pavement and walked up to the gate to the rear garden. She reached through the hole that had been cut in the board and opened the latch. She pushed the gate back and went inside. Abbas and Nawaz followed, Nawaz quietly closing the gate behind them.

Nadia paused to assess the way ahead. The garden was reasonably large for a suburban property, with a stretch of well-tended lawn running down to an oak tree that sheltered a garden office beneath its boughs. Nadia stayed close to the building as she made her way to the rear extension; there was a door there that opened onto the utility room, and she very carefully tried the handle. It was locked. She checked for wiring strips that might indicate an alarm and, seeing none, took out a set of picks. She crouched down and methodically set to work, sliding the pins into place and then trying the handle again; this time, the door opened. She pulled it back and stepped inside, waiting in the room beyond as Abbas and Nawaz came inside, too.

"Look for PIRs," Abbas whispered, pointing up to the corner of the ceiling where a passive infrared sensor might have been installed. There were none in here, but Nawaz nodded his understanding and stepped back so that Nadia could get to the door. The floor plan they had been given suggested that the kitchen was next to the utility room, and it proved to be correct. Nadia opened the door a little, looking for any sign of a sensor, and then, seeing none, opened it a little more. She looked up and around the door, but there were still none that she could see.

Nadia crossed the kitchen and opened the door that led to the hallway. There was a downstairs WC to her right, and the stairs that led up to the first floor were on her left. She waited for Abbas to nod his approval and then started up them, walking on the outside of each tread so as to minimise the risk of making an unwanted noise that might give her presence away. She reached the landing and waited for the others to catch her up. The stairs led up to the two bedrooms on the second floor. There were four more bedrooms on the first floor and, from the colourful poster on one of the doors, it was easy to work out which one belonged to the child. Abbas pointed to Nawaz and then to the child's door and waited as he crept across the hallway to stand outside it.

Abbas signalled that she should move. Nadia crept across to the door opposite the one with the poster and very gently rested her fingers against it, pushing it back just enough for her to look inside. It was gloomy, with a little illumination filtering through the thin curtains from the streetlamp outside. She took a step inside, and then another, until she was close enough to see the shape of the woman in the bed. She was turned away from Nadia, facing the window, and, as Nadia took another step and then another, she could hear the sound of her breathing. Nadia quickly looked around the room: she saw a framed photograph of the woman and her husband at their wedding and another photograph of the husband in his uniform. There was a clay pot that the child must have decorated, red and yellow splotches shining with the glaze.

Abbas waited in the doorway, his pistol in his hand. He nodded that Nadia should proceed. She held the Glock in a loose grip, stepped right up to the bed and reached down to rest a hand on the woman's shoulder. She shook her gently until she mumbled in her sleep, then shook her again until she rolled over and opened her eyes.

The woman started to scream, but Nadia reached down

and muffled the noise with her left hand as she pressed the muzzle of the pistol against her forehead with her right.

"No noise, please," she said, her voice firm and even.

The woman's eyes bulged as she looked up from the bed and saw Abbas.

"We don't want to hurt you, Elizabeth," Nadia said. "You or Nathaniel."

The mention of the boy's name caused her eyes to bulge even more.

Nadia held her hand in place and shook her head. "No screaming. Do exactly as I say and you have my word that you'll both be fine. Nod if you understand."

Fear swam in the woman's eyes, but she managed a jerky nod of her head.

"Good," Nadia said. "Now—if I take my hand away, are you going to be quiet?"

She nodded again.

Nadia withdrew her hand. The woman lay frozen in the bed, staring up at her, tears gathering in the corners of her eyes. Nadia had studied her file and had given consideration to how she might react to the ordeal she was about to be subjected to. Her name was Elizabeth, and she had worked as a legal secretary before putting her career on hold following the birth of her son. Her life revolved around the boy; she was with him more or less constantly, apart from when he went to day care, when she would go to the local gym or meet other mothers for coffee and cake in one of the several cafés near to the house. Nadia's assessment was that she would be terrified in the first few minutes, but that, as she realised that she and her son were not in immediate danger, she would find her balance. It would be so much easier if she cooperated.

"What do you want?" she said quietly. "Money? I don't have any in the house."

"Not money," Nadia said. "We just need to be with you today—that's all."

"Please—leave my son alone."

"We will. My partner is outside his room now. We don't want to frighten him. You can wake him up at the usual time and then, provided you do as we say, the day need not be all that different from normal."

"I don't understand. If you don't want money, what do you want?"

"We need your husband to do something for us," she said. "I'm going to need you to make a telephone call to him in a little while. I'll tell you exactly what to say. If you do that, and if he does what we tell him to do, I promise nothing will happen to either of you."

30

Milton was woken by the gentle murmuring of the lagoon washing against the struts of the villa. He reached over to the bedside table and fumbled for the clock, bringing it closer to his face so he could squint at the display: it was six in the morning. His eyes ached, and his muscles throbbed with fatigue. He lay back and tried to remember what time he had finally managed to get into bed earlier that morning. He had watched from the perimeter of the party until four a.m., when Huxley had finally gone to bed. The others had shown no inclination to bring proceedings to an end, and Milton had drifted away to sleep with the thump of the bass still audible from the other side of the island.

He rolled out of bed and, instead of showering, went out onto the terrace and climbed down the steps into the warm water of the lagoon. He drifted in the water for ten minutes, watching the fish darting left and right all around him, a pair of rays sliding just beneath the surface. Milton submerged himself and scrubbed the water through his scalp and into his whiskers. He found his thoughts turning back to the party. He was uncomfortable with a lot of what he had witnessed last night, but didn't know what he should do about it. The younger men and women seemed to be having fun, but there was something about some of them that made him uneasy. It was the way that they outnumbered the older guests, as if they had been ferried to the island for entertainment, and the lasciviousness with which they had been regarded. It felt as if they were part of the entertainment rather than being there to enjoy themselves on their own accounts.

He exhaled, but couldn't dismiss the unease. There was something about the island and the party that bothered him, a darkness behind the bacchanalia that he knew would gnaw at him if he thought about it for too long. It wasn't his way to turn the other cheek—especially not recently—but the lines were blurred enough for him to be unsure of himself and his loyalty to Huxley.

He swam back to the steps, climbed out of the lagoon and washed off the salt with a cold shower. Huxley had said that they would be returning to London at some point today. It seemed incredibly extravagant to travel all this way for a night and part of a day. How much would it have cost just to fuel the 767? How much would it cost to run the island? Did it matter? Huxley was on a different level now, one where questions like that were mundane and boring and irrelevant.

Milton looked out over the perfect blue and decided that, although this was paradise, he would be happy to put it behind him.

31

Nadia had watched the mother and child for the first three hours, and now Nawaz had taken over. Nadia went downstairs to the kitchen. Abbas had boiled the kettle and had found two mugs, a jar of coffee and a bag of sugar.

"Everything okay?" he asked.

"They're frightened."

"That's to be expected. Coffee?"

"Please."

He prepared drinks for both of them, scooping coffee into the mugs and then pouring the water over it. He handed one of the mugs to her. It was decorated with the silhouette of a passenger jet and had a slogan across the enamel: 'Getting high is part of my job description.'

"Have you heard anything from Islamabad?"

Abbas sipped from his mug and then set it down. "I have. Timofeyevich arrived at the island yesterday afternoon. There was a party last night—we have no reason to believe that Huxley didn't offer his usual entertainment."

"And Timofeyevich would be stupid enough to take advantage of it?"

"He is a powerful man. Well protected. And weak. He has no reason to think that Huxley would take advantage of him, but he will, just as he always does. And then we will take advantage of him."

She sipped from her mug. She was tired, and the hardest part of the assignment was still to come. The taste gave her a lift and she needed the boost that the caffeine would provide.

Abbas eyed her. "Are you ready to do what must be done afterwards?"

She nodded.

"And Nawaz?"

"Of course."

Nadia had killed before, but not a civilian and not in cold blood. She had no choice in the matter. Abbas would do it if they didn't, but they would have a limited future if they showed squeamishness now. Nadia was too ambitious to contemplate that.

"This has gone well," Abbas said. "See that you bring things to a satisfactory conclusion and you will be rewarded when you return home. I see a successful career for you, Nadia."

"Thank you," she said, feeling the heat in her cheeks. Abbas was usually stinting with his praise.

"The brigadier will be pleased. You know he has taken a special interest in this matter."

Brigadier Subhani Rashid was one of the senior leaders in the ISI, and Nadia was very well aware of how quickly her prospects would improve with someone of his stature as her patron. Abbas had been Rashid's protégé when he had graduated from the academy, and Nadia had tried hard to ensure that she could become Abbas's. Perhaps she could secure both of them? Nawaz would compete for the same favour, but Nadia knew she was better than he was. If earning their partisanship depended on her killing the woman upstairs, Nadia would do it.

She would kill the child, too, if that was what it would take.

Abbas put his coffee down. "We should get to it. It's time. We need to make the call."

32

Milton changed into fresh clothes and set out to walk the island. He reached the main house and the pool. The staff were on hand to clear up the detritus from the night before: a man was dragging a net through the pool, trapping cans and bottles and other trash that bobbed on the surface; uniformed maids were scrubbing the tables and loungers; a man was jet-washing the marble slabs. There were still a handful of revellers about. Two young women slept on the loungers, and a man whom Milton thought he recognised was dangling his feet into the water from the side of the pool while he listlessly spoke on the phone. The party had looked glamorous and fun at night, but now, with everything exposed by the morning sun, it looked shabby and tawdry. Milton knew what it felt like to party all night and remembered the shame he had always felt as he had taken taxis home to see the normal world rousing itself for another day. The glitter and enchantment of the night before had always inevitably been replaced by the mortification of memories lost in the haze of blackout and the arrival of another bone-aching hangover.

Huxley came out of the house, his phone pressed to his ear. Milton ambled around the water's edge and waited for him to see him. The staff had evidently been busy in whatever time they had been given between the end of the party and now. Apart from the ongoing efforts to clean things up, tables had been set on the terrace and draped with white cloths, and a large trestle near to the main building was laid out with plates of fresh fruit, platters of pastries, pitchers of juice and pots of yoghurt. The doors of a nearby sitting room had been thrown wide, and Milton saw Dutch Colonial furniture and mosquito netting that rippled in the breeze.

Huxley saw him; he raised a hand in greeting, finished his call and put the phone into his pocket.

"Morning," he called. He gestured to the table. "Want some breakfast?"

A member of staff appeared as if by magic as the two men arrived at a table, pulling back Huxley's chair and then Milton's and asking whether either of them would like anything from the kitchen.

"Coffee," Huxley said.

"Black?"

"Please. John?"

"The same," he said.

Huxley got up and led the way to the buffet table. He snagged a croissant and a selection of fruit and served himself a large dollop of fresh yoghurt. Milton took slices of mango and coconut and a glass of orange juice and returned to the table.

"I saw you last night," Huxley said, resuming his seat opposite him.

"Did you get any sleep?"

"An hour," Huxley said, with a laugh. "Doesn't matter. I promise the flight home will be a lot quieter than the one out here. Everyone's cooked. I'll take an Ambien, get ten hours' sleep and be fresh as a daisy when we get home."

"I noticed your Russian guest."

"Timofeyevich? He likes the parties we throw out here. Lots of privacy, no prying eyes. So I sent my Gulfstream to Moscow and flew him out here. Made sure he had a few drinks, had a chat with him, and presto." He clicked his fingers theatrically. "No more misgivings about the deal. You can tell MI6—they'll be relieved. The Indians will get their missiles."

The butler returned with two cafetieres of black coffee. He turned over their cups and poured.

Milton picked his up and sipped it, gratefully anticipating the buzz of caffeine.

"We'll stay here until the afternoon," Huxley said. "You really should take advantage of it and relax—call the spa and get a massage, go for a swim, lose some of that tension. The boats will be at the jetty to take us back to the mainland at three. We'll get to the airport at six, wheels up at seven. Should be back in England this time tomorrow."

They ate some of their fruit, both men gazing out over the pool to the ocean beyond. The staff finished cleaning and, with the efficiency that came from experience, disappeared from view. The terrace was calm and peaceful once more.

Huxley nibbled a bit more of his fruit and then set it aside. He finished his coffee and put the cup back in the saucer. "I've got a couple of things I need to sort out before we leave. But I'm serious—*relax*. I'm not going to come to harm if you let someone work on those knots in your shoulders for a couple of hours." He stood. "I'll see you on the boat."

Huxley crossed the terrace to the main building and disappeared inside it. Milton watched him go. He ate the rest of his fruit, then leaned back in his chair and looked out over the water of the pool. It was peaceful, but then a flock of cawing house crows shot up from the canopy, their angry chatter breaking through the calm and reminding Milton of what he had watched here just hours earlier. He felt the same disquiet again, but then the crows settled back into the trees, and the peace returned, leaving just the rumble of the ocean and the whir of an antique brass fan that circulated cool air inside the nearby open room.

33

Abbas and Nadia went up to the bedroom where Nawaz was guarding the woman and her son. Elizabeth sat on the edge of the bed, holding her young son in her lap. Both of them looked up at Abbas and Nadia with wide, fearful eyes as they came in.

"Hello, Elizabeth," Abbas said. "I'm sorry that this has been necessary, but it'll all be over soon."

"What do I have to do?"

"It's your husband."

Her eyes went wider with panic. "What? What's happened to him?"

Abbas smiled as reassuringly as he could. "Nothing. He's in his hotel in Colombo, waiting to fly home. He's due to leave tonight, isn't he?"

"Yes."

"Have you heard from him?"

"Yesterday," she said. "Before..." She gestured at them, the sentence dying on her lips.

"What did he say?"

"Just that he was expecting to be home tomorrow."

"Good. Very good. He might be delayed for a day or two, but that's it. There's no reason anything else should happen to him. We just need your help to make sure. Do you understand?"

"No," she said. "I don't."

Abbas sat down on a wooden chair that they had brought up from the kitchen. "Your husband is due to fly from Colombo to London."

"Why is that relevant? I still don't understand."

"He's going to get new instructions. If he follows them, then you have my word that nothing will happen to him, to you, or to your son. We have no reason at all to hurt any of you. We just need you both to cooperate."

"What new instructions?"

Abbas smiled. "I'll speak to him and explain. I just need you to make a call and tell him what's happening here, then pass the phone to me. All right? Can you do that for me?"

She nodded, her eyes wide with fear and uncertainty.

"That's good," Abbas said.

"When?"

"I think now is as good a time as any, don't you?"

Abbas unzipped the bag that he had brought with him and took out a satphone. He switched it on, put it on speaker and pressed the button to dial a preprogrammed number. Nadia heard the tone as the call connected.

A male voice answered. "Hello?"

Abbas held the phone up so that Elizabeth could speak into it. "Darling? It's me."

"Are you okay? It's early there, isn't it? Is Nathaniel—"

"There are some people with us," she cut over him. "They broke into the house."

The torpor in his voice vanished at once, to be replaced by panic. "What?"

"They have guns. They've threatened us."

"Are you all right?"

"They want to speak to you. They're here—right next to me."

Abbas moved the phone away from her. "Hello, Mr. Maidment. I'm sorry for disturbing you, but it is very important that we speak before your flight today."

"Who are you? Let me speak to my wife."

"Who I am is not important, and you'll be able to speak to your wife again once we've finished. I need you to listen *very* carefully and do as you're told. It'll be much easier for everyone if you do that. Do you understand?"

"Yes," he said. "I understand."

"Are you still flying back today?"

"As far as I know."

"What does that mean?"

"I have to be flexible. Things can occasionally get changed at short notice."

"But not this time?"

"Not yet."

"Good. Everything I'm about to tell you needs to stay between us. You mustn't tell anyone else—not your co-pilot, not the air crew, not your employer and certainly not the police. We have people watching you in Colombo, and your phone and your room are bugged. If you tell anyone—if we even *think* you've told anyone—then there will be unpleasantness here. Tell me you understand."

"I won't tell anyone. I swear I won't."

"Very good. We want you to prepare for the flight just as you normally would. No one should suspect that anything is different from how it normally would be. Okay?"

"Yes."

"Your route would normally take you northwest over the Arabian Sea. Correct?"

"Yes."

"There will be a change today. Wait until you're just south of Karachi and then change course."

"To where?"

"Afghanistan."

"What?"

"You'll be landing in Jalalabad."

34

Phillip Maidment hadn't known what to do with himself. The telephone call from his wife had terrified him, and the more he thought about it, the more frightened he had become. His first thought was to call the police, but he was thousands of miles away from his family, and that felt less of an option than it might otherwise have been. He supposed he could call Mr. Huxley; the demand that he divert the flight to Jalalabad must have been made with Huxley or one of the other passengers in mind, and beyond giving him a warning, perhaps he could involve his security. Maidment had flown them before and knew that they were not to be trifled with—several of them, especially Cronje, were seriously frightening—but what would they be able to do?

They have my wife and child.

He paced the room for fifteen minutes, unable to settle the riot of panic and fright and confusion that fought through his mind. He picked up his phone, thinking that he would call his wife so that he could reason with the man who was with her, then dismissed it as foolish. He had been told what he had to do. They had been very clear. He couldn't see how he had any choice but to follow the instructions.

He went to the window and stared out of it, his eyes not focussing on anything. He looked at his watch; the car that would take him and Cross to the airport was due in thirty minutes. The room felt stuffy and airless and hot, and he had to get out. He turned, grabbed his phone and his glasses from the bedside table, and went to the door. He took the elevator to the lobby and went outside, fumbling with his shades and then pausing, looking left and right, unsure what he was doing and where he should go.

"Mr. Maidment."

His attention snapped back into focus. The man was to his right. He was dressed in shorts and a colourful polo shirt that was open at the neck. His hair was black and slicked back, and he had a neat moustache. He, too, wore dark glasses, and Maidment couldn't see his eyes. His tone was mellifluous, although there was something to his white-toothed smile that felt fake.

"Who are you?"

"A friend."

"How do you know my name?"

He didn't answer that. "Where are you going, Mr. Maidment?"

Panic rolled through his gut and, for a moment, he thought he was going to be sick. "I... I was just going for a walk."

"Is that all?"

"I need fresh air."

"You were told to stay in your room."

Vomit bubbled up his throat. He swallowed it down. "I... Please, I didn't... I mean, I..."

"Let's not make a scene."

The man took him by the elbow and guided him away from the front of the hotel.

"I wasn't going to do anything. I was just going for a walk. I swear that's all."

The man aimed them toward a bench that overlooked the beach. He pressed down on Maidment's shoulder, impelling him to sit.

"You're being picked up in twenty-five minutes," the man said.

"I know. I was just—"

He spoke over him firmly. "Perhaps I need to remind you what's at stake if you don't do as you've been asked."

He reached into his pocket and took out a phone. He woke the screen, pressed his finger against the scanner, and opened his gallery. He swiped to the photograph that he wanted and turned the phone so that Maidment could look at it. It was a photograph of his wife and son. They were staring at whoever had taken the picture; Elizabeth was white with fear, and Nathaniel looked sleepy and confused. He recognised their bedroom behind them.

The vomit rushed up his throat, and he was unable to stop it. He bent forward and let it out, the remnants of his breakfast spattering out between his legs, hot splashes against the sides of his calves and across his shoes.

The man put a hand on his back, as if comforting him. His voice, though, had no solace in it at all. "This is serious. You need to realise that, and do exactly what you've been told."

"I will," Maidment muttered.

"You were told to stay in your room."

"I just needed some air."

"And now you've had it."

"Who are you people?"

"That doesn't matter. You just need to know that we're watching. We're here, at the airport, on the plane, at your house. We're *everywhere*. Do as you've been told and there's nothing to worry about. You can start by waiting in your room until the car arrives to take you to the airport."

"I will," he said. It felt like there was an iron bar laid across his chest. "I'm going to do what they asked. I'm not… I'm not messing around."

"I'm pleased to hear that." The man took a handkerchief from his pocket and held it out for him. "Now—please— clean yourself up and go back to your room. The car will be here soon. You need to be ready for it. You need to be on the plane, just as normal. If you're not—for any reason—well, I'm sure I don't need to explain what will happen."

"Please," he begged. "Please don't hurt them."

"We don't want to—but that's entirely up to you. Now—go."

35

Milton was taken to the airport in an SUV. The other passengers were all subdued, some of them taking the opportunity to sleep. All of them wore sunglasses against the glare of the midday sun and those who were awake drank greedily from the bottles of water in the seatback pouches in a vain attempt to slake thirsts worsened by their hangovers. The driver turned through a gate in the fence and brought the SUV to a stop next to three of the others that had departed before them. Milton opened the door and got out. Thorsson was waiting on the taxiway.

"What time did you leave the party?" he asked as Milton joined him.

"Just after four."

"Get any sleep last night?"

"Never had a problem with that," Milton said. "Force of habit from the military. Sleep when you can."

"Did you see Timofeyevich?"

"He was there."

"And?"

"He was having a very good time."

"Not what you'd expect for a business meeting." Thorsson paused and checked to make sure no one else was nearby. "Think the younger ones were paid to be here?"

Milton nodded. "The thought had crossed my mind."

An SUV pulled up. The doors slid back, and Cronje and then Huxley stepped down.

"Afternoon, everyone," Huxley called out. "How are we feeling?"

A few of them groaned in response.

"Some of you certainly look as if you could do with some sleep. We'll be on our way soon."

∽

It was Nadia's turn to watch Elizabeth Maidment and her son. They kept the bedroom curtains drawn, but had opened the curtains in the sitting room so as to avoid attracting unwanted attention to the house. Abbas and Nawaz were in the kitchen, and Nadia could hear the muffled sounds of conversation through the open bedroom door.

Nadia had holstered her pistol, but she kept it visible in the event Elizabeth might decide to take her chances and try to overpower her. Nadia wouldn't have needed the gun to subdue her—the woman had a softness about her that was impossible to miss—but Nadia much preferred the threat of it to keep her docile and compliant.

Nadia was sitting on the wooden kitchen chair now. Elizabeth was sitting on her bed, the boy snivelling as he curled up with his head in her lap. The boy was only young, and, although he couldn't have understood what was happening to them, he must have felt his mother's fear.

"*Please*," Elizabeth said. "He's scared."

"Everything's fine," Nadia said, smiling.

"Look at him—he's terrified. Are you a mother?" Nadia didn't answer. "No," Elizabeth said. "You can't be. If you had kids, you'd understand."

Nadia forced a smile. "Please, Mrs. Maidment. Try to relax. It won't be long now."

∽

PHILLIP MAIDMENT CONDUCTED his exterior check of the jet, walking around it from front to back. The ramp was busy with tugs, baggage carts, fuel trucks and belt loaders. Luggage was being sent up one of the belt loaders into the hold and, as he looked up at the window at the top of the jetway, he saw that the passengers were boarding. He paused, ignoring the woozy feeling from the sun and the smell of the fuel, waiting until the fresh wave of panic at what he had been told to do had passed. He continued the walk-around, looking for leaks, bird strikes or anything else that was out of place. He almost hoped that he would see something; a delay might give him the time he needed to work out what to do. But there was nothing wrong; everything was as it should be.

He had managed to keep it together in the car to the airport. His co-pilot—Colleen Cross—had commented that he looked pale, but he said he had had trouble sleeping, that he was a little tired but otherwise fine. She had picked up a copy of the *Times* from the hotel lobby and lost herself in its pages, her concern about Maidment quickly assuaged and forgotten as she read up on what was happening at home.

He made his way back up to the flight deck.

"All okay?" Cross asked him.

"All fine. Have you got the flight release?"

She held up the document that confirmed the exact routing that had been filed, the fuel calculations—the predicted burn, plus fuel to the alternate, plus forty-five minutes extra, plus the contingency—and the altitude that had been filed. He checked the deferred maintenance and saw a notification that one of the airport's ground transmitters was inoperative. He reviewed the passenger and cargo load, saw that it was within agreed tolerances, and handed the document back to Cross.

"We good to go?"

"We are," he said.

36

Brigadier Subhani Rashid looked out of the window of the helicopter as it approached Jalalabad. The airport was three miles southeast of the city. Jalalabad was located at the junction of the Kabul and Kunar Rivers and spread out across a plateau to the south of the Hindu Kush mountains. It had fallen to the Taliban as soon as the Americans had withdrawn and the Afghan army had pulled back to defend the capital. Everything looked dusty and dirty, cooked beneath a blazing sun that shone out of a cloudless sky.

The helicopter was an AW139 that belonged to the Army Aviation Corps. There were three hundred kilometres between Islamabad and Jalalabad, and the helicopter had covered the distance in just over an hour. They had left prosperous Pakistan behind them, flown over the mountains and crossed the border into Afghanistan. The differences between the two countries were stark and very evident from above. The towns and villages here had suffered through decades of war, with wrecked buildings left to collapse and the burned-out husks of vehicles still littering the roads. The airport, too, had suffered. The terminal building had been shelled, as had the runway; the patched-up sections were marked by fresh asphalt that had yet to be bleached by the ferocious sun. Two ancient passenger aircraft—a Tupolev and a Yakovlev from the 1970s—had been left on the edge of the runway, scavenged for parts and slowly covered over by sand as the desert claimed them for itself. Two technicals—flatbed trucks with .50-calibre guns fixed in the back—were parked at the entrance to the facility, bored-looking Taliban fighters lounging next to them.

The pilot brought them down next to the tower and powered down the engine. Rashid unclipped himself, pushed his sunglasses on and disembarked. Farooq Afridi, his number two, was waiting for him.

"How was your flight, sir?"

"Fine," he said, impatiently waving away the small talk. "Is everything ready?"

"Everything is fine."

He gestured to the technicals. "Any more of them?"

"No, sir. That's all. There are seven of them. Do you think that will be enough?"

Rashid would have preferred more, but seven men armed with Kalashnikovs ought to be plenty. They just needed to remove Huxley and transfer him to the helicopter.

"It should be fine," he said. "Do you know what you need to do?"

Farooq pointed over at a mobile bowser. "I will plant the device in the hold while the jet is being refuelled."

"Good," he said. He set off toward the tower with Farooq alongside. "Where are they now?"

"Still at Colombo. The passengers have boarded. They should take off shortly."

There was no point in trying to fool himself: Rashid was nervous. Maidment's family had been secured and contact had been made with the pilot. He knew what he had to do, and, from what Rashid had been told, he had agreed. Once Huxley was in the air, things would develop quickly. There were just over two thousand miles along the route that would take Huxley from Colombo to Jalalabad; that ought to take around four hours.

He looked at his watch.

Not long now.

37

Milton and Thorsson climbed the airstair, crossed the sill and stepped into the 767. Milton put his luggage into the overhead bin and sat down. There was a copy of today's *Times* on the table, and he opened it, watching over the top of the pages as the other passengers embarked. The atmosphere was more subdued than it had been on the outbound flight. Milton looked through the window at the tarmac below. Huxley's security was with him as he paced back and forth with his phone pressed to his ear.

Thorsson appeared beside Milton's seat. "Can I talk to you for a moment?" he said quietly.

Milton nodded and slid the newspaper into the cubbyhole beside his seat. Thorsson sat down so that they could speak. He kept his voice low so they were not overheard.

"I've been trying to focus on the job, but the more I see of what's been going on out here, the more I doubt myself and what we're doing."

"What does that mean?"

He exhaled. "There are some things you don't know," he

said. "About Huxley. I know you've seen the Group Three report. You had a redacted version. I'm talking about things that go beyond that. I sat in on a briefing by the analyst who put it together for Control. She said that Huxley's been dealing with complaints about his behaviour for years."

"What kind of behaviour?"

"From women, mainly—the way he treats them. They found evidence of eleven complaints, all settled with money paid under NDAs, all brushed under the carpet and forgotten about. They go back fifteen years. Sexual harassment. Group Three decided not to approach the women in case it got back to Huxley, but they were able to get into the servers of the law firm that acted for him and found statements from some of the women backing up what they said. They all said he took advantage of them."

Milton looked up as Cronje boarded the plane. The South African paused in the doorway, looked over at them, and then continued inside. Thorsson waited until Cronje took his seat before continuing.

"You saw what went on upstairs when we flew over here. And what happened at the island last night."

Milton was silent for a moment as he thought about what Thorsson had said, and what he had seen. "I didn't know about the complaints against him."

"You didn't see anything when you worked for him before?"

"Nothing like that," Milton said. "He was always with women, but he was young and rich." Milton stopped and cast his mind back. "There were moments when it was a little awkward, I suppose, but it wasn't like last night."

"It makes me uncomfortable."

"What do we do about it? You must have worked with people you didn't like before this."

"Plenty of them. But there's something about him that makes my skin crawl. What if the dossier only gets the surface of things? How much more has been hidden? What else don't we know?"

Milton looked at Thorsson. He looked troubled. "Why are you telling me this?" he said.

Thorsson bit his lip, and Milton wondered whether his duty would overpower his desire to relieve himself of the burden he was obviously carrying. "I had a sister," he said. "She was murdered."

"I'm sorry," Milton said. "I didn't know that."

"Why would you? You don't know anything about me."

Thorsson looked out of the window as the vehicle that had transferred their luggage into the hold was driven away.

"Huxley reminds me of the man who killed my sister."

∼

THE DOOR to the cabin was open, and the purser put her head through. "Evening. Are we all okay?"

"We are," Maidment said, busying himself with the instrumentation so that he didn't have to turn back to look at her. "Final checks."

"Passengers are almost all aboard," she said. "Just waiting for Mr. Huxley."

Maidment worked through the switches and levers and confirmed that they were all in the right position. He woke the flight management computer and checked that air traffic control had sent the route that they had been cleared to fly, the initial altitude and the expected cruising altitude. The routing would have taken them northwest, over the Middle East, and he looked at the Arabian Sea and knew that was where he was going to have to make the decision whether to deviate or not. He would have to think how to get Cross out of the cockpit. He took the unique code from the FMC and entered it so that the transponder would correctly identify them on the radar.

"Flight plan and FMC data match ATC clearance," he reported.

"Check," Cross responded.

Maidment tried to focus on the tasks at hand so that he could ignore the creeping fear that every passing minute brought him closer to the point where he was going to have to betray Huxley and everyone else on the plane. He took Cross through the departure briefing, running through the departure flight path, the obstacles to be aware of in the vicinity of the airfield, the flight path in the event of an engine flame-out and aborted take-off procedure.

"Here we go."

He turned to see the fueller holding the fuel slip, and waited as Cross matched it to the dispatch release fuel and the actual amount of fuel on board. She said that it did, and the man departed, his place taken by the agent from the airport who confirmed the actual passenger count.

"Is Mr. Huxley on board?"

The woman checked her list, but before she could answer the question, Maidment looked up to see Huxley standing in the doorway behind her.

"Good evening, sir," Cross said.

Maidment tried to speak, but found that his throat was dry.

"What's up, Phillip? You look worse than I feel."

"Sorry, Mr. Huxley," he managed. "Frog in my throat."

"Are we all good to go?"

"Yes, sir. Final checks. Pushback in five minutes if that's all right."

"Perfect. Just thought I'd pop my head in and say hello."

"Thank you, sir. Probably best to go and strap yourself in."

"Will do. Have a good flight."

The attendant used the intercom to report that the cabins were ready for flight. Maidment radioed down to the ground crew that they were ready for pushback, and the tug pushed them away from the stand. Maidment waited for their hand signals to confirm they were out of the way, and then turned the 767 on to the runway and taxied out to the far end.

He reached into his pocket and took out his wallet. He flipped it open and looked down at the pictures of Elizabeth and Nathaniel, both taken during happier times.

"This is Flight N898TH," Cross reported to the tower. "We're ready for take-off."

The local controller gave her clearance, and Maidment advanced the throttles to take-off power. The big jet rumbled down the centreline, picking up speed until they reached V1, the velocity beyond which there was no turning back. Maidment didn't have a choice; he *never* had. He was committed now. He would do whatever they asked of him and hope for the best.

The front wheels lifted, the jet tipped back, the back wheels lifted, and they were aloft.

Maidment thought of the pictures in his wallet and tightened his grip on the controls.

38

Thorsson gazed out through the porthole window as the ground rushed away from them. "Her name was Gudrún. The man's name was Finlay Karsh. Too much money and influence. It made him think he could do anything he wanted, just like Huxley. She found out about someone he'd murdered, and he killed *her* to keep her quiet. Paid a man to shoot her in the head. I chased him to a castle in Scotland and..." He paused. "I made sure he would never do to anyone else what he did to her. I started to work for the Group just after that. They offered me the man Karsh hired to do it. I followed him to France and told him who I was before I choked him. I don't think he even remembered Gudrún's name."

Thorsson took a breath to centre himself.

"I got back to London, and I couldn't get it out of my head. Group Three put together a dossier for me about Karsh in case there were others—there were things he'd done that remind me of Huxley. The same attitudes—money can get you whatever you want, people are just things to be bought and sold. The same sense that the usual rules don't apply when you're at that level. But Karsh was dead, there were no others, and I didn't have to think about him anymore. I got on with life. Did my job. And then Control gave me Huxley's file, and all the old nightmares came up again."

Milton saw Huxley in the doorway and held up a finger to indicate that Thorsson should stop. Huxley scanned the cabin, saw Milton and raised a hand in greeting. He didn't come over; instead, he turned left and made his way into his private suite. Two women followed, their faces obscured by huge sunglasses. The door closed behind them.

"See?" Thorsson said.

"I know," Milton said.

"I told myself that the complaints that came up about him were all in the past, that Huxley would've changed his behaviour, but I knew I was kidding myself. Men like that don't change, do they? They get richer; then they get worse. Yesterday proved it. I've seen enough. He *hasn't* changed. He's got *worse*. How many more complaints have there been that we don't know about? How many other women has he bought off?"

The flight attendant began making her way down the cabin with a trolley full of drinks and snacks.

Thorsson stared at Milton. "You were in the Group for years. How did you stomach it for so long?"

"Can I get you anything, gentlemen?" the flight attendant asked.

"Not for me," Thorsson said.

Milton smiled and shook his head, and the flight attendant moved on.

"I got drunk," Milton said.

"I've tried that," Thorsson said. "It doesn't work for long, does it?"

Milton thought of the nights that he had lost to the bottle, and the memories that still kept floating up no matter how hard he tried to drown them.

"No," he said. "Not for long."

39

Maidment looked at the flight computer and toggled across to compare the waypoints along the route with his present location. The sky was split into different geographic coordinates that were denoted by way of capitalised five-letter words that were pronounceable to any pilot regardless of the language that they spoke. They were often tied to geographical features and were most frequent over land, often matching the landmarks below. Over open sea, or over land masses that were lightly populated, it was possible to fly for an hour and hundreds of miles between each of them. The majority of the waypoints were found in the first and last minutes of a flight, when the pilot was required to make a series of turns to transit from the runway to the route and then back again as they lined up for their final approach. This flight, one that Maidment had made dozens of times before, had begun with the usual list: ITAWT, ITAWA, PUDYE, TTATT and IDEED.

The next one, fifty miles ahead, was ANNII. That waypoint marked the gentle turn to port, taking them from the Arabian Sea to the transit across the Middle East. They would reach it in a matter of minutes, and Maidment reflected grimly that ANNII was now more than just a geographical marker: it had become the pivot around which the rest of his life would turn. He could ignore the instructions he had been given and follow the route that he had programmed into the computer, and accept whatever consequences that might bring for his family. Or he could do as he was told, turn the plane and follow a new path to a different destination. There was uncertainty in whichever decision he made, but he knew he was kidding himself if he thought he had a choice.

He didn't.

"It's quiet back there today," he said to Cross.

"Makes a change," his co-pilot said. "They're probably still hungover from the flight out."

"Could you do me a favour?"

She looked over at him. "You want a coffee?"

"Gasping."

"Me too," she said, unclipping her belt.

"And a sandwich?"

"I'll see what they've got in the galley."

She stood and went back to the door. The procedure on normal commercial flights was that a flight attendant should wait in the cockpit when either pilot left, to prevent the other pilot from locking the door and then crashing the plane. The rules were not followed quite so religiously aboard Huxley's 767. Cross unlocked the door and stepped out, closing it behind her. Maidment reached for the toggle. It had three settings: UNLOCK allowed authorised people, usually the cabin crew, to open the door; NORMAL locked the door and kept it locked unless the access code was entered on the keypad outside; and LOCK was effectively a deadlock that could only be disengaged by flicking the switch again.

He chose the latter setting.

The door locked.

Maidment turned the knob to switch off the transponder and then disengaged the autopilot and took control, turning the plane to starboard so that they diverted from their route. He put ANNII to port and picked out a line to the next—MOBEE—that would give them landfall over Pakistan.

His hands were wet on the controls, and he wiped them on his trousers. His heart was racing and, for a moment, he felt faint. He breathed in and out until the moment had passed.

He wondered how long it would take for someone to notice what he had done.

40

"What do you want to do about it?" Milton asked.

"I don't know," Thorsson said. "I'm probably overreacting."

"Because if Control ever found out—"

"I *know*," he said, cutting him off. "I'm not going to do anything. He's an unpleasant man, but that's it. Right? We don't know that he's doing anything wrong now. I just want to get this over and done with so I don't have to see him again."

The plane turned to starboard. It was a sharp turn, and Milton had to reach out to stop his glass of water sliding toward the edge of the table. He looked out of the window and saw the wingtip descend as the pilot held them in the turn for five seconds, straightening them out again afterwards.

That was odd.

He looked up at the flight attendant who was circulating through the cabin with a jug of water. There was a look of confusion on her face, but it was only momentary; she noticed that Milton was looking at her, and the frown was quickly replaced with a professional smile.

"Is everything all right, Mr. Smith?"

"I was just wondering why we turned like that."

"Nothing to worry about. The captain's probably taking us around some weather."

Milton wondered if that could be right. It was possible. He asked her to refill his glass and waited for her to head back to the galley.

"We turned east, didn't we?" Thorsson asked.

"I think so."

Thorsson leaned forward and tapped the screen to switch off the movie that was playing. He selected the moving map icon and tapped it. They were over the Arabian Sea, with Oman just to the north. They should have been heading northwest, across Saudi Arabia and then over the Mediterranean and into Europe, but they were not. Instead, the icon of the plane was pointing east.

"That doesn't make any sense," Thorsson said.

Milton watched the screen as the plane slowly headed to the right. "Pakistan?"

And then the screen went dark.

"Shit," Thorsson cursed.

"It's been switched off."

Milton looked around the cabin; everything else appeared to be as it should be.

"We need to speak to Huxley," he said.

41

They went to the front of the plane, into the foyer with the stairs that led up to the cabin where the party had taken place on the outbound flight. The cockpit was ahead of that cabin and also accessed by the stairs; Milton stopped as he heard the sound of a raised voice from above. He changed course, climbing the steps with Thorsson behind him. The door to the cockpit was closed, and one of the two pilots Milton had seen before they took off—the woman—was banging her fist against it. The other passengers in the cabin were watching, fearful expressions on their faces.

Milton went to the cockpit door. "What is it?"

The woman turned. "It's locked."

"It's supposed to be."

"Of course it is," she snapped. "But with me *in* it. He's locked me out."

Milton knew the door would be the most secure on the plane: reinforced and bulletproof, rendered impregnable after 9/11.

"What's the procedure for getting back inside?" Thorsson asked her.

She pointed to the keypad next to the door; it was similar to one that would be used to access a building on the ground. "I buzz the interphone," she said. "Then I press the hash—it sounds the chime inside the cockpit. He checks that it's me on the camera and flicks the toggle to unlock the door."

"Don't you have a code for the keypad?"

"I tried that. He's set it to lock. It can only be opened from the inside."

"Why would he do that?" Thorsson said.

"I have no idea."

"What's his name?" Milton asked her.

"Maidment."

"And how did he seem when you left the cockpit?"

"What do you mean?"

"Did he do or say anything unusual?"

"No. He asked me to go and get him a coffee and a sandwich."

"That's standard?"

"Completely normal."

Milton tried to work out what might have happened. "Did you notice the plane changed course?"

"That's why I came back."

"So that was *after* you left the cockpit?"

She nodded. "Why?"

"It was a manual adjustment—he's not incapacitated."

"No. He locked me out, and then he made the turn."

Milton pointed at the keypad. "Can I speak to him?"

She nodded, tapped in the code and gestured that he should speak.

"Mr. Maidment?"

There was no reply.

Milton looked up into the camera; the black lens was inscrutable.

"What's his first name?"

"Phillip."

"Phillip," Milton said, "my name's John. I need to speak to you."

There was no reply. Milton laid his palm on the door and felt the solidity of the metal beneath the layer of fabric that covered it. He turned to Thorsson.

"We need to tell Huxley."

42

Those passengers seated in the upper deck had been able to witness the consternation at the cockpit door, and now the word had passed throughout the rest of the plane. Hushed conversations took place, and the atmosphere was fraught. Milton left Thorsson at the door while he descended the stairs to go and get Huxley. The flight attendant who served the lower deck was in the foyer, pale faced.

"What's going on?"

Milton took her to the side. "The pilot's locked himself in the cockpit."

Her mouth fell open. "God."

"You need to keep everyone calm."

"Why's he done something like that?"

"Listen," Milton said firmly. "It's Genevieve, isn't it?"

"Yes."

"You need to do your job, Genevieve. Make sure the passengers don't panic. I'm going to get it sorted, but it'll be more difficult if everyone's excited. Do you understand?"

"What do I tell them?"

"There's been a malfunction," he said, "and we're fixing it now. All right?"

She nodded.

Milton gestured to the door to Huxley's suite. "I need to see him. Is the door open?"

"Yes," she said, "but he's not alone."

He was going to ask her to elaborate, but he remembered seeing the two young women follow him inside earlier. Genevieve's shrug and the little shake of her head told him all he needed to know.

Milton knocked on the door. "It's John. Can I come in?"

He heard muffled conversation from inside.

"*Tristan*," Milton said, "I need to speak to you."

It took another few seconds before the door was unlocked and opened. Huxley peered out from behind it, wearing a dressing gown with a monogram of his initials on the breast. Milton glanced over his shoulder to see two young women sitting up in bed, the sheets pulled up to their necks.

Huxley noticed Milton's eyes and stepped forward, pulling the door closed behind him. "What is it?"

"There's a problem. The pilot's locked himself in the cockpit and changed course. We should be on a northwestern track. We're heading northeast."

"Heading where?" He paused, working out where the new course might lead. "Jesus. Pakistan?"

"That's what I'm worried about."

The colour drained out of Huxley's face. "Oh, *shit*."

⁓

Huxley made his way through the cabin in his dressing gown, climbed the stairs and went to the cockpit door. Thorsson was still there, and Cronje had joined him.

"Anything?" Milton asked him.

"Not a word."

"Out of the way," Huxley said, sliding between Thorsson and the wall so he could get to the intercom. He pressed the button. "Maidment? It's Tristan Huxley."

Milton was expecting the same silence, but this time, the speaker crackled into life.

"I'm so sorry."

"Open the door!"

"I can't. They've got my family. My wife and son. They'll hurt them if I don't do what they want me to do."

Milton leaned in closer to the microphone. "What do they want you to do?"

"Land in Jalalabad."

Cronje cursed under his breath as Milton closed his eyes. He knew now, for sure: it *was* the ISI. They wouldn't land a hijacked plane on Pakistani soil, but they maintained influence in Afghanistan. They'd set them down there, and Huxley would be whisked away into the badlands on the border. They'd smuggle him into Islamabad, and that would be the end of him.

"We can't go there," Huxley said. "They'll—"

Milton held up a finger to stop him. "Mr. Maidment, it's John again. I work for the government. We can help you. You don't need to do this."

"Didn't you hear me? They have my wife and child. They had a man watching me in Colombo. He threatened me at the hotel. He said they'd be hurt if I didn't do what they told me. I don't have a choice. There's no point trying to persuade me to change my mind. I've already turned the plane. We'll be there soon."

"You can turn it back," Milton said.

"No," Maidment said. "I can't. Please—it'd be better if you went and sat down. You won't be able to force the door. Let's just get it over with."

Milton stepped back away so that he was away from the microphone and out of the sight of the camera. The passengers on the upper deck were staring at him.

Huxley turned on Cronje. "Don't we guard the crew?"

"We've never felt it necessary, sir."

"'Never felt it necessary?' *Look!*"

Cronje shuffled uncomfortably.

"Hindsight will get us nowhere," Milton said. He turned to the co-pilot. "How long until we get to Jalalabad?"

She was pale. "I don't know."

"Guess."

She closed her eyes. "It's about four hundred miles from the waypoint to Karachi." She screwed up her forehead into a frown. "It's probably three times that to get from here to Jalalabad."

"Call it nine hundred miles," Milton said. "How long will that take?"

"We're cruising at four hundred and fifty knots."

"So two hours?"

"Give or take."

"And how long to land?"

"Depends on ATC. You can probably add twenty minutes."

Huxley grabbed Milton's arm. "You can't let him land there," he hissed.

"I don't intend to."

"So what do we do?"

"Force the door?" Cronje suggested.

Thorsson shook his head. "It's too strong."

Milton had an idea. "Is the Wi-Fi still active?"

The co-pilot took out a phone and checked her screen. "Yes. The gear for it is in the cupboard in the galley. He can't access it from the cockpit."

"We need to get word to London."

43

Control sat back and scanned the report from Number One that had been passed to her for review. It had arrived overnight and detailed the events that had taken place at Huxley's island in Sri Lanka. The extent of Huxley's work for the government had not been shared with her, and her visibility of what was taking place was limited to what One told her. He reported that he had seen Nikolay Timofeyevich, and included a series of photographs of the Russian that he had shot on his phone. The pictures had since been verified by the specialists in Group Three, but it was the other names that stood out to her now: Maxwell Stanley, a private-equity manager reputedly worth half a billion dollars; Aiken Jacobs, the press baron who owned a series of newspapers and websites in the United States and United Kingdom; Eugene Barton, a former president of Yale Law School and a former attorney general; Barry Hurford, the supermarket magnate; and Harold Stiles, who had, until recently, been minister for trade and industry. Control knew that the scope of Huxley's black book was vast, and that he had relationships with men and women—although mostly men—in dozens of different industries and fields in countries all over the world. That was what he offered those with whom he worked: he was a fixer, able to move between countries and continents, connecting different networks so that tasks that might otherwise be impossible could now take place. The classified background files that Control had read did not reveal how Huxley had been able to nurture such a disparate array of relationships. It seemed, to her, that he was a collector: these weren't real friends, but chattels. He nurtured relationships until he had use for them, and then he called in his favours.

The intercom buzzed. Control laid the file down and pressed the button to speak. "What is it?"

"Could I have a word, ma'am?" Weaver said. "There's been an issue with Huxley."

"Come in."

She stood and stretched her legs as Weaver opened the door and came inside.

"What issue?" Control said.

"We just had an email from Number One. He's on board Huxley's plane."

"And?"

"It's been hijacked," he said. "By the pilot. Number One says that the ISI are using the man's wife and child as leverage. They've told him to divert to Jalalabad."

"Where are they now?"

"The transponder's been switched off. Our best guess is that they're over Pakistan."

"The wife?"

"Thames Ditton."

"Do we have anyone near there?"

"Number Six is closest, ma'am. Huxley didn't have space for her on the flight out. She's at his mansion."

"How far is it from there?"

"Thirty miles."

"Tell her to go."

"I took the liberty of doing that straight away," he said. "She's en route."

"Who else?"

"Three and Twelve. They're inbound, too, but they won't be there in time."

"We'll need to tell Latimer and the others."

"I've done that. They've requested an urgent briefing."

Control pressed her palms together in front of her face. "How long do we have before the plane lands?"

"Less than two hours."

"So you can tell them they'll have to wait. Make sure Six calls in when she gets there."

PART V

SUNDAY

44

Six had been cruising at no less than a hundred and twenty ever since leaving Guildford, and now she touched one hundred and sixty as she raced the bike in the outside lane of the A3. They had been fortunate twice: first, there were only twenty-eight miles between Huxley's mansion in Chiddingfold and the pilot's house in Thames Ditton; second, Huxley had a thing for fast cars and motorbikes, and there was a Kawasaki Ninja H2R in the garage with the keys in the ignition. The motorcycle was insanely powerful; Six mainlined the adrenaline as she opened the throttle and fed the supercharged inline engine.

She was wearing an earpiece that connected her with HQ and the operator from Group Three who was providing remote surveillance. Weaver had explained what had happened: Huxley's plane had been hijacked by the pilot, and they did not have long before it was due to land in Jalalabad. Weaver told her that the pilot's family was being threatened in order to secure his obedience, and, unless she was able to remove them from danger, they would lose Huxley for good.

"Six, this is Weaver. Come in."

"Copy that, Weaver. This is Six."

"Where are you?"

The wind rushed around and over her, and she had pressed herself down as low as she could to try to avoid its hungry fingers. She carved around a truck as if it were stationary and looked up to see a sign approaching and then disappearing to her left. "Sandown," she said.

"Good," Weaver said. "ETA's ten minutes from there."

"Copy that."

Six lowered herself to the bike again and cranked the throttle around a little more. The engine whined, and the Kawasaki surged ahead, the traffic to her left melting into a blurred line of white and yellow headlights. London's glow lit up the darkness in the distance. She passed a sign for Thames Ditton and squeezed the brakes, bleeding off enough speed so that she could make the turn.

"Six, this is Weaver. I have Control for you."

"Six, this is Control."

"Copy that, ma'am. Go ahead."

"It is very important that you find the family and neutralise any threat against them."

"I understand, ma'am."

"Lethal force is authorised."

"Copy that."

"Good luck, Six. Control out."

Six buzzed with anticipation and nerves. This kind of assignment, loaded with so much uncertainty, was not one that would normally have been given to a single agent. She had been routed directly to the house, but the others—Three and Twelve—were due to arrive thirty minutes after her. Control had chosen her by dint of being the closest; Six would do her best to make sure that she didn't regret the choice.

45

Milton had told Huxley to keep trying to engage Maidment in conversation, to try to persuade him that it wasn't too late. Milton returned to the front of the plane and saw that his efforts had not been successful.

"He said he was sorry again," Huxley said, "and now he won't answer."

"Keep trying."

"He's made up his mind. It's pointless."

"Keep trying."

"You were supposed to stop this from happening," Huxley said sourly.

"And I told you travelling was a bad idea. We should've stayed at the house. They wouldn't have been able to get to you there."

"Easy to say that with hindsight."

"It's not hindsight. It's common sense. You didn't listen."

Huxley's face was white and pinched, and Milton half expected to receive a broadside of invective, but it didn't come. Instead, Huxley aimed his fury at the cockpit. He thumped his fist on the door. "Open up!" he yelled, not bothering with the intercom. "Open this fucking door right *now!*"

Milton thought Huxley looked ridiculous in his monogrammed dressing gown and slippers. The Pakistanis would throw him in the back of a four-by-four and disappear into the desert. That would be the last image that anyone had of him: a spoilt billionaire in his dressing gown who would soon be swapping the gilded opulence of his own 767 for a dank cell somewhere in the bowels of the ISI's headquarters.

Huxley thumped the door again and again.

"That won't help," Milton said.

"We've got to do *something*."

"We are. London got our message."

"But we don't even know if his wife and kid are still there. What if they've taken them somewhere else? Or they can't do anything about it? What then?"

"It won't come to that."

Milton tried to imbue his words with as much conviction as he could, but he knew that it was no more than a long shot. There would need to be an agent in the vicinity, and Huxley was right: it was entirely possible that the ISI had taken their hostages somewhere else. A long shot, then, but it was the only shot they had. Milton looked at his watch and saw that they were likely an hour away from Jalalabad and maybe less. He had been in Afghanistan before, during the war, and had no interest in returning. He had been involved in operations against the Taliban, and he knew that he faced an unpleasant future if they became aware of his identity.

Thorsson climbed the stairs and signalled to Milton that he should come over. Huxley was busy with the intercom and didn't notice as Milton turned away.

"Anything back from London?" he asked.

"Six is on her way," Thorsson said.

"How long?"

"She'll get there in ten minutes, but there's no guarantee that they'll still be there, or that she'll be able to get them out. It's just her."

"It's the best we can do," Milton said.

Thorsson nodded. "There's another thing. I spoke to Colleen."

"Who?"

"The co-pilot. Even if we don't land, she says we won't have enough fuel to get back home without stopping."

"We'll deal with that when we have to."

46

Six cruised down the road, passing the house that belonged to Phillip and Elizabeth Maidment. She looked up into the sky and saw the dark shape of a drone. The aircraft was equipped with technology that muffled the noise of its engine, with the result that its operator had been confident enough to bring it down reasonably low. She brought the bike to the kerb and parked it, then opened a channel to London.

"Weaver, this is Six."

"Six, this is Weaver. Go ahead."

"Update, please."

"Group Three have had a Watchkeeper on station for ten minutes."

"I saw it. Anything?"

"Negative. No activity outside the house."

"Inside?"

"We've been luckier there. The Maidments have multiple Echo devices. We've been able to piggyback off them and listen in."

"How many?"

"We think five: Elizabeth Maidment and her son in one of the bedrooms on the first floor."

"And the tangos?"

"Three," he said. "Two male, one female. We've run voice matches. Two of them are unknown, but the other one is Abbas Kader. He's a serious player in the ISI. Worked all around the world, including wet work in India, Kashmir and Saudi Arabia. You'll want to be very careful with him."

"Copy that. Do you have a plan of the house for me?"

"Sending it now. Huxley's plane will be on the ground in fifteen minutes. We need to secure the family and tell him that they're safe before the wheels are on the ground, or Huxley will be lost."

"Copy that, Weaver. Six out."

She took out her phone and opened her email. There was a message from Weaver with a plan of the property attached. The house had a dining room at the front, facing the street, with a sitting room, breakfast room and kitchen completing the ground floor; the first floor had four bedrooms, with another two up in the eaves. There was a large garden at the rear with a garage. She zoomed in and saw that there were doors to the garden in both the kitchen and sitting rooms; she would access the property there.

Six slid off the bike, feeling the bulk of the TacPro armour that she wore underneath her jacket. It was equipped with lightweight panels that allowed for ease of movement, yet still offered the benefit of acceptable stopping power. It wasn't the most comfortable, though, and she adjusted the Velcro strap so that it fitted her a little more snugly. She set off, walking briskly along the street, very aware that to give herself away would be to put the mother and child inside the house in the gravest possible danger.

She stayed on the pavement and glanced at the houses

as she passed them. They were all identical: mock Tudor, with white render and fake black beams, hipped slate roofs, and small walled gardens to the front with the suggestion of larger gardens at the rear. Number twenty-eight was just like the others. Six slowed her pace just a little so that she could give the property extra attention, but there was nothing to suggest anything beyond what they already knew.

She turned and walked back down the street toward the house. Both it and the street around it were as quiet and peaceful as one would expect of a suburban, middle-class area like this. She would have liked to establish a cordon a hundred yards on either side of the property, but apart from the fact that she didn't have backup, she couldn't take the chance that anyone inside might notice.

She paused a moment longer and then turned off the path and walked quickly up the drive and along the side of the house.

47

Huxley and Colleen kept trying to engage Maidment, but they met with the same lack of results. Milton tried to think of another way into the cockpit, but he knew he was wasting his time; the door was designed to withstand the blast from a grenade, and if Maidment didn't want to open it, it was going to stay closed. The passengers were growing frantic, with Genevieve's efforts to keep them calm becoming less and less effective.

Huxley hammered his fist against the door. "Open up!" he hollered again.

Milton signalled that Thorsson should come over where they could talk without Huxley hearing them. He looked at his watch. "How far out are we from Jalalabad?"

"Thirty minutes," Thorsson said.

"The ISI will be there when we land."

"You think we could keep them out?"

"We could lock the doors," Milton said, "but what good would that do? We have to think about the passengers. I'm not putting them at risk to keep Huxley safe."

"But if we delayed them..."

"There's no point," Milton said. "We'll be on the ground in Afghanistan. No one will come to help us. If we land, it's over. We'll have no good options. The best thing to do will be to hand him over and hope they'll let the passengers leave."

Milton looked out of the nearest window. The desert was everywhere beneath the jet, an expanse of yellow and grey and brown that ran all the way to the horizon.

"Ladies and gentlemen," Maidment announced over the PA, "we will soon be commencing our descent. Please return to your seats and fasten your seat belts. Crew to your positions, too, please."

Milton looked at his watch: twenty minutes until they were on the ground.

∽

NADIA AND NAWAZ were in the kitchen, looking out into the garden. Nadia was looking forward to being told that the plane had landed and that they were free to conclude the operation. It had been a long, long, *long* day. The mother had been stoic, showing a bravery for her child that she obviously and understandably didn't really feel, but as the evening turned to night, she was finding it harder and harder to present a positive front. She had tried to put her son to bed, but the boy had been disturbed and would shriek and scream as soon as he was left on his own. They had the upstairs windows closed, but Nadia wasn't prepared to risk the possibility that the screaming would attract the attention of a neighbour or someone passing the house. She told the mother to go and keep him quiet and, after a moment when they could hear the sound of lullabies through the open door, the child had settled.

"I can't wait to get out of here," Nawaz said.

"It won't be long. Abbas said it was nearly on the ground."

Nawaz stretched and reached for the packet of cigarettes that had been left on the kitchen counter. "Fuck it," he said, noticing Nadia's raised eyebrow. "I'm stressed. One won't hurt."

Nawaz lit a cigarette from the hob, opened the door and took it outside. Nadia opened the curtains and looked out into the darkened garden, noticing the glowing red tip of the cigarette as he inhaled. She was running through the details of their exfiltration again when she thought she saw something. It was dark outside, with just a little of the light from the kitchen reaching the trees and neatly trimmed plants and bushes, but there had been *something*. Movement, she thought, a lighter shade of darkness skimming across the black. She stared, straining her eyes for anything that might tell her that she had seen something, that it wasn't a question of tired eyes playing tricks, and there it was: a dark grey next to the tree at the rear of the garden.

Nadia reached for her pistol and went to the door.

Nawaz turned back to the house, saw her framed in the light that fell through the kitchen door, and took a step back in her direction.

But only one.

Nadia heard the *thwip* of a passing round and then the muffled thump of a suppressed gunshot.

48

Rashid brought the binoculars to his eyes and scanned the sky to the south of the airport. Rashid had cultivated excellent relationships with several of the key tribal chiefs, and, in return for his forbearance when it came to their activities in the borderlands between the two countries, he was able to call on the Taliban's assistance when he needed it. This operation had been an example of that. He had needed somewhere to land Tristan Huxley's jet. He couldn't bring it down in Pakistan, for obvious reasons. The operation had to be deniable; the ISI couldn't be proven to be behind the hijacking, even though it would be obvious that they were responsible. Jalalabad was remote, in an area that was under friendly control, and had a runway that was—just about—long enough to land such a large aircraft.

Rashid was in the control tower, a rickety building that had been damaged during the country's gruelling war. One of the windows had been shot out, and not all of the equipment worked. It was high up, though, and offered clear sightlines out to the mountains and beyond. Despite that, he still couldn't see the jet.

"Where *is* it?" he said impatiently.

The radar operator checked his screen. "Still on approach."

Farooq took his own set of binoculars and looked out to the south. "There, sir. Just coming into view now."

Rashid looked and, this time, spotted the jet. It was a speck of white against the blue of the sky, and, as he watched, it grew larger.

"What's he doing?" he said.

"He wants to get a look at the runway before he tries to set it down," the operator said.

Rashid looked back out of the window as the jet reached the edge of the runway. It was low—no more than a couple of hundred feet off the ground—and the engines thundered as it approached. Rashid looked at the cockpit window at the front of the bulbous top deck, but the sun sparked off it and made it impossible to see inside. The jumbo roared overhead, rattling what glass remained in the windows.

Rashid turned as it continued to the north, the pilot pulling up and slowly turning to starboard. He looked down at the Taliban waiting on the runway. They would move quickly, removing Huxley and subduing the passengers while the plane was refuelled. Farooq would plant a small explosive device in the hold and set it to detonate once the jet was airborne once more. Maidment would be the fall guy for what had happened. They had already built the story that they would use: a mental breakdown had caused him to murder his wife and son, and then, his state of mind unbalanced, he had crashed the plane.

The bodies of his family would be found later, burned up in an abandoned car so that it would be impossible to determine the time of death. It wasn't perfect, but it didn't have to be. There would be an investigation, but there would be little for it to find. The jet's transponder was switched off, making it difficult to demonstrate its route or establish that it had landed before it crashed. The witnesses on the jet would all be dead. Huxley would be assumed dead even as he and the *kompromat* that he held were being smuggled across the border. They would use him to kybosh the deal between the Russians and the Indians and who knew what else besides. He would be an intelligence asset of the most exquisite value.

Rashid lowered the binoculars and turned to the controller. "Tell him he needs to land *right* now," he said. "Remind him what will happen if he doesn't."

The man nodded his understanding and flicked his radio to transmit. Rashid left him to it, descending the stairs so that he could check that the team on the ground was ready to move.

49

Nawaz fell backward onto the lawn.
Nadia shut the door and backed away.
"Abbas!"

She heard the sound of the toilet flushing, but he didn't reply.

"Abbas!"

They'd found them. She had no idea how, but they had.

The window next to her exploded, and a small black cylinder bounced off the counter and onto the floor and rolled against the wall.

She looked down and shielded her eyes.

The grenade exploded in a riot of noise and light. The detonation was deafening and disorientating. Nadia was blinded, her retinas bleached with the bright white of the flash.

The boy shrieked in terror upstairs.

It didn't matter now.

Nadia bounced off the door frame as she staggered into the hallway. She squeezed her eyes shut and opened them again, willing her vision to return.

"Abbas!"

She crashed into the side table and knocked it over, tripping over the leg and falling to her knees.

She blinked frantically, her vision returning in time to see an arm reach through the smashed window in the kitchen door and turn the latch. She scrabbled back, finding her feet and lunging for the stairs. She heard another suppressed gunshot, and the wall to her left spat bits of plaster against her face. She climbed the stairs on hands and feet, throwing herself onto the landing and rolling clear as another bullet blasted into the wall ahead of her.

∼

MAIDMENT TRIED to ignore the banging on the door. Huxley was angry now, his voice muffled but loud enough to hear without the interphone. He bellowed out that he would see that Maidment was punished for this, that he would go to prison for years for what he had done, that they would throw away the key. He felt terrible about what he was doing, but there was nothing that Huxley could say that would change his mind. They had his wife and child. They had promised to hurt them if he didn't do what he was told. He had no choice. Couldn't Huxley see that?

He *had* to land.

Maidment felt the sweat on his palms. The runway wasn't much more than a dusty strip that cut a brown line through the desert, and it was very short. He guessed it was between six and seven thousand feet from one end to the other. He wasn't confident that it was long enough. He looked at the fuel gauge and saw that he still had three-quarters of the kerosene that had been loaded in Colombo. He tried to add that to the payload and work out the maximum landing weight for a runway as short as this one. It would have been impossible to land here if the jet was fitted out for commercial flight, with a full complement of passengers and cargo. But he was only carrying fifty-two passengers today, the jet didn't have rows and rows of seating and a full hold, and it helped that the runway was dry. If he jettisoned some of the fuel, he might be able to touch down and stop if he slammed on the brakes hard.

Maidment flicked the switch to dump the fuel. The kerosene was pumped out of nozzles in the wings and dispersed, creating a fine mist that was visible on the backward-facing cameras. He circled for five minutes until the tank was just a quarter full and then lined up with the runway for the second time. He decreased speed to two hundred knots with the autothrottle and checked the GPS to confirm he was on the correct approach. He decreased speed to one hundred and sixty knots and applied the flaps to full. He lowered the landing gear, waited for the instrumentation to stabilise, and then set the auto-brake and armed the speed brake.

He opened the channel again. "This is Flight N898TH. Inbound on approach."

He checked the altimeter. They were four hundred feet above the ground and descending.

Almost there.

50

Abbas heard the *crack* of the flash bang, Nadia's panicked warning and then the sound of a suppressed gunshot and knew: the British secret service had located them. He was wearing his pistol in a shoulder holster and reached around to draw it, stepping quickly to the door and then carefully unlocking and opening it.

Nadia reached the top of the stairs, throwing herself down and then rolling out of the way as another gunshot cracked into the wall. She crawled to the wall and put her back against it.

Abbas drew his pistol and aimed at the top of the stairs.

"They shot him," Nadia said. "Nawaz—they shot him."

"How many of them?"

"I don't know," she said.

The boy was crying and, when Abbas reached out to try the door, he found that it did not move. He put his palm against it and pushed; it still didn't open. The woman must have barricaded it. Abbas could have tried to force it, but that might take time, and it would certainly be noisy enough to attract attention to his presence. He backed away from it and waited at the top of the stair, hidden from the floor below by the angle of the wall.

Abbas held the pistol in both hands and risked a glance around the corner.

The bullet fizzed just past his head, crashing into the wall and producing a shower of plaster.

"Toss your weapon," a female voice called up to him.

"I don't think so."

"You're outnumbered. You've got nowhere to go."

Abbas bit his lip. Nawaz was dead. He had no idea how many enemy agents had been sent, but it seemed unlikely that they would send only one. He knew they would start on the ground floor, clearing that before moving up to secure the floor above. They would be deliberate. Their uncertainty and caution *might* buy him and Nadia the time they needed to get clear. They might prevail in a firefight, but the odds were not in their favour, and even if they did make it out, there was almost no chance that they would do so uninjured. Exfiltrating with a bullet wound would be much more difficult, perhaps impossible.

He discounted that strategy and decided on another.

"We need to run," he whispered to Nadia.

"What about Nawaz?"

"There's nothing we can do about him."

"One more time," the voice shouted from the foot of the stairs. "Throw it down the stairs."

"We have the mother and child up here," Abbas said.

"Give up. There's nowhere for you to go."

"Stay where you are, or we'll shoot them both."

"What do we do?" Nadia whispered.

He pointed to the main bedroom. "Go," he hissed. "Out of the window."

She nodded and stood, putting her weight on the boards at the edge of the landing where they were laid across the joists. She moved silently, reached the main bedroom and continued inside.

"Last chance," the woman called up to him.

Abbas followed Nadia to the bedroom, closing the door behind him. She had already opened the window. He looked down and saw Nawaz's body, a square of light from the kitchen window falling over his left leg. The rest of the garden looked empty and, as he looked straight down, he saw the roof of the shelter where the bins were stored. He indicated that she should go first, aiming down and ready to fire if a target presented itself. She swung one leg over the sill and then the other and, with her pistol holstered, lowered herself down and then dropped, the bins rattling as she thudded onto the roof of the shelter.

He followed, sliding out of the window and dropping onto the shelter. He rolled forward, landing on the grass, and sprang to his feet.

"*Run,*" he said.

51

Six heard the sound of an impact from outside and spun to face it, bringing the gun up.

"Weaver, this is Six. What's happening?"

"They're running."

Another impact followed, the same as the first.

"Let them go," Weaver said.

She walked warily into the kitchen and then the boot room, her pistol raised. "How far away is my backup?"

"Ten minutes away."

Six paused at the door. She had taken out one of the intruders and was operating on the basis that the woman she had shot at and the man who had answered her were the last of them. Should she give pursuit?

"Six, this is Control. Let them go. Your priority is the wife and child. We're running out of time."

"Yes, ma'am."

Six went back to the stairs and very carefully climbed to the landing above. She checked the rooms one by one, clearing each until she was left with one that, given the colourful decoration on the door, was used for a child.

"Hello?"

She heard movement inside, but there was no response.

"I'm with the police," she said. It was far easier to be liberal with the truth than explain for whom she really worked. "The people who were here have gone."

There was a pause and then an uncertain voice. "How do I know you're telling the truth?"

"I'm afraid you're going to have to trust me," she said, "and you'll have to be quick. They were using you to get your husband to do what they wanted him to do, weren't they? They wanted him to divert his plane to Afghanistan."

There was another pause—shorter this time—and then a timorous, "Yes."

"We think he's in serious danger. We need you to speak to him so that he knows you're both safe. It'll be very dangerous if he lands—for him and the passengers he's flying. He probably won't be allowed to leave."

Six heard movement from inside and then the sound of something heavy being dragged across the floor. The handle turned, and the door opened. A woman stood just inside the room, a child clutching her legs. She looked at Six's pistol, her eyes going wide.

"Sorry," Six said, holstering the pistol and smiling. "You must be Elizabeth." She looked down and winked at the boy. "And you're..."

"Nathaniel," the boy answered timidly.

"Can I speak to him?" the woman said. "My husband, I mean?"

"Yes," Six said. "Just a moment."

She turned her head and spoke into her throat mic. "Weaver, this is Six. The house is clear, and I've secured both Elizabeth and Nathaniel Maidment. We need a line to Number One, ASAP."

"Stand by, Six. I'll patch you through now."

∾

MILTON LOOKED out of the window and saw buildings and vehicles and then, a mile or two beyond, a city nestled in the desert. They were losing altitude and, as they did, the details of the buildings began to be a little clearer.

Thorsson had his phone to his ear. Milton watched as the Icelander's face broke into a grin. He nodded at Milton, and Milton pressed the button to activate the interphone.

"Phillip," Thorsson said, "you need to listen to me. Your wife and child have been freed. They're both fine."

The pilot's reply was thick with disbelief and suspicion. "I don't believe you."

"We have them on the phone. Your wife—Elizabeth—she wants to talk to you."

"I don't..." he started; then the sentence tailed off.

"Here—wait." Thorsson put the phone on speaker and held it up. "You can speak to him now, Elizabeth."

They heard a female voice. "Phillip?"

The suspicion in Maidment's voice was replaced by a torrent of relief. "Elizabeth? Are you all right?"

"I'm fine."

"And Nathaniel?"

"We're both fine."

"Do you swear?"

"I swear. The police are here. The people who broke in are gone. Don't land, Phillip. They said it'd be dangerous if you did."

His next question was almost lost amid the welter of words, so quickly did he speak. "Where did I ask you to marry me?"

"What?"

He managed to slow down a little. "Quickly—where did I ask you to marry me?"

"Corfe Castle," she said. "And *I* asked *you*, not the other way around."

Milton heard a sob over the interphone and then the sudden roar of the engines as the power was increased. He had to put out a hand to steady himself as the nose tipped up and they climbed.

Huxley whooped.

Thorsson moved the phone nearer to his mouth. "Thank you, Mrs. Maidment. He listened to you. We're gaining altitude. Just give him a moment, and then I'll make sure you can speak to him again."

He lowered the phone and leaned against the fuselage, exhaling with relief. Milton braced himself with one arm, and Huxley, alongside, beamed his gratitude.

"Is that it?" he said.

"I think so," Thorsson said. "Let's just get the door open and work out where to go."

"I need a drink," Huxley said.

Milton dropped down into the nearest seat. "Don't tempt me."

52

Rashid stood next to the tower and brought his binoculars to his eyes once more. The 747 was lined up dead straight with the centreline of the runway, the flaps were fully extended, and the landing gear was down. He watched as the big aircraft descended: four hundred feet, three hundred feet, two hundred. The wheels touched down once, but before they could touch for a second time, the engines roared angrily, and the nose of the jumbo was pulled up. The jet lumbered back into the air, slowly gaining altitude. As it roared past the tower, Rashid involuntarily cupped his hands over his ears and let the binoculars fall down to be suspended on their strap. He dashed back to the entrance and bounded up the steps to the control room.

"What is he *doing*?"

"He's not landing, sir," Farooq said.

"I have eyes. I can *see* he's not landing. I want to know why he isn't."

"I don't know."

"Get him on the radio," he said.

The air traffic controller opened the channel, but before he could speak, Rashid yanked his headset away from him and put it on himself. "Flight N898TH. Mr. Maidment? Are you there?"

There was no reply save the crackle of static.

"You need to land your plane at once," he said. "At *once!* Have you forgotten what will happen if you don't do as you've been told?"

There was still no reply.

Rashid dragged the headset off his head and threw it at the controller. "Get him to answer," he said.

Farooq's face was grave. "I've just had a flare from Islamabad," he said. "They've heard from Abbas."

Rashid's stomach fell. "And?"

"The operation has failed. They've managed to release his family. That's why..." He gestured to the departing 747 already carving away to the west.

Rashid raised a hand to his head and clawed at his temples. He remembered the meeting at the compound before he had flown out to Jalalabad. Ali Khan had invested a lot of capital—financial and political—into this operation and had chosen Rashid to lead it. The director general had impressed upon Rashid how critical it was that it be brought to a successful conclusion. He had promised that Rashid stood to gain if he could deliver Huxley; the unsaid implication was that his career would suffer if he failed.

He followed the 747 as it continued to gain altitude, putting Jalalabad and Afghanistan and all of Rashid's carefully wrought plotting behind it.

PART VI

TUESDAY

53

Milton's return to the building on the banks of the Thames was more auspicious than the occasion of his previous visit. Instead of being driven into the underground car park in the boot of a car and taken downstairs to one of the holding cells with his hands in restraints, this time he was able to go in through the main door. The receptionist worked behind a desk that was branded with the Global Logistics logo, but upon seeing Milton, she told him he could proceed to the lift and go up to the top floor.

Weaver was waiting for him when he stepped out of the car into the lobby.

"Take a seat." He gestured to the red light that was lit above the door. "She'll be with you in a moment. Wait for it to go green."

They had been back in London for some thirty-six hours after a long and circuitous flight home. Maidment had purged most of the 747's tanks in an effort to reduce the weight for landing. He had—fortunately—left enough fuel to climb back to cruising altitude, but there had not been nearly enough to get them home, and Maidment and his co-pilot had quickly assessed their options. Dubai was a thousand miles away and likely just out of range. Tajikistan was six hundred miles to the north, but Huxley had vetoed it on the grounds that the ex-Soviet country was now a little too friendly with Pakistan. They had settled on Delhi, having just enough fuel to cover the eight hundred miles to get there. The main argument against the choice was that they would need to transit across Pakistan, between Multan and Faisalabad, but they had concluded that the Pakistani government would not attempt to interdict them in so brazen a fashion. Ultimately, although those hours had been nervous ones, the choice had been right. Milton had been relieved as they had crossed the border west of Bahāwalnagar, and even more so when they'd finally touched down.

They had been accommodated at the Indian government's expense overnight while the 747 was refuelled. Huxley had decided to remove Maidment from the flight deck so that Cross could take charge, with assistance from a new co-pilot who had been flown in overnight. Maidment was not even allowed back on the plane, and was sent home by way of an Air India flight. Milton had spoken to Huxley and urged mercy. Huxley had said that he would consider it.

Milton looked up. The light went green.

"She'll see you now," Weaver said.

54

The office beyond the door had changed in the years since he had last been here, but the view out of the wide window was just as spectacular as he remembered it. Control was standing on the other side of her desk, hands clasped behind her back as she gazed out onto the wide stretch of river beyond. Björn Thorsson was sitting down in one of the armchairs.

Weaver followed Milton inside and shut the door.

Control turned. "Milton," she said, "thank you for coming. Please—take a seat."

Milton did as he was told.

"Tea?"

"No, thanks, ma'am." He wasn't interested in platitudes. He wanted to be told that his work was done, and that he could leave. "Have you heard from Huxley?"

Control took her chair. "I have. He's grateful. As am I. You both did well."

"Do we have a better idea of what happened?"

"MI6 is still investigating, but we know most of it. It was

the Pakistanis—they're absolutely sure about that. Senior management in the ISI is very keen to scupper the deal that Huxley's been working on between the Indians and the Russians. We didn't think they'd go to these kinds of lengths, though. That was a surprise."

"What about the agents here?"

"There were three: two men and a woman. The senior man was Abbas Kader—he's one of their more dangerous operators. We believe he's been in the country for two weeks. The Border Force have no record of him, but we found evidence that suggests he might have got in aboard a boat from Rotterdam."

"And the others?"

"Cleanskins," Weaver said, taking over. "They only entered the country the day before. Nawaz and Nadia Khan, a married couple here to take up places to study at LSE. We don't know who they really were, of course. I doubt we'll ever know. Nawaz Khan was shot and killed by Six. Nadia escaped with Kader."

"Where are they now?"

"We don't know," Control said. "Six had no backup, so we had to let them run."

Weaver took over. "We had a Watchkeeper overhead. We know that they hijacked a car and drove to Hersham, and that they got on the last train into London. We had the Transport Police stop the train at Clapham Junction, but they weren't there. Group Three went back and checked the CCTV along the line, and two people were seen jumping from the train as it went into the tunnel outside Earlsfield. They lost the drone there."

"And then?"

"That's the last we saw of them," Weaver said.

"It does beg another question," Thorsson said. "How did they know his itinerary? Putting an operation as complex as that in place would have required a lot of preparation. The trip to the island had only been planned just before he went. Where did they get their intelligence?"

"We're not sure about that," Control said. "It's either someone here or someone in Huxley's operation."

"Who's probably still in place," Milton finished.

"Quite," Control said. "That's not lost on me. Either way, Huxley has been told that he is not to leave his property. I know you've had problems with his stubbornness, but it seems this latest escapade has helped him see the light. He's agreed to do as he's told until the deal is done."

"When will that be?"

Thorsson chuckled. "So you can disappear again?"

"That was the agreement. I keep him safe while he gets that over the line, and then I walk."

"But it's *not* over the line, Milton," Control said. "The terms have been agreed, but there are still small details left to take care of."

Milton felt his stomach fall. "How long?"

She leaned back in her chair and shrugged. "A day or two. A week at the outside."

Milton shook his head. "You've got until the end of the week."

Control pursed her lips. "It's done when it's done, Milton."

"The end of the week," he insisted. "This was never open ended."

The atmosphere was strained. They stared at each other for a moment until Thorsson intervened.

"We need to get back to the house. They tried to get at

him once. Kader and Khan are in the wind. There's nothing to say they won't try again."

"There's a car waiting downstairs," Weaver said. "Get over there now. Number Six is with Huxley, but he's already asked for the two of you. It appears that you've both made an impression on him."

55

The driver took them from London to Huxley's property in Chiddingfold. He had the radio tuned to a channel playing music from the eighties, and Milton was happy just to sit and listen. Thorsson reviewed notes on a tablet that he had collected from Weaver.

"It wasn't just the Russians on the island," he said quietly. "I took some photographs, and Group Three ran them. Look."

Thorsson handed Milton the tablet. The screen showed a series of thumbnails that, when Milton tapped them, enlarged to fill the screen with a caption denoting the subject.

"I don't recognise the names," he said.

"He's from Silicon Valley," Thorsson said, gesturing to the man on the screen. "He works in AI."

Milton swiped.

"On the front bench of the last Labour government."

"I know him," Milton said, swiping again.

"Owns a bank in the British Virgin Isles."

Milton swiped.

"Hollywood."

Milton swiped.

"Art collector."

He swiped again.

"Owns half a dozen newspapers."

"What's your point?"

"What were they all doing there?"

"He's rich," Milton said. "Birds of a feather flock together."

Thorsson shook his head. "They don't need to go for the sake of a party, do they? Most of the men in those photographs probably have islands of their own. They're not all doing business with him, either, at least not now. I don't think it's that."

"So what is it?"

"Maybe it's the chance to meet other people like them somewhere discreet, away from prying eyes. I had an assignment to babysit a billionaire at Davos last year. That was all about the networking, the elite maintaining the status quo. What if it's something like that, just with added discretion?"

Milton flicked through the photographs again and saw the same thing repeated over and over: older white men surrounded by glamorous younger men and women. There was a context behind those pictures, but neither he nor Thorsson were prepared to raise it. He thought of Huxley and how he had changed in the years since he had seen him last. His rise had been meteoric. He had been a fixer then, but could he have generated the stratospheric boost to his status with his network alone? What else might he have done?

Milton handed the tablet back to Thorsson. "I'm going to make sure no one puts a bullet in his head, and then I'm going to disappear. That's it. I don't ever intend to have anything to do with him again."

"Be careful," Thorsson advised. "Control is stubborn. She'll follow through on her promise, but you might have to give her a little extra leeway."

"I've worked for people like her before. You give them an inch and they take a mile."

"It might be worth giving an inch."

Milton leaned back in the seat and breathed out. He knew Thorsson was right. "I hear you."

∽

Huxley was waiting for them as the car pulled up next to the house. He opened Milton's door and stood back.

"A sight for sore eyes," he said, extending his hand.

Milton took it. "How are you?"

"Suitably chastened. I should've listened to you. I thought I knew best, and I quite plainly do not. It won't happen again. I'm going to do exactly as I'm told."

"I'm glad to hear it," Thorsson said.

"Thank you—both of you."

"It's not really us you need to thank," Thorsson said.

"Yes, I know—it was your similarly unresponsive colleague. I thanked her, too."

"Where is she?" Thorsson said.

"Inside."

The driver popped the boot, and Thorsson went around to unload the bags. They were heavy, and they rattled as he lowered them to the ground.

"What's in there?" Huxley asked.

"Some extra gear," Thorsson said. "I'm not taking any chances."

"You think they'll try again?"

"Probably not, but I'd rather have everything I might need and not have to use it than need it and not have it." Thorsson heaved the bags up, hooking the straps over his shoulders. "I'm going to find somewhere to get set up."

"Anywhere you like," Huxley said.

Thorsson grunted and set off.

"Does he ever smile?" Huxley said when he was out of earshot.

"Very rarely," Milton said.

"You know Iceland only gets four hours of sun each day in the winter?"

"I do," Milton said.

"Explains a lot."

The driver got back into the car and started the engine. They watched as he turned around and set off along the drive.

"I was going to go and see the horses," Huxley said.

"I'll come."

"You really don't think I'm safe here?"

"You said you'd learned your lesson."

"I have. Really—I'm taking it very seriously. Cronje's stepped things up, and I meant what I said about taking your advice." He pointed. "The stables are over on the other side of the wood. Come on."

56

Rashid was flown back to Islamabad in the same AW139 that had delivered him. The helicopter landed at the airport and, when he disembarked, he was greeted by a man who worked for Ali Khan.

"You need to come with me," the man said.

"He wants to see me?"

The man nodded and held the door of the car open for him to get inside.

There would be no cigars this time. The director general would want to know what had happened, and why Rashid was not returning with the intelligence asset that he had promised.

∼

The same three people were waiting for him in the same conference room. Lieutenant General Chaudhury Ali Khan was sat on the other side of the table, with Nazimuddin and Qamar to his left and right. The three of them presented as a tribunal, with Rashid told to sit facing them on the other side of the table. If he was in any doubt as to the displeasure with which the three of them viewed his failure, their *froideur* would have quickly disabused him.

"What happened?" Khan said without preamble.

"The operation in the United Kingdom failed."

"We know," Khan said. "How? You said it would be easy."

"I'm waiting to speak to my agents."

"You haven't managed that yet?" Qamar said.

"Not yet."

"What do you know?" Qamar asked him.

"Very little, I'm afraid. It's still early, and—"

"Let me help you out," she said. "At least one of your team was killed at the pilot's property."

"So we still have two agents in the field."

"Injured? Uninjured?"

"Obviously, I don't—"

"Captured, perhaps?"

"As I say, I don't know."

"Do you know *anything?*"

"Why don't you ask your source?" he snapped at her, forgetting, for a moment, to whom he was talking.

She paused for a moment, allowing the foolishness of his outburst to hang over the table. "A single Group Fifteen agent attacked the property, killed one of your agents and freed the pilot's family. Contact was then made with the pilot, and he was persuaded not to land. Huxley was flown to India, the plane was refuelled, and then he returned home. He has been taken to his property, where security has been increased."

She laced her fingers, rested her hands on the table and tilted her head to the side as she looked across the mahogany at him. Ali Khan and Nazimuddin watched him, too. They didn't speak, and, the silence unbearably heavy with tension, he shrugged and tried to grasp at a way forward.

"We still have ROOSTER," he said.

"Do you think he would be prepared to do more than just pass on the details of Huxley's itinerary?"

"He is a greedy man, and he knows that now is the time to abandon Huxley."

"And if he still says no? He knows that there are other ways we could ensure his cooperation?"

"Of course. He's no fool."

"Make contact with him. Find the agents who survived and make sure that they can get to Huxley. The deal with the Russians has not been signed yet. It must be stopped."

"I understand," he said.

Ali Khan waved a hand, and Rashid knew that he was dismissed. He got up, the back of his foot catching against the leg of the chair, and awkwardly made his way to the door. He escaped into the corridor and wiped his wet palms against his trousers. It had been an excruciating five minutes, but, as he closed his eyes and waited for his heart to settle back into its normal rhythm, he knew that he had been fortunate. They could have removed him from the operation, demoted him, sent him to work at an inhospitable outpost until he gave up and retired. But they had given him a chance to redeem himself. He took out his phone and called Farooq.

"Yes, sir?"

"Find Kader," Rashid said. "And make contact with ROOSTER—at once."

57

The stables were on the other side of the house and, like everything else on the estate, were of the highest possible quality. A collection of stone-and-block buildings were arranged around a cobbled courtyard. There were eight horse stalls, a feed room, a tack room, a loft and wood store. There was a large sand barn, an indoor arena with mirrored walls for dressage and a large hay barn. Like everything else about Huxley's property, it was brand new but built to look as if it had been there for years. The house was styled as if it were a Georgian pile, and this yard had been built to recall a rural idyll that might once have existed here.

"We've got seven fields," Huxley said as he led the way along the track to the stables. "Fifty acres on the south side of the valley. We keep them in grass. You've got different contours, drops, water crossings, and grass gallops. It's perfect."

Milton was left with the impression that Huxley kept the horses because that was what rich people did. Milton knew that he had come from a humble background, and those beginnings—parents who worked long hours, not much money to go around—had left a mark that looked as if it was going to be indelible. Huxley had told him once how he felt like an imposter when he mixed with those who had always had wealth. He had never shaken off the need to impress. Milton had seen the impulse in him before, all the way back when he was starting to accumulate his fortune, and the vast piles of money he had amassed since then had evidently not cured him of his insecurities.

They reached the stables. There were two horses here, and Huxley explained that both had been lame and were being kept out of the paddocks until they recovered.

Huxley scooped a handful of horse nuts from a bag, went to the nearest stall and held out his hand. The horse—a big chestnut mare—ducked her head and took the nuts, allowing Huxley to scratch her behind the ears.

"What did you decide to do about Maidment?" Milton said.

"I thought about that," Huxley said as the horse nuzzled him. "I was going to fire him."

"But?"

"You told me I should sleep on it, so I did. I can't have him flying me again. I know it wasn't his fault, but for a role like that, you have to have complete trust, and I don't—I can't. Not anymore." He took another handful of nuts and offered it to the horse. "I've told him he can't work for me, but I put together a severance package that means he won't have to worry about money. Seven figures. You're right—it wasn't his fault, and I don't want to see him punished for it." He looked over at him. "Does that sound fair?"

"It does," Milton said.

"The wife and child, too, what they went through... it's

awful. I've said they can go and have a week on the island while the police finish up at their house."

"That's a nice idea."

The horse whickered for more nuts.

"I don't know what they told you," Huxley said, "but the Indians and the Russians are coming to London to sign in two days. You won't have to worry about me for much longer."

He gave the mare another handful of nuts and then turned away from the stall. His expression changed to one of confusion; Milton turned and saw a man walking toward them. He was wearing a large rucksack on his back and holding something in his fist.

"Rufus," Huxley said, perplexed, "what are you doing here?"

Milton automatically stepped forward, putting himself between the newcomer and Huxley.

"Back off!" the man yelled, holding out his hand.

Milton tried to see what he was holding, but whatever it was, it was clenched too tightly in his fist to make out.

A wire ran from his hand over his shoulder and into the rucksack.

Milton tensed. "Stay behind me," he said to Huxley.

"Time's up, you piece of shit," the man said. "Time to pay for what you did."

58

The man was pale and sweating, but there was a determination in his eyes that was unmistakeable.

"What did you say your name was?" Milton asked.

The man blinked the sweat out of his eyes.

"His name's Rufus Lewsey," Huxley said, his voice wound as tight as wire.

"Rufus, then," Milton said. "I'm John."

"You need to get out of the way," the man said. "I don't want to hurt you."

"I'm not going to do that, Rufus. I'm going to stay right where I am, and you and I are going to talk."

"Talk?" He shook his head. "There's nothing you could say that would make me change my mind."

"About what?"

"This," he said, holding up the trigger. He jabbed it toward Huxley. "And him."

"I don't understand."

"Ask him. He knows."

"Calm down, Rufus," Huxley said. "This isn't necessary."

"I had a life. I was happy. *We* were happy. Everything was good. You took it all away."

Milton held up his hand, more to silence Huxley than the man with the bomb. He gestured to the rucksack. "That's not fake, is it?"

"No. I know how to make an IED."

"You're ex-army."

"How do you know that?"

"You never lose the look. What were you in?"

"RLC."

"So you *do* know. Okay. Good. At least we know that it's real. No one is going to do anything sudden. We don't want it going off accidentally."

Lewsey chuckled bitterly. "It's going off. You need to walk away."

"I told you," Milton said, "I can't."

"Get out of the way!"

Milton stared at the man's right hand. He was holding the trigger tightly. Milton knew that if he opened his fist, the trigger would pop open, the circuit would be completed, and the detonator would fire. The blast would be practically instantaneous and, at this close range, the shrapnel that he guessed was packed in the bag around the explosive would cut him, the bomber and Huxley to ribbons. That thought did not particularly concern him; he had no wish to die, but he knew that death would find him eventually. It was a surprise that it hadn't happened yet. He accepted it, but as he held up his hands in an attempt to placate the man, the wisps of a thought he hadn't really been aware of stitched themselves together: he didn't mind the prospect of death, but he wasn't sure that he wanted to go out in defence of Tristan Huxley.

Milton wasn't armed, but he doubted it would have

made a difference even if he was. The man would be able to trigger the device in an instant. The only way he was going to be able to navigate the situation was by talking the man down.

"Please, Rufus, just talk to me. Tell me what this is all about."

Milton stepped back, hoping that Huxley would do the same. The man—Lewsey—took a corresponding step forward. Milton recalled the layout of the stable and didn't need to look back to refresh himself; they were close to the entrance to one of the stalls. The stable had been constructed from brick. If he could get Huxley through the door, it might be strong enough to protect him from a blast, but that wouldn't do them any good if the man followed them inside.

"He used to work for me," Huxley said. "He ran the yard for me. Right, Rufus?"

Milton stepped back again; Lewsey stepped forward.

"Tell him what you did!" he yelled, spittle and sweat mixing on his lips. "Tell him what you did to my daughter!"

He raised his fist and, for a moment, Milton thought he was going to release the trigger. Milton stepped back, and again Lewsey mirrored him. The man was beyond reason, and Milton knew he was losing control of the situation. He was out of ideas, helpless to do anything beyond telling Huxley to run, when he saw Thorsson come around the corner of the stable block with a pistol in his hand.

"*Tell him!*" Lewsey yelled at Huxley. "Roxanne would still be here if it weren't for you!"

Milton backed up again.

Lewsey mirrored him.

Thorsson stayed where he was and aimed the pistol.

Huxley must have seen Thorsson, too. Milton couldn't

see Huxley's reaction, but he hoped against hope that he wouldn't do anything stupid to give him away. Milton risked a quick glimpse over his shoulder and saw the stall a step or two behind them. Huxley was still behind him; Milton hoped that he would anticipate what was about to happen.

"Stop moving!" Lewsey yelled.

Thorsson held his aim.

"I'm going to count to three," Lewsey said.

His hand shook.

Milton glanced behind the man and saw Thorsson give a single nod of his head. He was fifty feet away from Lewsey. It would be a difficult shot from that distance, but Thorsson dared not draw any nearer; he was already well within the blast radius of even the smallest bomb, and, with no cover, the odds that he would receive shrapnel wounds were so high as to be almost certain.

"I mean it," Lewsey shouted. "*One.*"

Milton readied himself to move.

"*Two.*"

Now.

He spun on his heel, located the open stable door and, as fast as he could, barrelled into Huxley and shoulder-charged him backwards.

There was a single gunshot.

And then the huge *crump* of an explosion.

59

Control had been summoned to see Latimer in the River House. The meeting was attended by other members of Latimer's team from MI6, together with Control from Group One, whose agents were responsible for the intelligence gathering in the wake of the failed ISI operation. The government was represented by Everett Burt, the liaison officer who had replaced Vivian Bloom. Control sat down and looked around the table. Everyone here would have known that Latimer was the sort of ambitious operator who would ensure that none of the opprobrium from what had *almost* happened to Huxley besmirched his reputation. He was well versed in the art of spreading the blame around, and Control was ready to fight her corner. Her opposite number as Control of Group One —a man called Clarendon, studious in wire-framed spectacles and a three-piece suit—fidgeted with his papers in a way that suggested he was nervous about the update he would be asked to deliver. Control could guess why; Group One had been charged with finding Abbas Kader and Nadia Khan, and, as far as she knew, they had been chasing ghosts.

Latimer rapped his knuckles against the table to bring the room to order. "Thank you for coming," he said. "You've all seen the agenda. Let's start with our friends Kader and Khan. What do we have?"

Clarendon shifted in his chair. "Not very much, I'm afraid. They've both dropped off the map. We've tried all the usual channels, and no one is saying a thing."

"That's disappointing."

"I agree. The embassy is under twenty-four-hour surveillance. If either of them is stupid enough to go there, we'll pick them up."

"But Kader's *not* that stupid, is he? He's experienced. A professional."

"Unfortunately, yes."

Control might have felt sorry for Clarendon if he didn't annoy her so much.

Latimer wasn't ready to move on. "So? What else are we doing?"

"We're watching their agents, too. They'll need help if they're in the field."

"And if they try to leave the country?"

"There's an All Ports Alert out."

"They're not going to be stupid enough to get caught like that," Control said, annoyed more by the certainty that Kader and Khan would be able to get clear than by the lack of originality in the attempt to find them.

Latimer turned to her. "You have agents ready if they are found?"

"On five minutes' notice to move."

Latimer's phone buzzed on the table with an incoming message. Control watched with annoyance as he was distracted by it.

"We've opened a backdoor channel with the Pakistanis," Burt said. "We've protested against what they did in the strongest possible terms."

"And they denied it," Control said.

"Of course, but they know we're on to them."

"I'm sure that'll stop them from doing anything like this again," Control said. "Perhaps, if we ask them nicely, they'll hand Kader and Khan over to us."

Latimer swore under his breath and then stood. "I'm afraid we're going to have to postpone. There's been an explosion at Huxley's property."

"What?" Burt said.

"A bomb, apparently."

"Huxley?"

"I don't know." He looked over at Control. "You still have agents there?"

"Two, plus Milton."

"I'll be interested to hear why they didn't stop this from happening and why I'm learning about it an hour after it happened."

He stood and stalked out of the room. Control pushed her chair back and stood. She gathered her things, sweeping the papers into her bag, and followed in Latimer's wake.

Weaver was waiting for Control in the lobby downstairs.

"Have you heard?" she asked him as they passed through security.

"Yes, ma'am. Just now. Milton called it in."

She pushed through the doors and emerged outside. "Huxley?"

"Uninjured."

"One and Six?"

"Six was inside, but One's been hurt. They took him to

the Royal Surrey in Guildford. They're stabilising him now, but they say he's going to need surgery."

"We need to be there," she said.

"Yes, ma'am. My driver is waiting for us outside."

60

Milton bought a cheap cup of black coffee from a vending machine and took it to drink in the hospital canteen. He *hated* hospitals; it was the smell of them, mostly, the cloying antiseptic stink that seemed to be everywhere, evoking memories that he would much rather forget. He looked around the room and saw patients in wheelchairs who had been pushed down from their wards for a change of scene, a woman in tears as she passed upsetting news to a friend, an elderly man with dementia who was rocking back and forth on the edge of a plastic chair. The coffee was unpleasant, but it was strong and hot, and he needed the jolt of caffeine to stop him from cadging a cigarette from the smokers who had lit up in the shelter outside the entrance.

He had hitched a ride in the back of the ambulance that had delivered Thorsson to A&E. The Icelander had been woozy from the sedative that the paramedics had administered, but as he drifted in and out of unconsciousness, he mumbled that Milton owed him. Milton had agreed before Thorsson's grin dissolved into a grimace of pain as the medic prodded and poked at his chest in an attempt to assess how badly he had been hurt.

It *was* true, though. Thorsson had saved his life; he had saved Huxley's, too.

Milton had called London and had spoken to Weaver. He had told him to wait at the hospital and had called back five minutes later to say that he and Control were on their way. Milton knew that Control would want to know what had happened, but he wasn't sure that he could give her any answers. The bomber had been lucid and had obviously been convinced of the justness of his cause. That, though, was the question that would go unanswered: why had he done it? He had spoken of his daughter, but had not elaborated.

Milton could ask Huxley, but he doubted that he would get an answer. He thought of what he had seen on the plane and on the island and felt that same sense of foreboding that he had felt before.

∽

MILTON WAS FINISHING a second cup of coffee when Control and Weaver strode briskly through the entrance to the hospital. Milton raised a hand as they went by the cafeteria, and they diverted across to him.

"What happened?"

"Someone tried to blow him up."

"The ISI?"

"No," he said. "Definitely not. Huxley knew the bomber. He was English—Rufus Lewsey. He used to work for him. Something to do with his horses."

"So this is a coincidence? After everything that just happened?"

"That's what it looks like. There was some sort of issue between them. Lewsey lost his job."

"And tried to *kill* Huxley over it?"

Milton decided not to mention what Lewsey had said about his daughter. "There was more to it than that," he hedged. "I don't know what, though—you'll have to ask Huxley."

"What about Number One?"

"Lewsey had a dead man's switch. I got Huxley into cover, Thorsson shot Lewsey, and the bomb went off. He was a distance away, but still close enough to take some of the shrapnel."

Control raised a hand to her head and massaged her temple. "Where is he?"

"They're going to operate."

"I need to speak to him before that. Show me where he is."

~

Milton took them to the ward where Number One had been waiting.

"He was over there," Milton said, pointing to an empty bay. "They said they were getting ready to operate. They must have taken him to theatre."

The doctor who had updated Milton on Thorsson's condition was writing up notes on a clipboard. Milton pointed to her, and Control strode ahead of them.

"Excuse me," she said.

The doctor frowned. "You shouldn't be in here."

"I work with one of your patients," she said.

"Which one?"

"Mr. Guðjohnsen."

"He's being prepped for surgery. Please—you'll have to wait downstairs."

"I work for the government," Control said. "National security. So does Mr. Guðjohnsen. How is he?"

The doctor looked as if she might protest, but, perhaps anticipating that Control could make things difficult for her, relented.

"He was struck by small pieces of shrapnel down the left-hand side of his body: the side of his head, his neck, his chest, his legs. Nothing particularly serious, but we need to make sure everything is out. I need to know whether he's got internal bleeding, and there's a chance the foreign objects will cause an infection if we leave them in. I've seen embolisms from wounds like these before—I don't want to take the chance."

"Is he lucid now?"

"Yes," she said.

"Take me to him, please."

"It would be better if it could wait. I'd much rather—"

"No," she cut over her. "It has to be now."

61

The doctor led the way through the hospital until they reached the preoperative ward. It was close to the theatre complex to allow for the quick transfer of patients, and was staffed by anaesthetists, resident doctors and preanaesthetic nurses. Thorsson was in bed while an anaesthetist reviewed his notes. The anaesthetist turned to Control and Milton and frowned his disapproval, but the doctor spoke to him, and the two medics, albeit reproachfully, left them alone.

Milton walked to the side of the bed. They had cleaned Thorsson up, washing away the blood. The wounds had been treated with dressings and bandages.

"How do I look?" Thorsson said, his voice slurred with the effects of the preanaesthetic painkiller he'd been given.

"You've looked better," Control said.

"You should see the other guy," he said, more thickly now.

Weaver took the chart from the end of the bed and scanned it. "He's on morphine."

"It's good stuff," Thorsson managed.

"Milton said Huxley knew the shooter."

"He worked for him." Thorsson winced, then shuffled around to make himself more comfortable. "Don't remember much more than that."

The doctor made her way back inside. "We need to anaesthetise him now. We can't really wait."

Control nodded and stood back. Thorsson reached out, grabbed Milton's wrist and pulled him down so that he could whisper in his ear.

His voice was weak. "Find out what he meant... about his daughter."

Thorsson let go, his hand falling limply onto the side of the bed.

"Look after him," Control said to the doctor, pausing on her way out. "And let me know when he's awake."

∽

MILTON, Control and Weaver took the lift down to the foyer.

"What did he say to you?" Control said.

"A running joke," Milton said. "I said I didn't need his help to keep Huxley out of trouble. He disagreed."

Milton wasn't sure why he felt compelled to lie, but he did.

"Number One's not usually one for jokes."

"I'd noticed."

The lift reached the ground floor, and the doors parted.

"I'd rather we had him at our facility," Control said.

"Does he have family?"

She tutted. "You know better than to ask that. Weaver will make sure someone's here once he's out of theatre."

"I'll stay," Milton said.

"No. I need you and Six to watch Huxley."

Milton was reminded about her predecessor as Control, the man who had been responsible for sending Milton into the field. He had been completely dispassionate about the agents who worked for him. Milton had quickly determined that he saw them as tools; they were useful to him only as long as they were in good working order. When they were not, they were discarded and replaced. His own history bore testament to that.

"Nothing else is to happen to Huxley," she said. "*Nothing*. Lock him inside his house if you have to. There's a panic room—put him in there. I don't care. The sooner that deal is signed, the better."

62

Milton watched Control and Weaver as they made their way back to the car that had delivered them from London. He had arrived at the hospital in the back of the ambulance with Thorsson, and now he was going to have to find a taxi to take him back south. There was one waiting at the rank outside the hospital, but on impulse he decided to delay his journey and, instead, crossed over the road and made his way into a Tesco Superstore.

He bought a cheap Android phone with a Pay-As-You-Go contract and took it to the store café, where he ordered a coffee and a cheese roll and found an empty table. He plugged the phone into an outlet next to the table, woke it up, opened a browser window and navigated to Google.

He remembered what Lewsey had said during the confrontation: he had wanted Huxley to admit to something that had happened to his daughter. He closed his eyes and tried to recall exactly what he had said.

Her name was Roxanne.

He tapped in her name and searched.

The results included two pages of women with that name.

He narrowed the search to show results from the United Kingdom.

There were six possible results, but one of them stood out. The search pointed back to the website of a local newspaper in Aldershot. Milton tapped it, waited for the website to load and then read.

A woman died by suicide two days after her twenty-first birthday; an inquest into her death has been heard. Roxanne Lewsey was found on December 23 last year in the attic of the house at Bercow Road in Aldershot that she shared with her parents, Rufus and Hazel.
Her mother told an inquest into her death, which was held at Surrey Coroner's Court in Woking, that her daughter had mentioned feeling suicidal in the past.
"She had been battling demons for some time," she added.
Felicity Alexander, area coroner for Surrey, recorded a conclusion of suicide.

There was a picture of Roxanne with her parents. Milton opened another browser window and searched for Hazel Lewsey. The first few hits were of different women, but the result at the top of the second page had a photograph that matched the newspaper report. It was the About page of a website for an architect's practice in Godalming, a town south of Guildford and close to Huxley's house in Chiddingfold.

Milton put the burner phone in his pocket and powered down the phone that Thorsson had given him. He made his way back to the taxi rank at the hospital and slid into the back of the car at the front of the line.

"Where to?"

"Godalming, please."

"Right you are."

The driver started the engine and pulled out.

Milton had been told to go back to watch Huxley, and he would. Six was there already, and she would be able to manage while he took a short diversion.

63

Hazel Lewsey Architecture had an office listed on Coopers Rise, a road that was close to Eashing Cemetery. It was a residential area. Milton guessed that the practice must have operated from Lewsey's house. The driver pulled up outside number eight. Milton paid him, took a card so that he could call another cab when he was finished, and stepped outside. Coopers Rise looked to be an estate from the seventies or eighties. The houses were semi-detached and set back from the road behind generous driveways. Wheelie bins were pushed out to the pavement, and cars were parked with the wheels up over the kerbs.

It was a grey and overcast day that promised rain. Milton turned up the collar of his jacket and climbed the shallow slope to the front door.

He knocked, and after a moment he saw the shape of someone approaching through the frosted glass. The door opened, and a middle-aged woman looked out at him.

"Hello?"

"Mrs. Lewsey?"

"That's right. Who are you?"

"My name's John Smith. Do you think I could have a word with you? It's about your husband."

Her shoulders slumped. "Ex-husband," she corrected. "What's he done now?"

"Do you think I could come inside?"

"I don't want anything to do with him. I'm sorry. I think you're wasting your time."

She gave an apologetic shrug and started to close the door.

Milton put out a hand to stop it. "Your husband died earlier today, Mrs. Lewsey."

She stopped, and her mouth fell open. "No. What?"

"I'm very sorry."

"You must be mistaken."

"He died at the property of Tristan Huxley."

"Oh, God," she said, steadying herself with a hand against the frame of the door. "He said he was going to go after him. I thought it was just talk. I didn't believe it."

"Please, Mrs. Lewsey—I'd really like to talk to you. Could I come in?"

64

There were photographs of Roxanne Lewsey everywhere: there was a framed photograph on the wall with her wearing a purple dress; another photograph in a smaller frame showed her riding a horse. The house was neat and tidy and clean; the vacuum cleaner had been propped up against the back of a sofa in the sitting room.

"Sorry," Hazel said, gesturing to it. "I was just hoovering up."

"I'm sorry for disturbing you."

She collected the vacuum and put it into the cupboard under the stairs. "Who did you say you were again?"

"John Smith."

"Police?"

"I work for the government."

She looked confused. "How does that have anything to do with Rufus?"

"I've been working with Mr. Huxley. I was at his property when your husband arrived today."

"And he's..." She closed her eyes.

"He had a bomb," Milton said. "He said he was going to kill Mr. Huxley. He was shot by one of the men guarding him. The bomb went off."

"He said he was going to do it," she said. "I never believed him."

"Kill him?"

She nodded. "After what Huxley did. Is he dead?"

"No," he said. "He's not. But that's why I'm here. Your husband mentioned something about Mr. Huxley and your daughter. Could you tell me what he meant?"

"I don't really want to go over it all again."

"I'm sorry to have to ask, but it's important."

"I've been here before. I know what happens—I tell you, you say how awful it is and that something will be done and then it all gets swept under the carpet."

"It won't," he said. "Not this time. I know you don't know me, and you have no reason to trust me. But that's what I'm going to ask you to do—trust me. I want to understand what happened. Maybe I could help."

She clenched her jaw. "I doubt it."

"Your daughter took her own life, didn't she?"

She nodded, just a little, then exhaled. She looked away and dabbed a finger at the corner of her eye. "I need a coffee," she said without looking back at him.

She went into the kitchen. There were more pictures of her daughter, a line of small portraits that were arranged on the windowsill. Hazel ran the tap and filled the kettle with water.

She still didn't look at him. "My ex-husband blames himself for what happened. He said that if it wasn't for him, then she would never have met Huxley and none of this would have happened. I told him that he shouldn't blame himself, that there was no way he could have known what

Huxley was like, but it didn't do any good. It ate him up. It was bad enough when Roxy was still alive, but it tore him to pieces when she died. It's why we split up." She sighed. "You have to have a strong relationship to stay together after the death of a child, and, if I'm honest, we didn't. We've been separated since before the inquest, and my solicitor had just sent the papers to him." She paused. "God. That might have been why he actually decided to go through with it."

"Don't blame yourself."

"Why not? I've been blaming myself for months. Both of us have."

She went to a cupboard and took out a jar of instant coffee and a bag of sugar. She unscrewed the top of the jar and spooned coffee into two white china mugs.

"What happened to her?"

She turned to face him, leaning against the counter, and bit down on her bottom lip as if searching for the right place to start. "Rufus was in the army."

"He told me," Milton said. "Royal Logistics Corps."

"That's right. He was decorated, too—the Queen's Gallantry Medal. While he was in Afghanistan, he helped a Danish armoured vehicle that was hit by an IED. They put a second device on the rear door to trap the soldiers inside, and he was defusing that when a third went off. One of his mates was hurt. Rufus cleared a route for medics to reach him. He was shot a month after that while he was disarming a bomb under a bridge in Helmand. The injury healed, but there was the PTSD, and he couldn't do it anymore. He was discharged after that." She poured hot water into the coffee mugs. "He'd been a rider when he was younger, and his therapist suggested he take it up again to help with his treatment. It helped. He took the compensation he got through the AFCS and used some of it to study equine management at college. Huxley had just built his stables and was looking for someone to run them. Rufus got the job. He was as happy as I've ever seen him for the first few months. He never forgot what had happened in Helmand, but now he was able to deal with it. It felt like we'd turned the corner on it all." She laughed bitterly. "Sounds stupid saying that now."

She slid one of the mugs across the counter to Milton, together with a container of milk, the sugar and a spoon.

Milton pointed to one of the photographs on the windowsill. "Your daughter loved horses, too."

She collected the photograph and handed it to Milton. It was of her daughter sitting atop a large chestnut bay. "She was good. Confident. She was saving up for university and looking for a weekend job. Rufus asked whether Huxley would take her on as a groom at the weekends, and he said yes."

Her voice had become a monotone. She sipped her coffee.

"That's when Huxley met her?"

Hazel nodded. "She was looking after one of his horses. It had gone lame, and they had to keep it in the stables. She said they got talking. She wanted to work with animals, and she told him that she was hoping to study to be a vet. He told her that he had a foundation that helped students get experience before they went to college, and that they had an annual expedition to Sri Lanka. He said that he could get her a place if she was interested. She asked us whether she could go. I can remember it like it was yesterday—she was so excited. We said yes, of course. We had no reason to think that there was anything to be worried about. Rufus asked Huxley what it would be like, and he said that there'd be treks into the wilderness; they'd see leopards and elephants and go whale watching on the coast. He asked about supervision, and Huxley said that there would be local rangers plus chaperones from the foundation."

"So you said she could go?"

"Of *course* we did. How often do chances like that come around? There was no way we could ever have afforded to send her to something like that, and we knew it would make a big difference on her CV. She took a gap year and went out there—she was gone for three months. She emailed us twice a week to start, then once a week and then once every other week. We knew something was wrong—the emails were long to start with, with pictures from the treks they'd been on, the animals that they'd seen. But they got shorter and shorter. The tone changed, too. Rufus managed to get through to her on the phone, and he said that she was bad tempered with him. That was out of character—she was always a daddy's girl."

Milton flashed back to the party on the island. He knew where Hazel's story was going, but he needed her to finish it. The feeling of unease that he had tried to ignore was stronger now, an ache in the pit of his stomach.

You knew what was happening. You pretended you didn't.

"She came back completely different to the girl who had gone out there. She was surly. She didn't speak, just locked herself in her room. We told her that she had to apply to college, but she said she'd changed her mind and didn't want to go. We told her that wasn't going to happen, but the next thing we knew, she'd applied for a job at McDonald's. She had all this enthusiasm, all this potential, and she was going to throw it all away. That was bad enough, but then I noticed the burns on her arms and thighs. She'd started wearing long sleeves, but I saw her coming out of the shower one morning, and I saw them. She'd started smoking, and she'd put the cigarettes out on her arms. Rufus and I confronted her about it. It was this massive blow-up, her shouting at us, blaming us, and then tears, and it all came out. She'd been on the trek, but it had only been for a month. Huxley had flown her to his island." She paused, and, when she spoke again, her voice was as cold and hard as iron. "He told her she had to have sex with the men he brought out there. We had no idea." She stared at Milton with cold, flinty eyes. "He ruined her life. He ruined ours."

65

Hazel turned back to the window and the photographs of her daughter.

"What happened then?"

"We told her that we had to go to the police. She said we couldn't. Huxley had told her that no one would believe her if she said what'd happened. What he'd *done*. He told her if she said anything to us, then Rufus would lose his job, and then he'd go to his lawyers and ruin us. You must've read what he's like when it comes to that—he has a reputation for dragging people through the courts. How would people like us stand a chance against someone like him? He's a billionaire. He'd have *buried* us. We'd have lost everything." She bit her lip. "Well, I didn't know what to do. I wanted to go to the police, but Roxy begged us not to. Rufus just went into himself. He started getting nightmares again, the ones from Helmand, and he shut himself away. He stopped going to work and started drinking. We were really struggling—we couldn't manage on the money I was bringing in, so we had to spend the college fund we'd saved for Roxy to pay the bills. And then, a month or so after Roxy came home, I got a call from a doctor saying that Rufus was in hospital. He'd been beaten up. His nose and wrist were broken, and he was concussed. He wouldn't say what happened. He came home and went to sleep, and I found a message on his phone. I recorded it—I thought I should, in case we needed it later. I'll play it to you."

Her phone was charging on the counter. She fetched it and played back the recording of the message.

"That was just us messing around. It'll be worse if you come around again. Don't forget we know where you live."

Milton recognised the South African drawl.

Christiaan Cronje.

"After that?"

"It got worse. Huxley fired Rufus, not that he would've wanted to work there after that. We started arguing. Roxy got worse. We got her to see a therapist, but she stopped going after the second session. She stopped eating, and then I found hash in her bedroom. I told her that wouldn't help, so there was another argument. She told me she hated me, that we were to blame for everything, and that she couldn't live with us anymore. She moved in with a boy she'd been seeing. We did our best, but she wouldn't see us. She broke up with him and found someone else. She was arrested for shoplifting—the police said they suspected she was doing heroin and stealing to fund the habit. They let her out with a warning, and she did it again." The story and the anticipation of its conclusion were difficult for her to manage; she was pale, and her voice was quiet. "Roxy was a good girl. She'd never got into trouble before, and now it just felt as if she was throwing her life away."

She put her mug to her lips and held it there, forgetting to drink.

"I know what happened next," Milton said. "You don't have to say."

She either didn't hear Milton or ignored him. "We persuaded her to move back. Both of us were petrified that she'd do something, so we made sure that she was never on her own. She seemed to be getting better, turning a corner, and then one evening she told us that we should go out together. She said she was fine and that we had to do something for ourselves. But she was just pretending. She waited until we'd gone, and then she killed herself. Rufus found her in the attic when we got back. She'd hanged herself."

She robotically lowered the mug and set it back down on the counter. There were no tears, and her face was a blank mask.

"I'm sorry."

"Why? It has nothing to do with you."

"I'm sorry that he was able to do what he did and there haven't been any consequences for it."

"That's how the world is for men like him and people like us."

Milton felt the anger in his stomach, a tight, malignant knot. "Not this time."

"You believe me?"

He stared at her and nodded. "I've been to his island. There were younger men and women there. I didn't do anything—didn't say anything—and I should have. I will."

"A man like him, with all that money and all those resources... How do you start?"

"There are ways."

"I've heard that before."

"Do you have anything that proves what you've said?"

"Beyond the fact that my daughter killed herself because of it?"

"I'm sorry—I have to ask."

"I don't have proof beyond what Roxy told us. Huxley's too clever to leave anything incriminating. But there are other girls." Hazel chuckled bitterly. "He's been doing it for years."

She opened a cupboard and took out a cardboard box. She set it on the counter and removed a notebook. She handed it to Milton, and he opened it, flipping through the pages. Each page was headed with a name, written in capitals and underlined, and, beneath that, more names—Milton guessed that they were parents—together with contact details, locations and dates.

He turned the pages and read the names.

Mona Carline.

Wendy Cunningham.

Imogen Gutierrez.

Joy Clark.

Hatti Ray.

Kate Wells.

Emma Rodgers.

Rosa Castillo.

"How many are there?" he asked.

"We know of twenty-two."

"How did you find them?"

She took out a folded piece of newsprint, opened it and handed it to him. "The newspapers covered Roxy's death. We had a reporter come around and ask for the details of what happened. We told her everything, expecting it all to get published, but it didn't happen that way." She pointed at the newsprint. "Look at it—they took out everything. All they said was that she'd been looking forward to a trip to the Galapagos Islands that had been sponsored by Huxley's foundation. He comes out of it looking like a saint. We were furious—the reporter wouldn't answer her phone, so Rufus went to London to confront her. She said that she couldn't speak about it—it was obvious that someone had leaned on her to keep the details out. We thought that was the end of it, but then we got a letter from a couple in Middlesbrough. They said that their daughter had been involved with Huxley, too, and could they speak to us about it? We said yes, of course, and we called them. It turns out that they were in charge of a kind of victim support group—it wasn't just Roxy and their daughter. There were twenty of them, and they all went back years."

"How long?"

"Ten years, at least. And that's just the ones they were able to find. I think there'll be dozens."

Milton felt sick.

Hazel noticed. "What is it?"

"I worked for him a long time ago," he said. "I should've noticed."

"Maybe if you'd done something then, things would be different now?"

"Yes."

"I've heard that before. We said it, and so have the other parents."

Milton didn't know why he felt compelled to be honest with her; she was a stranger, after all. He could see now that the memory of what he had seen from the first time he had worked for Huxley had stayed with him. He had almost forgotten it, but not quite. The visit to the island and the things he had seen there had revived it. He knew himself well enough to know that, unless he was careful, he would dwell on the regret and the guilt until he blamed himself for what had happened.

She must have seen it, too. "I don't blame anyone for

what they did or didn't do. They all tell the same story—the women were abused, then, when they complained or threatened to go to the police, they'd be threatened by his lawyers, or, if that didn't work, they'd get threatening phone calls late at night or a visit from his muscle. And it's obvious he has friends in high places—someone like him is untouchable when it comes to people like us. You know what he said to Rufus when he confronted him? He said he was bulletproof."

"He said the same thing to me," Milton said. "But it's not true. He's not. I've dealt with men like him before. There are always ways." He looked at his watch. He needed to get to Huxley before Control realised he wasn't there. "Would the others speak to me?"

"I don't know. You're a stranger—you say you're on our side, but we only have your word for that."

"I understand that," he said. "I hope they'd let me prove it. Would you ask for me?"

She paused and then nodded.

Milton thought of the young men and women he'd seen on the jet and on the island. "As soon as possible. His behaviour hasn't changed. He needs to be stopped."

She looked at him, then gave a nod. "Come back here tomorrow at midday. Two of the women live nearby. I'll try to persuade them to come."

66

Nadia reached for her pistol as she heard someone climbing the stairs. She raised it and took aim at the door, her finger on the trigger. There was a knock, two knocks, then a pause, and then a further three knocks. Nadia exhaled in relief, lowered the pistol and unlocked the door. Abbas was outside. She stepped aside so that he could come in.

They had been in the safe house since the failure of the operation. They had split up and conducted separate dry-cleaning runs; Abbas had told her to be especially thorough, and, with that in mind, she had taken seven hours to confirm that she was black. Even so, on the final leg of the journey back to the apartment, she had been fraught with nerves. London was a cosmopolitan city, and it had been easy enough to blend in, but, even as she acknowledged that, she was still frightened. Every sight of a police car or anyone who looked as if they might be tailing her had filled her with dread. Abbas had been waiting for her, and they had stayed inside until he had gone to check the dead drop earlier that day.

He took off his coat and hung it on the back of the door. It was raining outside, and drips ran down the leather and fell to the floor.

"Was everything okay?" she asked.

"It's fine," he said.

"Was there anything there?"

"There was," he said.

Abbas had been to the reserve dead drop. Nadia knew how the information would have been passed to them. They were using a method that had first been developed by the British. A transmitter disguised as a rock, hidden beneath a particular tree in Regent's Park, would transmit data to devices that connected to it. There was a bench nearby, and Abbas would have been able to wait there while whatever had been left for them was transferred to his phone.

"What did they say?"

He sat down at the kitchen table. "There was an explosion at Huxley's property after he returned. The details are unclear, but it appears that it was an attempt to kill him."

"Not by us?"

"No. We want him alive." Abbas scrubbed his eyes with his fists. "But they've increased his security. He's going to be more difficult to reach."

"They still want us to try?"

He nodded. "He's too important for us to give up. They've spoken with ROOSTER. He'll deactivate the security tomorrow night. We'll do it then."

"Just us?"

"ROOSTER will help. We'll need to make a plan. It'll be difficult, but not impossible. At least we're well equipped."

He gestured to the arsenal that had been provided for them by the quartermaster. There were handguns, three carbines, submachine guns and the ammunition and spare magazines to go with them all. There were flash-bangs and fragmentation grenades, restraints and sets of head-worn Gen3+ image intensifying night vision goggles.

"How do we get him out of the country?"

"There's an aerodrome seven miles east of the house. They'll send a plane, and we'll fly him to France." He stretched out his legs. "We should get some sleep. I don't know when we'll next get the chance."

67

Milton took a taxi back to the house. He paid the driver and buzzed the gate, then decided to walk through the grounds so that he might have a chance to compose himself before seeing Huxley again. It was a pleasant evening, and the walk would have allowed Milton to enjoy the grounds if it weren't for the riot of thoughts that he was struggling to control. He was angry —with himself, with the situation that he had found himself in, but mostly with Huxley—and he knew that he was going to have to keep that anger hidden. Huxley was astute, and Milton didn't know whether he would be able to hide his disgust.

Milton would investigate the allegations that Hazel Lewsey had made, but he didn't expect to find anything that would cause him to doubt the conclusion that he had already reached. He had witnessed Huxley's behaviour at first hand. He'd look for more evidence to be completely sure, but he had enough.

Huxley would pay for what he had done, and Milton needed to stay in his good graces until he was ready to act.

He had access to him now, but Huxley would be impossible to reach once the assignment came to an end with the signing of the deal.

He had two days.

He was going to have to move fast.

∽

IT TOOK fifteen minutes to walk up the drive. Milton saw that security had been upgraded in the hours following the attack. Two Range Rovers had been parked outside the house, with one vehicle occupied by a man with binoculars. Milton noticed two other men as he approached; they patrolled the grounds, both armed with automatic weapons. He saw new cameras and motion sensors in the grounds, and those were just the ones that had been left in the open; there would be others, too, including laser tripwires that would make an undetected approach to the house almost impossible. They were reminders that Milton needed to remain free of suspicion from Huxley or the other Group agents. He could get into the house now, and that would make it easier to take action against its owner.

It would be very much more difficult if his access was revoked.

Milton saw the man with the binoculars check him out from the Range Rover, raising a radio to his mouth so that he could confer with the patrolling guards. One of them diverted across the lawn and intercepted Milton on his way to the stables.

"Private property," the man said.

"I've been looking after Huxley," he said.

"ID?"

"I'm John Smith. You should have my details."

The guard took out a phone and swiped across it, comparing the images on the screen with Milton's face. He still had not given him permission to proceed as Huxley jogged over to them from the house.

"Let him through."

The man turned to Huxley. "Best stay inside, sir."

Huxley thanked him and then, when he had turned away, rolled his eyes at Milton. "He's one of mine. Cronje's brought in another half dozen to beef things up."

"That's not a bad idea," Milton said.

The two of them started back toward the house.

"How's Guðjohnsen?"

"They're operating on him," Milton said.

"Will he be all right?"

"It's not serious—just cleaning out a few bits of shrapnel. He was lucky he was a good way back. Any closer and he would have been blown to bits."

"Thank God for that. I asked about him, but they wouldn't say. Is there anything I can do to help?"

"No. He's getting excellent care."

Huxley carried on as if Milton hadn't spoken. "I have concierge medicine. Do you know what that is? I have specialists on call twenty-four hours a day. I should make a call."

"There's no need. If he needs anything, they'll take him to a facility they use in London."

"I'll send him a bottle of something," Huxley said. "What is he again? Finnish? What do they drink? Vodka? What about his family? Is he married? We should send something to his wife."

Milton saw through it all now. The extravagant generosity, the lavish gestures, all designed to take centre stage so that the focus was on Huxley's largesse rather than the malignancy that festered beneath the baubles and glitter. Milton recognised it and wouldn't be fooled, not anymore.

"I had London on the phone," Huxley said. "They say they're not going to take any chances. I tried to explain that what happened with Rufus Lewsey isn't connected to the deal, but they're not listening."

"What *did* happen?" Milton said. "Why did he do what he did?"

"Lewsey?" Milton was looking for a reaction and caught the barest flicker of unease before Huxley hid it with a sad shrug. "He ran the yard here. We had a disagreement, and I had to let him go."

"Something like that had him coming after you with a bomb?"

"He was in the army—Afghanistan. Cronje had him investigated after we let him go. PTSD. He was wound tight. It didn't take much for him to snap. I understand there were problems at home, too."

"What kind of problems?"

"His daughter killed herself. We looked into it, too—she had mental problems. Self-harming."

"I was going to ask about that—he mentioned her."

"She worked here too. We had an issue a few months ago. One of the stables caught fire. We looked on the CCTV and saw she'd been smoking dope in there. We think she dropped a roach on dry hay, and it all caught fire. We put it out quickly, but it could have burned everything down and killed the horses. We had to let her go. Her dad needed to blame someone for what happened, and he blamed me. The truth of it is—and I hate to say it—he ought to have looked a little closer to home."

Huxley was completely credible. He knew the truth of what had happened to Roxanne Lewsey and his own role in it, yet he lied as easily as he breathed. There were the tiniest little tells, but Milton only saw them because he knew to look for them. The way he tapped his thumb and forefinger together, a momentary glance away, a lick of the lips. He was almost convincing, but Milton knew too much to be taken in.

Huxley was a sociopath.

"To be honest," Huxley said, "I'm not complaining if they want to increase the security. The last couple of days have been crazy. Right? I'm happy to stay here for as long as it takes." He clapped Milton on the shoulder. "You going to have dinner with me tonight?"

Milton shook his head. "I'll pass. It's been a long couple of days. I'll make sure the security is in place, and then I'm going to get some sleep."

Huxley nodded his understanding. "Fair enough. Maybe tomorrow?"

Milton said that he would.

They reached the door to the house. "I know you don't do this anymore," Huxley said. "You didn't have to say yes, but I'm glad you did."

"Forget about it."

"I just want you to know how grateful I am."

Huxley's false praise and urge to ingratiate himself made Milton's skin crawl. He just wanted to get away from him, but he knew that he couldn't afford to give any reason for suspicion. "I'll see you in the morning."

PART VII

WEDNESDAY

68

Milton spent the morning patrolling the grounds of the house. The security was much more stringent now; he saw Six inside and the two other armed men whom he had seen last night standing sentry by the front and back doors. They were well equipped beyond the weapons they carried; Six and the two newcomers each wore earpieces and microphones that would be connected to tactical radios. Milton had not been afforded the same privilege, not that he'd expected it.

Huxley was in the entrance hall as Milton came down the stairs.

"Missed you at breakfast," he said.

"I got an early start. Went and had a look around the grounds."

"And?"

"You're about as safe as you can be."

"I told you—I'm going to be good. I just got some excellent news, too. The Russians are flying in tonight, the Indians first thing tomorrow. They'll sign the deal at the Russian embassy, and that'll be that."

"Good."

"And then you get to go home."

"That's the plan."

He put his arm on Milton's shoulder and guided him deeper into the hall, away from the door. "Let me bend your ear one more time. Between you and me, I think I'm going to let Cronje go. The situation on the plane and then what happened with Lewsey yesterday—I don't know. I think he's lost his edge. Do you know what I mean?"

"That's a decision for you."

"Let me at least have another try to talk you around. Money's no object, obviously, and maybe there's a way that it could be more of a supervisory role. You could train the others and pick Cronje's replacement."

There was no way that Milton would work for Huxley—not now—but there was no profit in closing that door today. Dangling the possibility that he might waver made better sense. "Fine."

"You'll do it?"

"No, but we can talk about it. Get your deal out of the way, and then we can sit down."

Huxley beamed with boyish enthusiasm. "Perfect."

"There's one thing you can help me with," Milton said. "I need to go and see Guðjohnsen, but I don't have a car. Could I borrow one of yours?"

"There's a Range Rover in the garage. The keys are in the ignition. Help yourself."

∽

MILTON LEFT the compromised phone in his room and went to the garage. The car was where Huxley had said. Milton climbed in and started the engine, rolled it outside and turned the wheel to aim along the drive. He saw movement in the mirror.

"Hey!"

It was Six. She was jogging toward him from around the corner of the house. Milton left the engine running and waited for her to reach him.

"Where are you going?" she asked.

"I need to speak to Number One."

"What about?"

"There are a couple of things about what happened yesterday that I want to clear up."

"Such as?"

"If it's relevant, I'll share it with you when I get back."

He put the car into gear and pulled out. He glanced into the rear-view mirror as he set off down the drive and saw her standing there, staring after him. She would report it to Control, he knew, but that would be something that he would deal with later. He looked at his watch and saw that it was coming up to eleven. He had an appointment to keep, and he didn't want to be late.

69

It was ten minutes before midday when he arrived back at Hazel Lewsey's house. There was a car that hadn't been there before, together with another car parked with its right-hand wheels on the pavement. Milton slotted the Range Rover behind it and climbed the sloping drive to the front door.

He knocked on the door and waited for it to open. He knew that he was going to have to move quickly if he was to do what he meant to do. The assignment could come to an end tomorrow, and, besides that, he knew that Control would be told of his absence and might very easily remove him from the security detail. Thoughts about how to deal with that, though, could wait. He believed what Hazel Lewsey had told him the day before, but, given that the only possible response to it was a radical one with consequences for his future, he needed corroboration.

Hazel opened the door. "Come in."

She led the way into the sitting room. Four women were arranged on the sofa, the armchair and one of the chairs that had been brought in from the dining room.

"This is John," she said.

Hazel went around the room, pointing to each of the four women and telling Milton their names: Wendy, Imogen, Emma and Hatti.

"Thank you for coming."

"You've got ten minutes," said Wendy. She was in her early thirties. She was small, but gave out the sense of high voltage. She was dressed in black trousers and shirt, and wore a colourful headscarf around her head; Milton guessed she was being treated for cancer. "Hazel says you've got good intentions, or else I wouldn't have come. I don't mean to be rude, but we've been here before, and nothing has ever come from it."

Imogen—small and delicate featured, of a similar age to Wendy and pretty in a flawed kind of way—nodded her agreement. "To be honest, from my point of view, just coming here and talking about *him* rakes it all up again."

Milton looked from woman to woman until his eye settled on the one who had been introduced to him as Hatti. She was also small, but lacked the healthy colour of Imogen's complexion and was skinny to the point where Milton suspected she might be anorexic. Her hair was cut short, her nose was pierced, she was dressed all in black—black leather jacket, black T-shirt, black jeans, black DMs—and gave out the impression that she wanted nothing to do with anyone, and that she was very much here on sufferance.

She was staring at Milton hard.

"I know you," she said. "I've seen you before."

Milton looked at her. He didn't remember her face.

"You were younger then, but it's you. Hazel said you worked for him."

"That's right," Milton said.

"You were there."

There was a murmur of discontentment from the others.

"I worked for the government," he said. "I was given the job of keeping him safe, but it was a long time ago. More than ten years."

"*Fourteen* years," she corrected. "I could give you the day if you wanted. It's not the sort of thing that you forget. You didn't do anything then. Why should we believe that you'd do anything to stop it now?"

"I didn't know what was happening," Milton said. "And I'm very sorry about that. I'm sorry about what he's done to all of you."

Hazel stood up. "It's not his fault," she said. "We all know what Huxley is like. He's a con man. He fooled us when he came for our daughter. He fooled most of your parents, too. I wish someone had done something about him years ago, but the fact of the matter is that he is very, very good at hiding what he is behind the image he puts out. I wish John had seen something and stopped him, but he didn't. It is what it is—I don't blame him for it. But he's willing to do something now when he doesn't have to. I think it's worth hearing him out. If you don't like what he has to say, that's fair enough. But at least give him a chance."

The murmur of disquiet continued for a moment, then stopped. The atmosphere still felt antagonistic, but Milton knew that was to be expected. He was nothing to these women, and the revelation that he had been involved in Huxley's circle before was a fact that gave them a good reason to suspect him. But it was clear that they respected Hazel. She had lost everything, after all—her daughter and her husband—and if she was prepared to give Milton a chance, it was difficult to argue that the others shouldn't.

Hazel suggested they tell Milton what had happened to

them, and, one by one, they did. Hatti went first, recounting a series of assaults that had taken place in London and then Paris. The others followed, and Milton couldn't fail to pick out the common threads that tied them all together: they had all been young, with vulnerabilities that a man as clever and manipulative as Huxley could take advantage of. There were offers to pay for an education for those who didn't have the money to afford it; the suggestion that introductions could be made to people Huxley knew in the music business and modelling industry; money for clothes and make-up; invitations to parties that would be attended by people they'd recognise from the newspapers and television. Once ensnared, the pattern was the same: they would be pimped out to the men—and sometimes women—that Huxley brought to them. They had all sought to get away, but Huxley had threatened them: all the things that he had promised would be taken from them, and, worse, their families would suffer the consequences that a man with unlimited wealth could unleash. When that didn't work, there was always the unvoiced threat that Cronje, the frightening ex-soldier with a reputation for violence, would be sent to 'persuade' them to comply.

Milton listened in silence. They were reluctant to talk, and the pain they felt at having the memories dredged up was plain on their faces. He listened and let their words sink in and, when Emma finished, any doubt that he might have harboured about what he was proposing was gone.

"Thank you," he said.

"It doesn't mean we trust you," Hatti said.

"I know. But I'd like the chance to show you that you can."

"How?" Hatti said.

"You deserve justice. He needs to pay for what he's done. I can give you that."

"No one has ever shown any interest in even *listening* to what we have to say," Emma said. "I went to the police. They opened a case and said they'd make sure he was prosecuted. You know what happened next? They said there wasn't enough evidence to charge him, and they closed it. His thugs came to see me a week later and threatened to hurt me if I ever did it again."

"I won't go to the police," Milton said.

"So what's the point?"

"There are other ways for him to pay."

They paused at that, perhaps wondering what Milton was suggesting. He knew the impression that he gave others; he was drenched in blood from the work he had done for the Group and, despite his best attempts to scrub it off, it was part of him now.

He told them what he proposed to do.

70

Milton waited in the hospital foyer for ten minutes so that he could get an idea of whether or not anyone had been left to watch Thorsson. He thought it was unlikely, but experience had taught him that caution was sensible. He couldn't see anything and, satisfied, he made his way up to the first floor and then followed the labyrinthine corridors until he was outside the room again. He glanced through the glass panel in the door and saw that Thorsson was alone. He rapped his knuckles against the glass and went inside.

Thorsson was awake. "What are you doing here?"

Milton sat down. "How are you?"

"Just sore. It wasn't as bad as it could've been. They're going to let me out today." Thorsson shifted back so that he could raise himself into a sitting position. "So? Why are you here?"

"You were right."

"About what?"

"Huxley."

"What did Lewsey mean about his daughter?"

Milton explained what he had learned from his interview with Hazel: how Lewsey had introduced his daughter to Huxley, how she had been tricked into travelling to the island, and what had happened there.

"She came back and wouldn't talk to anyone about it. Then she killed herself."

Thorsson's jaw clenched.

"It gets worse. The Lewseys found other women who said they were abused. Some at the island, some at his house. I met them this afternoon. Four of them. Their stories are all consistent and credible. You saw what I saw on the island—I think it's obvious what he's doing. Huxley finds young men and women who are vulnerable or want something that he can give them, tricks them to trust him and then takes advantage. I think he's using them to tempt whoever it is he's trying to woo at the time. We were wondering how he's got into the position he's in—this is how. You know what else we saw on the island and in the house?"

"Cameras," Thorsson said.

"They're everywhere. One of the women I met was given a job by Huxley at the house. She said he showed her a control room where all of the feeds from the cameras were displayed. It wasn't just the common spaces. He has hidden cameras in bedrooms and bathrooms, in places where they could only have been installed because he was after footage that he could use."

"For blackmail."

"Why else?"

Thorsson closed his eyes and breathed out.

"How much do you think Control knows?" Milton asked.

"She knew he had a reputation with women. She told me. Beyond that, though? You'd have to ask her."

Milton looked across at the Icelander and saw the anger in his eyes. Thorsson had always struck Milton as loyal to a fault, the perfect agent who did not suffer doubt or remorse about the nature of his calling. The kind of agent that Milton had been, once, before the guilt had been too much for him. But now, though? He was questioning Control openly, in front of him. Milton paused and thought about what he could say next. He knew that he had two choices, and that each presented its own risks and rewards.

He could tell Thorsson that he didn't have a plan, that he wasn't prepared to go up against someone of Huxley's wealth and influence, especially not when he was a ward of the Group. He would plan in secret and act with the benefit of surprise. But reticence would wall him off from any help that Thorsson might be prepared to furnish.

Or he could tell Thorsson that he was not prepared to stand aside, that Huxley's victims needed to see justice done. That choice bore risks. Thorsson's loyalty to Control might outweigh any anger that he felt; he would be able to stop Milton easily enough, and that would be that.

But if he was angry enough to act, he would be a valuable asset.

He thought back to what Thorsson had said about his sister and trusted that the anger over what had happened to her would be enough.

"What are you going to do?" Thorsson asked him.

This was it: if Milton was wrong about Thorsson, he was dooming his plan to failure before he had even had a chance to get started.

But he had already made his decision. There was no going back.

"I'm going to make him confess. And then I'm going to put him away."

Thorsson shook his head. "That won't work. He's too valuable. You know what'll happen—anything you start will get shut down."

"Not if I make enough noise."

Thorsson gave Milton a knowing look. "There are easier ways to get justice."

"And I haven't ruled them out. But I want to see the women compensated for what he did to them, and it'll be easier if Huxley's still alive."

"After that?" Thorsson said.

Milton shrugged. "What happens, happens."

"I meant what about you?"

"That doesn't matter."

"There'll be no amnesty."

"So I disappear." Milton shrugged. "I've been running for years. It's not a hardship."

"They'll send the Group after you again."

"You only found me when I got lazy."

"You won't be able to stay ahead of us forever."

"Maybe," Milton said. "But that's not going to stop me from doing what needs to be done."

Thorsson looked away.

"Are you in or out?"

Thorsson turned back and held his eye. "In."

71

Control put the phone down and stared out of the window to the river beyond. Six had called earlier to say that Milton had left the house, and she had just confirmed that he was yet to return. She looked at the clock on the mantelpiece: it was two in the afternoon. Milton had been gone for three hours.

She held down the button on the intercom and waited for Weaver to answer.

"Yes, ma'am?"

"I need to speak to Number One. Right away."

"I'll call him now."

Control had never been comfortable with the idea of inserting a man like Milton into a live assignment, but Huxley had made it a precondition before he would accept their protection. She went to the desk and picked up Number One's report on how Milton had behaved. There had been no red flags. One had reported how Milton had helped prevent the landing of Huxley's jet in Jalalabad, and there was nothing that he had seen—either before or after

—that had given any suggestion that Milton was not playing them straight.

But there was still something that nagged away at her.

The intercom buzzed. "Number One is on the line, ma'am."

Control picked up the phone and held it to her ear.

"How are you feeling?"

"I'm fine, ma'am," Thorsson replied. "The doctor says I'm ready to be discharged."

"Excellent. The shrapnel?"

"There wasn't much to get out. I'll live."

"Do you feel up to going back to the house?"

"Yes, ma'am. Of course."

"I'm not expecting you to play an active role, but I'd like you to take charge. I'm led to believe that the parties are due into London to close the deal. Huxley needs to be there."

"I'll see that he is."

Control stood. "There's something else."

"Ma'am?"

"I wanted to ask you about Milton. I understand he came to see you today."

There was a brief pause. "Yes," he said. "He did."

Control frowned. "Why?"

"He wanted to run through what happened with Lewsey."

"Why is he going after that?"

"He's thorough. Lewsey got through the security—he wants to make sure it doesn't happen again."

"That's what he said?"

"Yes, ma'am."

"When was this?"

"Just after lunch."

"It's two o'clock now. So where is he?"

"Isn't he back at the house?"

"No, Number One, he's not." She didn't bother to hide her irritation. "That's why I'm finding this a little perplexing."

"Then I'm very sorry. I don't know where he is."

She breathed out with weary resignation. "Do you trust him?"

"If you'd asked that a week ago, I would've said no. You know what I thought about him being put on the job."

"You thought it was a dreadful idea. You made that *very* clear."

"I did. But I've worked with him since then, and I've changed my view."

"You trust him?"

"I do—to a point."

She sat back down, drumming the fingers of her left hand against the table as she decided what to do. "Find him and secure him."

"Ma'am?"

"We can't take chances. Go back to the house and let me know when you have him. I'll have Weaver send a car, and we can put him back in a cell until we decide what to do with him."

"Do you think that's necessary? I haven't seen anything to make me doubt him."

"That's quite the *volte-face*."

"I realise that. But I may have been wrong about him."

"Not a gamble I'm prepared to take, I'm afraid. You have your orders—see that you follow them."

"Of course, ma'am. I will."

72

Milton knew that he had to get back to the house, but there was preparation to take care of first of all. It took him seventy minutes to drive into London and the hotel near Vauxhall Bridge where he had left his things. He opened the safe, took out the handgun that he had stowed there, and checked that the magazine was full and the weapon was ready to fire. He slid it into the back of his trousers and made sure that it was covered by his jacket.

He went back down to the car and drove to the mall he had passed on his way into London. He went to Tesco and bought a roll of duct tape, two packs of ibuprofen, a pack of wound dressings, crepe bandages, sterile wipes and microporous tape.

He went back to the car, took out his phone and opened Airbnb. He needed a particular kind of property: secluded, with no neighbours, yet within striking distance of Chiddingfold. There were several options, but he settled for a converted stable in Dunsfold. Milton opened the map to check that it was suitable. It was on a farm, but well away from the main building and screened by a line of elm trees. Milton paid for a week and left a message that he would arrive later that evening.

He looked at his watch: he had been away for nearly five hours. He knew that there would be questions to answer upon his return, but he just needed to stay the course until this evening. They could have their suspicions; by then, it would be too late.

73

Milton drove back to the house, reaching the gate and waiting there as his identity was checked. He meant what he had said to Thorsson; there was no time to delay. He was as sure as he could be about Huxley's guilt and knew that he wouldn't be able to live with himself if he turned away from the course that needed to be taken. This brief return to government employment had cast what he had done since he'd first quit in stark relief. Working for the Group felt wrong. This might not have been murder on behalf of the Crown, but he knew those assignments were still crossing Control's desk, and that men like Thorsson and women like Six were still being sent out into the world to action the files that they were given. The path that Milton had chosen was different: he helped people who would otherwise have been helpless. People like Hazel Lewsey and the women that she had introduced to him; people without the means to fight back against the monstrous injustices that had been foisted on them. Milton knew, too, that doing the right thing was dangerous, and that Thorsson had been right: the Group would find him again, no matter how far he ran, and, when they did, there would be no new offer of clemency.

Milton had decided to do the very thing that he had been charged to prevent—put an end to Tristan Huxley—and he knew that sort of disobedience came at a cost.

But he didn't care.

The gates buzzed and pulled back, and Milton edged the car inside and continued down the sweeping drive. He went up to his room and shut the door behind him, taking out the pistol and the phone that he had purchased earlier. He was halfway through drafting an email when he heard a soft knocking on the door. He opened it and saw Thorsson standing in the corridor. He came in, shut the door behind him and then put his finger to his lips while he went into the bathroom and ran the shower. The water was loud against the tray; Milton recognised the behaviour of someone who was warding against the possibility of their conversation being eavesdropped, and followed the Icelander into the bathroom.

"You're back," Milton said quietly.

"On orders," he said. "You have a problem. Control knows you left the house today."

"Six saw me drive out."

"And she called that in," Thorsson said. "You might have been a little more discreet."

"It would've been more suspicious if I'd climbed over a wall and disappeared."

"Control knows you came to see me earlier, and asked me what you wanted to talk about. I said you came to talk about Lewsey."

"I did."

"Yes, among other things. She's shrewd—and she doesn't trust you. I've got orders to have you returned to London."

"So pretend you couldn't find me."

"That's just delaying the inevitable."

"You won't need to delay it for long. I'm going to take care of this tonight."

"Meaning?"

"I'm going to get him off the property. I need a little time alone with him—somewhere I won't be disturbed. He's going to confess."

"Best not to ask what you'll do if he doesn't want to play along?"

"You know as well as I do that won't be needed. He's soft. I doubt I'll have to do anything more than give him a fright."

"And if you need to do more?"

"It won't be anything he doesn't deserve."

Thorsson bit his lip as he considered what he had been told. "All right. I'll cover for you for as long as I can."

"Thank you."

"How are you going to get him away?"

"I'll tell him there's a threat and that we need to get him to a secure location."

"When?"

Milton looked at his watch. "It'll be dark in an hour," Milton said. "I'll do it then."

74

Christiaan Cronje waited at the top of the stairs until the two guards who were loitering in the entrance hall below him moved on. He was nervous. He had grown comfortable with the role that he had assumed for most of the last year, providing what scraps of information he could find on Huxley's business in exchange for Pakistani money. Every month had seen him collect a bag of cash from a series of dead drops that he suggested to the man who had recruited him. It had been easy, and, once he had realised that working carefully removed most of the risk, he had even come to see it as easy money.

This, though, was different. This was more than passing on the scraps of gossip that fell into his lap. It was more than providing the details of Huxley's travel arrangements. They had asked him to take an active role tonight, and he knew that there was a chance—if he was not careful, or if he was unlucky—that he would be discovered, with all the repercussions that would flow from that. He had said no when they had asked him to do more, and he had discovered that his recruiter's affable and grateful nature could change. He had threatened him, told him that he didn't have a choice, that he must have realised that the enormous sums of money that he had been given would eventually require him to do more than whisper secrets. Cronje was a hard man and not prone to fright, but he knew when he was out of his depth. The consequences of saying no were more frightening than the risk of being caught, and, when the deal had been sweetened by the promise of the biggest payday yet, he had agreed to do what they wanted.

The guards finished their conversation and continued their patrol.

Cronje had approached the Pakistanis at the beginning. He had watched, disgusted, as Huxley's behaviour had become more and more brazen. Huxley had told him that his money and influence would protect him and, for the most part, he had been right. Some of the young men and women who had been sucked into Huxley's orbit had complained, and Cronje had been dispatched to persuade them that silence was a much better choice than making empty, pointless threats. Cronje had cajoled and threatened and, when that didn't work, had delivered the bags of money to shut them up. Huxley could pretend he was invulnerable, but Cronje knew better. Huxley's utility would be used up one day, and when it was, when he was shorn of the shield that his work provided, he would be brought down low. Cronje knew that anyone else who worked with him would be ruined, too, and he had no intention of being around when that happened. And so he had gone to the Pakistani High Commission and made his offer. He had socked away the better part of two million dollars, and he would use that to disappear.

Tonight.

Cronje descended, waited at the bottom and listened to confirm that there was no one else here. Huxley was in the entertainment wing, and the agents from London were elsewhere. He walked through into the office that accommodated the security equipment. The banks of screens on the wall showed the feeds from the exterior cameras; Cronje knew about the cameras inside the house—the bedrooms and bathrooms and all the rest—but they could only be accessed by Huxley. He closed the door behind him and went to the desk. The cameras, the motion detectors and the other exterior sensors were all controlled from a single computer. He woke it with a tap on the keyboard, scrolled the mouse to the menu bar and opened the settings. There were three sliders to move from active to inactive and, as he finished with the last, the feeds from the cameras all went black.

Cronje took out his phone and pressed send on the message he had already prepared.

75

Abbas and Nadia had hidden the car inside a farmer's field two miles to the south of Huxley's estate, and now they moved with elaborate care through the thick woods that bordered the paddocks to the north. Abbas was wearing night-vision goggles, and, as they paused before a large oak, he saw a flash of luminosity against the dark. It was a deer, and, as soon as it caught their spoor, it bounded away until all that was left was the fading green swipe on the lens.

They hadn't seen anyone as they moved into position. The road out of the village was a single track and, as evening began to change to night, there had been no other cars. These woods, too, were empty. They passed across a muddy track that bore the impressions of a horse's hooves and the tread of a mountain bike, but there was no one out at this hour. It was quiet and peaceful, but Abbas knew that it was likely to be the calm before the storm.

They reached a low dry-stone wall. Abbas had no need to check his map; he knew that Huxley's property was a mile to the northeast. The cameras and motion detectors would be inactive, but Huxley's guards would be on alert after what had happened over the course of the last week.

He turned to Nadia. "Ready?"

She nodded.

They pulled their balaclavas down and checked their weapons. Abbas did not want there to be bloodshed, but he knew that there was a realistic chance that it would be unavoidable. ROOSTER had provided details of Huxley's security: his men, together with armed agents from Group Fifteen and the ex-agent upon whom Huxley seemingly depended. Abbas hoped that they would be able to rely on stealth to get in and out without being seen, but they couldn't rely on that alone. ROOSTER's guards had been paid to look the other way, but the Group Fifteen agents would be a different proposition. Abbas had the element of surprise and would not hesitate to use it.

They vaulted the wall. A farmer's field lay beyond, and then the start of more woods.

His phone buzzed. He took it out and saw the message from ROOSTER.

"The security is down," he hissed to Nadia.

"I'm ready."

"Time check. I have eighteen hundred hours."

Nadia synchronised her watch. "Eighteen hundred hours."

"Thirty minutes to get into position. All good?"

She nodded.

Abbas gave the signal to proceed.

76

Six finished her patrol. It was dark in the grounds that encircled the big house. The sun had lingered for half an hour or so, but now that it had slipped all the way below the horizon, the night had rushed in. She had checked all of the outside doors, confirming that they were properly secured. Everything was as it should be. She reached the door to the boot room and went inside.

Cronje, the head of Huxley's personal security detail, was waiting to go outside.

"What are you doing?" Six asked him.

"Hourly check."

"No need," she said. "I've just been outside."

"No offence," he said, "but that's what I'm paid to do. Can't just defer it to you."

He opened the door and stepped outside.

Six's phone vibrated in her pocket, and she had to lower the zip to reach inside and fetch it.

"Hello?"

"Six, this is Weaver. Hold for Control."

She unzipped her jacket and took it off. It was cold outside, and she had appreciated the warmth.

"Six?"

"Good evening, ma'am."

"Where are you?"

"At the property."

"Is Number One there?"

"Yes, ma'am."

"When did he arrive back at the house?"

"Late afternoon. Why?"

"I've been trying to contact him—he's not returning my calls."

"Would you like me to find him for you?"

She didn't answer. "Have you seen John Milton?"

"An hour ago."

"Still at the house?"

"Yes, ma'am. Is there something you'd like me to do?"

"Number One was given orders to secure him, and, clearly, he hasn't. You need to do it. Number Twelve is on his way—he'll be with you in half an hour. He'll bring Milton back to London."

"What shall I tell Huxley? He won't be pleased that—"

"I don't care whether he's pleased or not," she snapped. "Just find Milton and give him to Twelve."

77

Thorsson returned to Milton's room just after six. Milton ran the shower, and they convened in the bathroom again.

"He's in the pool," Thorsson said.

Milton took his pistol and hid it in his jacket pocket. "What about a car?"

Thorsson held out his hand and opened his palm to reveal a key attached to a fob that bore the logo of Aston Martin. "Press the button at the front to open the garage doors," he said.

Milton took the key. "Thank you."

"Where are you going to take him?"

"Probably better you don't know."

"Once you've done this... there's no coming back."

"I told you—I don't want to come back."

Thorsson put out his hand. "Be careful. I still think you're old and slow."

CRONJE WAITED a minute before opening the boot room and confirming that the woman was gone. She was. He shut it again and squinted out into the darkness. The wooded area on the other side of the lawn provided a deeper shade of black and, as he peered into it, he thought he saw motion. Cronje held his breath as shadows detached from the black and hurried across the grass: two of them, moving quickly and low to the ground. They were dressed in black, with balaclavas covering their faces and the exposed skin around their eyes and mouths daubed with black camouflage paint.

They approached. Their faces were obscured by the balaclavas and the goggles that were pushed back onto their foreheads, but Cronje recognised the man from the embassy to whom he had delivered his intelligence. He had been told to call him Raamiz.

"Where is he?" Raamiz said.

"In the pool," Cronje said. "He usually swims before dinner."

"Are the doors unlocked?"

"I did it twenty minutes ago."

"Your men?"

"Verwoed and Kruger are on board, and the others are off shift. All three government agents are here, though."

"We saw the woman," Raamiz said.

"She just finished a patrol. The big one was in hospital until this afternoon."

"He's back?"

"With his arm in a sling—you won't have to worry about him. I haven't seen the other bloke."

"Do you have a car for us?"

"It's the Range Rover at the front. It's open, and the keys are under the seat."

Raamiz gave a nod. "We'll go around the house and

come into the pool from the outside. You need to make sure he can't get back to the safe room. Don't let anyone in, and don't let him out."

Cronje hadn't wanted to be so actively involved, but Raamiz had made it plain that he had no choice. His final payment was contingent on Huxley being flown out of the country, and he needed the balance of his fee to put his plans into effect. Verwoed and Kruger had been persuaded to help, their cooperation won by the promise of a generous lump sum once Huxley had been taken. Cronje had told them that their involvement would never be revealed; at best, they would just have to look the other way.

"Ready?" Raamiz said.

Cronje pulled his pistol. "Ready."

78

Thorsson left, and, after a minute to allow him to get clear, Milton set off too. He crossed the house to the wing with the bowling alley, cinema and pool. He passed through the gym and into the corridor with the sunroom to the left and the cinema to the right. He looked through the open door and saw Huxley in the water, carving back and forth as he swam lengths.

Milton had planned to tell Huxley that they had received a threat against him and that the decision had been taken to remove him to a safe house. He was thinking of the best way to deliver the news when he heard the door to the main house open behind him.

"Where have you been?"

He turned around: it was Six.

"I went to see Number One."

"All day? You were gone for hours."

"There were some things that I needed to do."

"Go on."

"I don't understand why that has anything to do with you."

She reached into her jacket and took out the pistol that she wore beneath her shoulder. "You need to come with me."

"Put that away."

She aimed the pistol directly at Milton. "Please don't make me ask again."

Milton raised his hands as the door to the house opened again.

"What are you doing?" Thorsson asked her.

Six turned her head to glance back at Thorsson, the pistol never wavering from Milton. "Control wants him back in London—Twelve's on the way to take him back."

"She hasn't told me that."

"She couldn't reach you, so she asked me."

"Let me talk to her. Put the gun down."

"No."

"Stand down, Six."

Milton saw uncertainty on her face. "There's no need for you to speak to her. I spoke to her fifteen minutes ago."

Thorsson reached a hand to his pocket. Six took a step back, swivelled and moved her aim so that she could cover them both.

"I'm just getting my phone."

"Leave your hand where I can see it."

"Lower your weapon," Thorsson said.

She didn't, holding her gun in a comfortable grip. "Not another inch."

Milton was out of options. He was going to have to be completely honest with Six. "Huxley isn't who we think he is. He's been abusing young men and women for years. We saw evidence of it on the island—he's a pimp. That's what Lewsey came here for—his daughter killed herself because of what Huxley did to her."

She shook her head. "That's not in the file."

"I found others," Milton went on. "Four other women, but there'll be more. He's been doing this for years. There might be dozens—maybe hundreds."

"He's been using them for blackmail," Thorsson said. "That's how he has his influence. It's not the money. That's probably where the money comes from."

"Tell Control that. He"—she jabbed the pistol at Milton—"is still going back to London."

It was a stand-off, but Six was the only one with her weapon drawn. Milton was not ready to concede without a fight, but with the pistol aimed at him and Thorsson caught between his duty to the Group and his decision to side with Milton against Huxley, there was no obvious way to break the stalemate.

Six was facing the pool, and suddenly Milton saw her frown in consternation.

"Shit," she said.

Milton turned and looked back. The door at the far end had opened, and a figure, dressed all in black, was stepping through it. The person—it looked like a man from the shape—hadn't seen them.

Huxley was oblivious to what was happening, continuing to stroke up and down the pool.

"This isn't done," Six said. She turned and aimed her pistol across the water. "Don't move!"

The figure was wearing a balaclava and was heavily armed. He was toting a short-barrelled carbine and, with an economy of movement and decisiveness that revealed his training, he raised the weapon and fired. Six fired, too, but the odds of hitting anyone at this distance were negligible. Her round punched through the window; the incoming volley studded the wall behind them, a round whistling close enough to Milton's cheek that he felt the heat in the air.

They saw muzzle flash from outside, and another fusillade crashed through the glass, pinning them down in a crossfire. The three of them dropped to the tiles. Milton drew, sighted the shooter outside from the rough location of the flash, and loosed a single round. The glass popped as the bullet sliced through it. Milton knew the odds of a hit were infinitesimally small, but he might give the shooter pause for thought.

Six had slithered on her belly until she was pressed up against the side of the raised jacuzzi. The first shooter took aim and fired, his volley slamming into the frame of the tub. Thorsson turned out of cover, aimed and fired. He was closer this time, and the man, perhaps unsure as to what he was facing, retreated into the darkness.

"It's Kader and Khan," Six yelled back to them.

"At least," Milton said.

"What do we do?"

"Get Huxley away from here," Thorsson yelled back.

"I'll do it," Milton said. "He trusts me."

Six popped her head above the tub. "I don't."

Huxley was at their end of the pool now, his hands on the side. He took off his goggles and a pair of waterproof earbuds and looked up at Milton, Thorsson and Six, all of them with their weapons drawn. He turned his head and saw the open doors and the shattered glass, and his eyes went wide.

Milton saw movement in one of the huge arched windows that looked out from the pool and onto the gardens beyond. He went to the corner where the corridor met the pool room, sighted along the frame of his pistol and aimed at the spot where he had seen the activity. A fist punched through the glass and reached down for the handle to open the door. Milton fired twice, both shots blasting through the glass. The hand jerked out of the window again, leaving the door still closed.

"Six," Thorsson called to her, "go with Milton. I'll cover you. Get Huxley and go."

79

Huxley braced his hands on the side and thrust himself out of the water. He went toward his robe and pool shoes, but Milton grabbed him and yanked him back toward Thorsson.

"Tango!" Six yelled. "Get down!"

Milton saw a flash from outside and tackled Huxley to the tiled floor as another volley blazed into the pool room, blowing chunks out of the marble that faced the windows.

"What's happening?" Huxley stammered.

Milton held him down and made a quick assessment. The shooters were in the gardens to his left. It was dark there, so, while he or she would be able to see inside the lit pool room, it was much more difficult for them to see out.

"Get him out of here!" Thorsson yelled.

"Down!"

Six fired again, and then automatic fire punched through the windows in response. Chunks of glass were blasted out of their frames to shatter across the tile.

"Kill the lights!" Milton called out.

"I've got it," said Thorsson, and, a moment later, all of the lights in the pool room went out.

That was better. They had been sitting ducks before, but now it would be more difficult for anyone outside to see when they made their move.

"The panic room," Huxley gasped. "I'll be safe in there."

"Agreed," Six said.

That was the last thing Milton wanted. If Huxley made it to the safe room, that would be the end of any chance that he had to bring him to account. Control had given the order that he was to be taken off the detail, and Six was ready to hand him over to the agent who would take him back to London. She was aware that Thorsson sympathised with him, too.

There was only one thing to do: Milton would have to disable Six between here and there.

"Take him," Thorsson said. "I'll hold them off."

∽

ABBAS WAS OUTSIDE, taking cover behind the trunk of a tree. He had hoped that it would be possible to collect Huxley and remove him without fuss, but it was clear that Huxley's guards had got to him before they had. Stealth would have been preferable, but if that was no longer possible, then force would have to do.

It didn't matter: as long as he left with Huxley, the ends would justify the means.

"Nadia," he said into his microphone. "Nadia—report."

She was at the other side of the pool building. "I'm here."

The lights in the pool room switched off. He lowered his night-vision goggles, and the view ahead was bathed in green as they switched on. He saw movement inside: Huxley, wearing his swimming trunks and barefoot, was running. Two of his guards, a man and a woman, were on either side of him.

"They're pulling back into the house," Nadia said.

"They'll run into ROOSTER. Go inside and follow them."

Nadia said that she would and, as Abbas watched, she pushed the door open and scurried into the pool room. A large figure—the bigger of the three government guards, he thought—slid out of cover and took aim at her. Abbas raised his carbine and fired, three rounds sent through the wrecked glass. The big man ducked, and then, as Nadia found shelter and fired too, he pulled back.

Abbas left the cover of the tree and hurried around the side of the building, staying low, keeping in cover where he could. He clutched his carbine in both hands and slipped into the shelter of a decorative wall, looking over it and through a doorway that led into what looked like an opulent sitting room. It was a good spot to observe: he could see all of this side of the house, including the garage. He would wait here until ROOSTER and his men had Huxley, and then he would lead them to the Range Rover and drive him away.

80

Milton led the way, with Huxley behind him and Number Six bringing up the rear. He remembered the door to the panic room; it was in the centre of the house, between the wine cellar and the elevator that accessed the first and second floors. He was going to have to find a way to get Huxley away from Six before they got there.

"Is it them again?" Huxley said.

Milton kept his attention on the way ahead and didn't answer.

"It's the ISI, right? Milton? *Milton!* Talk to me!"

"Be quiet," Six hissed.

Milton knew it had to be the Pakistanis. Two of their agents had escaped from Maidment's house, and it looked like they had been under attack from two shooters. He gave serious thought to just handing Huxley over to them. But there was no guarantee that he would be punished if he was taken to Islamabad. He had something that they wanted. They might extract it by way of unpleasantness in a damp and dark basement, but they might just as easily conclude that they would have more success by offering him something—a life of comfort, perhaps—if he gave it all up willingly.

Milton wasn't going to take the chance that they opted to be clement.

They reached the covered walkway that connected the entertainment wing with the rest of the house. The kitchen was ahead, and, after a left turn into the reception hall and then another left, they would be at the door to the panic room. Milton thought he heard something ahead of them and raised his hand to bring them to a halt.

Christiaan Cronje and two of his men were in the kitchen and coming their way. Milton took a step back, but Cronje had already seen him. He raised his arm, aimed a pistol and fired. The bullet whistled just to the side as Milton dropped. He returned fire, sending two bullets the other way. A saucepan clanged as one of the bullets struck it; there was another clatter as it crashed from the wall to the floor. Cronje grunted in pain as the second bullet tattooed him just below the right shoulder. He tumbled out of sight before Milton could fire again.

"The next person who puts his head where I can see it gets a bullet between the eyes," Milton called out.

"There are three of us," Cronje grunted through the pain.

"And one of you was stupid enough to get shot. I don't mind our odds."

"Send Huxley through here, and maybe you get to piss off in one piece."

"Him?" Huxley spat. "He sold me out? The fucking disloyal *shit*."

"We can't go that way," Milton hissed to Six, "and we can't go back."

"Agreed."

"So what do we do?" Huxley said, his voice tight with panic.

Milton flicked his pistol at the door that led into the gardens. "Outside. Through the woods."

Six nodded her agreement. It was the best that they could do. Milton would get Huxley away from the house and then leave Six behind.

She went to the door, opened it and glanced outside. "Clear."

Milton put his hand on Huxley's shoulder. "We're going to run and not look back. All right?"

"Okay."

"Ready?"

Huxley stammered out that he was.

"*Now!*"

81

They couldn't move as quickly as Milton would have liked on account of the uncertainty of whether there might be other hostiles in the gardens and, especially, because Huxley's feet were bare, and he complained every time he trod on a pine cone, thistle or any other piece of debris on the ground. Milton wanted to head due north, cutting through the wooded area and then breaking into the arable fields that surrounded the estate. There was a farm a couple of miles away, and he hoped to be able to find transport there.

"Slow down!" Huxley gasped out.

"We can't. Keep running."

"Stop!"

Gunfire rang out overhead. Indignant birds exploded from their roosts.

Milton reached for Huxley and brought him to a halt. Six stopped, too, hiding her pistol against her body so that it wouldn't be visible from behind.

They turned back to the house. The moon passed out from behind a cloud and cast just enough light for Milton to be able to see the two figures who had caught them up: both dressed in black, both wearing night-vision goggles, both toting short-barrelled carbines.

"Hands," the man to the right ordered.

Milton raised his hands above his head. Huxley followed suit.

The woman to the left aimed her carbine at Six.

"That's the one," she said.

"She killed Nawaz?" the man said.

"Yes."

"Do it."

The woman shouldered the stock and fired a single round. Six's head was driven back, blood sprayed out, and she fell to the ground. Huxley shrieked. Milton clenched his fists, but made sure to keep them up high.

The man gestured to Milton's pistol. "Throw it away from you."

Milton did as he was told, losing the pistol in the darkness as it thudded into the leafy debris on the ground.

"You," the man said, gesturing to Huxley. "You need to come with me."

Huxley's attention was fixed on Six. His mouth was open, and his eyes were wide.

The man took a step toward Huxley, the muzzle of his carbine aimed into his face. Milton saw that he had a cable tie in his hand. "Put your hands together and hold them out in front of you."

The woman was covering Milton. There was nothing that he could do. The two of them were well equipped and professional and wouldn't be the sort of operators who would leave witnesses. The woman had already shot Six in cold blood. Milton knew it would be his turn next.

Huxley lowered his hands and held them out as he had

been told. The man tossed the cable tie onto the ground and told Huxley to put his wrists through the loops.

And then Milton saw movement between the trees behind them.

Milton needed to distract them. "You won't get far."

It was too dark to make out, but he saw something coming toward them.

"Do we need him?" the woman asked.

Thorsson.

Clouds covered the moon again, and the light grew faint.

"No," the man said. "You can—"

A flash lit the dark. The gun barked.

The woman fell to her knees.

The man's reaction was instant: he ran.

Thorsson aimed.

Milton knelt down and grabbed the pistol from Six's hand.

Thorsson pulled the trigger.

The gun clicked, but didn't fire.

The man sprinted into the trees.

Milton aimed blind and fired.

His round hit a tree with a heavy thud.

They heard the noise of the bushes and saplings as the man rushed through them.

Milton aimed again, but he knew it was no use. The man was already out of sight.

Thorsson cursed. "I lost count."

"What the fuck," Huxley stammered. "What the *fuck!*"

Thorsson took the dead agent's carbine. He snatched the goggles and pulled them on, then checked that the weapon was ready to fire.

"I'll go after him," he said. "You need to get him out of here."

Milton grabbed Huxley by the shoulder and hurried him onward, following a faint trail that led away from the woods into which the man had disappeared. He kept the pistol in his free hand and hurried him on through the undergrowth toward the lane that marked the northern perimeter of the property. He would find the transport to get Huxley clear, and then he would do what had to be done.

PART VIII
THURSDAY

82

They trekked through the woods until they found the road that led back to the village. Milton reached the dry-stone wall and paused there, assessing his options. He could turn east toward the village, find transportation and get away. It would be easier to find a car there, but they would be exposed as soon as they left cover, and it was a too-obvious choice. Milton had no idea whether there were more tangos in the vicinity and, if there were, the odds of being found would be higher if he was predictable. On the other hand, he could turn west and head away from the village.

"What's down there?" he asked Huxley, pointing along the lane.

Huxley was still wearing his swimming trunks and had started to shiver as the water on his skin chilled in the cold air. "There's a farm."

"Anything else?"

"Another couple of houses."

"How far?"

"Half a mile?"

That made it easier. "We'll go that way."

"And then?"

"We'll steal a car and get you out of here. We have a safe house. Somewhere to take you in the event that something like this happened. They won't be able to find you there."

"You think there are more of them?"

"I don't know," Milton said. "There's at least one. I wouldn't be surprised if they had others. We'll have to be careful until we're clear."

Huxley put his hand to his head and muttered a curse.

"You'll be fine," Milton said. "Do exactly as I tell you and everything will be okay. All right?"

Huxley nodded, swallowing Milton's lie. There was no reason for Huxley to doubt him and, as panicked as he was, all he was interested in was the promise of escape. He would have felt very different if he had known that he was exchanging one peril for another, but Milton didn't care about that in the least. He would get him clear, get him out of reach of the Pakistanis and the Group, and then he would do what had to be done.

Milton set off. He stayed on the south side of the road, following a narrow animal track that picked a path between the trees and low bushes. The wood was dark, and there was no sign of traffic. He knew that he would see the headlights of any vehicle that might approach them, but, equally, doubted that any other agents looking for Huxley would be foolish enough to drive with the headlights lit. He knew, too, that the man who had escaped was still out there and that, if he was any good, he would have reached the same conclusion as Milton: the village was too risky, and the best chance of concealment was in heading to the west.

Huxley caught up with Milton. "That was them again, wasn't it?"

"Yes."

"Fucking Cronje," he cursed. "First they get Maidment and now him."

"No talking."

Huxley muttered another curse, but did as he was told.

The woods petered out as they reached a farmer's field. Milton stopped. He remembered that the agents who had attacked them had been equipped with night-vision goggles. The terrain ahead was open, without any cover save the hedge; they would be obscured from the road, but if anyone was in the field with them, they would be easy to spot. He bit his lip as he reassessed the good sense of his plan.

"What are we waiting for?" Huxley said.

"Hush."

"Can't we wait here? Won't London be sending reinforcements?"

That was certainly not an option. "The plan was to retreat to the safe house. We don't want to vary it now. You're a sitting duck out here."

Huxley was getting agitated. Milton determined that proceeding to the west was still the better course of action and, after closing his eyes and listening for anything that might suggest that they were not alone, and hearing nothing, he left the treeline and hurried on through the field. He saw the spectral shape of another line of trees across the field to their left, the naked branches picked out in the dim light of the moon. The field was damp, and they splashed through puddles, Huxley complaining under his breath that he wasn't wearing anything on his feet. Milton allowed himself a kink of a smile at the thought of the two of them, together, like this: the billionaire in his bathing costume, struggling through muddy puddles on the way to a fate that he would enjoy even less.

83

They reached the end of the field and the line of trees that demarked the boundary between it and the property beyond. Milton edged between the hedge and the start of the trees and emerged on a rectangle of lawn that was bounded by a rough wooden fence and an open gate. A track led to the south and, in the distance, Milton could see a square of yellow light from a window.

"What's down there?" he asked Huxley.

"A house," he said.

"We'll have a look," Milton said. "Stay close. No more talking."

They followed the lawn, staying close to the boundary. The drive extended for a quarter of a mile and ended at a pleasant-looking cottage. The light that Milton had seen went out as they approached the property, but Milton remained watchful. There would likely be spotlights activated by motion sensors, and, knowing that at least one of the occupants of the house was presumably still awake, he would have preferred not to trigger anything that would signal their presence. There was a garage before the house that did not appear to have any security measures. A Land Rover Defender was parked outside it. Milton crept up beside the vehicle and tried the door; it had been left unlocked.

"How are you going to start it?"

Milton swivelled and held his finger to his lips again, then turned back and reached up to the visor. He pulled it down in the hope that he might find the keys. They were not there, nor were they under the seat. It didn't matter. There was a small toolkit in the glovebox; Milton took out a screwdriver and slid it into the keyhole of the ignition. He turned it in the hope that it might start the engine, but it didn't. Next, he removed the screws on the steering column cover and then pulled out the access panels. He took out his phone, switched on the flashlight and used it to identify the yellow wires for the ignition and the red wires for the battery. He used the edge of the screwdriver to strip the wires and twisted them together: the radio and lights all turned on. He found the wire for the starter motor, quickly stripped that and touched it to the ends of the other two.

The engine grumbled to life.

"Get in," Milton said.

The light in the window of the house flicked back on again, and the curtains were pulled back to reveal the silhouette of a man or woman looking down at them. Milton hauled himself into the Defender's cabin, waited for Huxley to join him, put the engine into gear and pushed down on the accelerator.

Milton swung the wheel to head down the drive. He saw another square of light in the mirror as the main door of the house opened, and a man hurried out. He was holding a shotgun and, to Milton's horror, he aimed it at them.

"Down!"

Huxley bent at the waist, dipping down below the line of the sill. The shotgun boomed, but they were not struck; the man had either missed them or was firing a warning shot. Milton swore under his breath. The report had been loud, and he had no doubt that it would have been audible to anyone between them and Huxley's property. The owner of the Land Rover might not have done them any immediate damage, but he had given anyone who wanted them a decent idea of where to look.

Milton switched off the headlights and pressed down on the pedal. They reached the end of the drive. Milton had planned on turning right and heading back to the village, but now he decided on additional caution. He turned left and drove on, following the road for another mile until they reached a gate that blocked onward progress.

"It's the farm," Huxley said.

"What's on the other side of it?"

"There's a road."

That was good enough. Milton spun the wheel and drove through the hedge, the Defender making short work of the branches and the dip where a narrow culvert funnelled run-off water away. The front and then the back wheels bounced up and out of the culvert, and Milton pressed down on the accelerator, sliding the Defender to the left and jolting away across the uneven ground. The terrain was decent as Milton guided them around the farm buildings until he found the road on the other side. He switched on the headlights, found a gap in the hedge that the farmer used to bring his equipment into the field, and passed through it, turning to the south and accelerating away down the single-track road.

84

Milton rolled to a stop outside the gates to the cottage that he had rented. He got out, opened them, then climbed back into the driver's seat and drove through. He rolled the Defender around the corner of the building and switched off the engine.

Huxley breathed out. "This is it?"

"Yes."

"Thank you."

Milton opened the door and stepped out. Huxley did the same and followed Milton as he went to the door. The key had been left in a lockbox mounted on the wall. Milton thumbed the combination, took the key, unlocked the door and went inside. It was dark. When Huxley was inside too, Milton told him to shut and lock the door. He waited to hear the sound of the key in the lock before reaching across and switching on the lights.

"I can't believe that just happened," Huxley said.

Milton found a wooden chair in the dining room and brought it into the kitchen.

"The last week," Huxley said. "It's been crazy."

Milton took the roll of duct tape that he had bought earlier and set it down on the chair.

"I mean, come *on*," Huxley said. "How can I let you walk away? What's your price to stay on? I'm serious, John."

Milton took off his jacket.

"Name it," Huxley said.

Milton took his phone from his pocket, opened the camera and checked that there was enough light.

Huxley looked confused. "What are you doing?"

"Sit down," Milton said.

"What?"

"Sit," Milton said. "We need to record your confession."

Huxley's smile became hesitant. "I don't get it."

"I know what you've been doing, Tristan. I should've noticed it a long time ago, but I had my eyes closed. Things are different now. You said it yourself—I've changed. I don't ignore things anymore."

"You've lost me. What confession? What have I done?"

"The men and women on the island. You pimp them out, don't you? You trick them, offer them money or jobs or a chance to better themselves, and then you use them to get what *you* want."

"You're joking. This is crazy—"

"I'm not joking. *Sit down*." Milton opened his hand and drove the heel of his palm into Huxley's sternum, toppling him backward so that he landed in the chair. "You're blackmailing people. You throw parties at the island or at the house or on the jet and you film them. I've seen the cameras, but you have others—bedrooms and bathrooms."

"You've lost your mind."

Milton ignored him. "You entrap them, and then you blackmail them. You get them to do whatever you want them to do. Was that what the trip to the island was about?

Did Timofeyevich get cold feet? You needed to apply a little pressure?"

Huxley stared up at Milton and sneered. "You have no idea. You have no idea how the world works. Are you *that* naïve, John?"

"You betrayed people who trusted you, just so you could get what you needed and then get others to do what you wanted."

Huxley chuckled bitterly. "You're going to criticise me? *You?* Have you forgotten what you used to do? You're a *murderer*, John. 'Let him who is without sin cast the first stone.'"

"That's right," Milton said. "I am a murderer. But I've tried to make up for what I've done. I used to walk through life with my eyes closed, but not anymore. Lewsey blamed you for his daughter's death, so I looked into that. I found his wife, and she told me what you did. And then she introduced me to other girls you took advantage of—four of them. There are more, though, aren't there? How many more? A hundred? Two hundred?"

"Piss off, Milton. You're out of your depth."

Huxley got to his feet. Milton clenched his fist and struck him square on the nose. "Sit *down*."

Huxley squealed from the pain and stood again. "You're finished. I'm leaving."

Milton reached into his jacket and took out his pistol.

Huxley wiped the blood from his face. "Is that it?" he scoffed. "You're going to threaten me with that? No. You've forgotten who I am. I was someone when I met you before, but I'm more than that now. You know what I can do now? I can call MI6 and have them send one of their agents after you tomorrow. I can call the Home Secretary and have her declare you an enemy of the state. Or maybe I drop ten million to the Serbian mercenary I met in Odessa last year and send *him* after you. Or call the Russians—you know how much money I've made them in this deal? It's *billions*. Maybe I tell them what you've done. They'll send one of their teams and have them deal with you. Don't you get it, you fucking clown? I'm *bulletproof*. It just takes a phone—"

Milton had heard more than enough. He shoved Huxley down into the chair again. He grabbed Huxley's left wrist and pressed it down against the arm of the chair, then took his pistol and pressed it against the top of Huxley's left hand. "Bulletproof?"

He stared at Milton defiantly. "You wouldn't dare—"

Milton pulled the trigger, and the shot cracked out, echoing around the enclosed space.

Huxley shrieked in agony.

"Will you look at that," Milton said. "Turns out you're not."

Milton had aimed carefully. A shot to the thighs or upper arms risked damaging the femoral or brachial arteries and a swift bleeding out. But a bullet through a hand or foot, while excruciating, would not be life threatening.

Huxley stared at his hand and the bloody wound in the centre of it.

"You *shot* me! You fucking... you fucking..."

"That's right," he said. "I shot you." Milton took Huxley's chin in the fingers of his right hand and straightened his head out so that he could stare right into his eyes. "This is what we're going to do. You are going to confess to what you've done."

"I *can't*!"

Milton held down Huxley's right wrist and pressed the muzzle of the pistol against the back of his hand.

"You can." Huxley struggled, and Milton pushed down harder. "You are going to confess, and I'm going to record it."

"It'll ruin me," he said.

"It will, but, on the condition that you give me your blackmail material and enough money to make a difference to the lives of the people you betrayed, you'll have my word that it never sees the light of day."

"You want me to *trust* you?" He held up his bloodied hand. "After you did this?"

"It's up to you, Tristan. Trust me or don't trust me; it's the only way you get to decide what happens next. Do as you're told and you can walk out. But don't? I'll put a bullet between your eyes. You know me, and you're right—I *am* a murderer. You can tell me how much you think I'm bluffing, how much you don't believe me, but you know me better than that. I don't bluff."

Huxley's eyes bulged in their sockets. Milton took the pistol and pushed it against the top of Huxley's head.

"I've got a first aid kit over there. I can treat that wound and take the pain away. Or I can shoot you. Life or death? You decide."

Huxley breathed heavily, staring down at the floor.

"What do you want me to do?"

PART IX

FRIDAY

85

The coast of France was slowly revealed, the lights of Petit-Caux and Dieppe prickling the dark beyond the channel. The turboprop had a range of seven hundred nautical miles, more than enough for it to make the trip from the airfield at Ghyvelde across the channel to Dunsfold and then back again.

Abbas was the only passenger in the five-seater cabin. The plan had been for Nadia to be aboard, but she was dead in the fields outside Tristan Huxley's estate. Huxley should have been there, too. Abbas had been equipped with restraints and enough propofol to knock him out, but it would all go unused. He had tried to locate Huxley in the woods but had been unsuccessful until it was too late. He had seen the lights of a vehicle and had sprinted hard in the hope of being able to intercept it, but the vehicle—a Land Rover Defender—had turned the other way and had accelerated away from him. He had aimed his carbine at it but had not pulled the trigger. It was a hopeless case. He was alone, in a hostile country, any element of surprise long since spent. He had been thwarted, the mission had failed, and all that remained to him was to exfiltrate before even that, too, was lost.

Dunkirk was the nearest city to the airfield, and the pilot used that to line up for his approach. A car was waiting for Abbas for the hundred-mile drive into Belgium. Once they were across the border, he would adopt another new identity for the short hop to Dusseldorf and then the longer flight to Islamabad.

He was under no illusion that things would be simple as soon as he reached home. The operation to force Maidment to comply with their demands had failed, and now this final throw of the dice—desperate, perhaps, but still possible—had failed, too. The brigadier would have been hauled over the coals by the director general, and Abbas knew that Rashid would make him suffer because of it. He would want an explanation for what had gone wrong, and Abbas wasn't sure how he would give him one.

"Make sure you're strapped in," the pilot said into the headphones. "We'll be on the ground in five minutes."

86

Milton parked the car outside the bank in Knightsbridge and watched as Huxley waited to be allowed inside.

It had been a long night, and Milton had not slept.

Huxley had been wise enough not to call Milton's bluff, and, after Milton had treated the wound on his hand, he had answered all of Milton's questions. He spoke with his eyes on the floor, refusing to look into the camera, occasionally looking up to stare at Milton with a resentful but completely impotent anger. Milton had started the narrative from the time that he had worked for him before. He had him confess to taking advantage of young men and women, to how he had dazzled them with his money and fame until they were his to do with as he chose. Milton named the four women whom he had met in Hazel Lewsey's house; Huxley said he didn't remember them. Milton asked him about Roxanne Lewsey, and, perhaps sensing that ignorance would not be believed or tolerated, Huxley admitted that what her parents had said was true. He even professed regret at what had happened to her; Milton kept his attention on the video for fear of what he might do otherwise.

The recording, once it was finished, had lasted three hours. Milton saved it onto a memory stick, uploaded it to a Dropbox folder and then attached the link to an email that he had already prepared, and sent it.

The confession was thorough and compelling, but it wasn't enough.

Milton wanted corroboration and reparation.

He had bought Huxley a change of clothes and then driven him to the bank that they had visited before. Milton had asked what Huxley kept in the safe-deposit box and, after a little persuasion, Huxley had been forthcoming. He was too cagey to believe that the footage he used for blackmail would be safe if it was stored online. To that end, he had copied it onto several hard drives and stored those in a variety of places, which meant that if one location was compromised, he would always have another to fall back upon. There were drives at the house and on the island, although Milton couldn't very well go back to either of those places. He also kept drives inside the safe-deposit box, and it was those—together with a million pounds in cash and another million in bearer bonds that he kept as an emergency fund—that Milton had told him to go and get.

Huxley stepped back outside the bank. He looked a sight: he was wearing cheap jeans and a shirt that was too small for him, his left hand was bandaged, and he carried a canvas bag in his right. He looked up and down the street and, for a moment, Milton wondered if he was going to run. He reached across the cabin and opened the passenger door. "Get in," he called.

Huxley, jaw clenched tight, crossed the pavement and climbed into the Land Rover.

"Did you get it?"

He held up the bag with surly indifference.

"Show me."

Huxley unzipped the bag and parted it so that Milton could look inside. The money took up most of the space: thick bricks of fifties sealed with red paper bands.

"The drive?"

Huxley reached inside and took out a hard drive. Milton pointed to the laptop that he had purchased at the same store where he had provided Huxley with his new wardrobe. "Decrypt it and transfer the files."

Huxley knew there was no point in arguing. Apart from the threat Milton posed to his physical well-being, he had his confession. Milton had given Huxley his word that he would not release it on the condition that Huxley gave him the money and the files. He plugged the drive into the laptop, entered the password, and dragged the directory from the drive onto the laptop's home screen. He rested the laptop on the dashboard.

"Buckle up," Milton said.

"Where are we going?"

"There's someone I want you to meet."

∞

MILTON DROVE to King's Cross station. He parked nearby and checked that the laptop had finished transferring the files. It had. He put the computer back into its bag and got out, waiting for Huxley to join him.

"What are we doing?"

"I told you," Milton said. "There's someone I want you to meet."

"Who?"

Milton didn't answer, taking Huxley's forearm and impelling him forward. They crossed the road and entered the terminus. Milton led the way to Dishoom, a café that had been decorated at obvious expense to resemble a railway eatery from 1920s Bombay. They took a table at the back of the room, and Milton ordered tea from the waiter who darted efficiently between the numerous tables.

"Who are we here to see?" Huxley repeated.

Milton had taken the chair that faced the door, saw the newcomer, and raised his hand to attract his attention. "Him."

The newcomer was huge—almost as big as Björn Thorsson—but, whereas the Icelander was fair and blond, this man had a thick mop of dark hair and skin that had been scoured by the Highland weather. He crossed the restaurant and sat down between Milton and Huxley.

Huxley gaped at him in confusion. "Who are you?"

"This is Ox," Milton said. "He's a friend of mine."

"Good morning," Ox said.

"Ox is a freelance journalist. I met him in Scotland before I was persuaded to work for you. I've told him what you've been doing, and he's interested in writing a story about it." Milton corrected himself. "He's written it, actually —isn't that right, Ox?"

"Aye," Ox said. "The broad strokes, anyway. I just needed the evidence to back up everything John told me."

Milton took the laptop from the bag and opened it. He woke the screen and handed it to Ox. "Here you are. Everything you need is on here."

Milton had given cursory thought to holding onto the *kompromat* on the hard drives. It would have served as a useful insurance policy: there were gigabytes of material, and, from just a quick check of the file names, he had identified among them an actor with a fading career and a politician who had built his career on family values. Milton could have held back the footage with the threat that it would be released were anything to happen to him, just as Huxley had done. But he dismissed the idea. The men and women in the footage did not deserve to have their secrets kept. They all knew what they were doing; they would have known that their favours were being bought, and none of them would have spared a moment's thought for the playthings that Huxley provided to win their patronage. And Milton didn't care about himself. The promise of his own safety was not worth the price; he wanted to shine a light on Huxley and those who had sold themselves to him, and he couldn't do that unless he gave Ox everything.

Huxley's face dropped as he realised the scale of the danger he was in. "No," he begged. "You can't do that. You *can't*. That's... that's not—"

"You're not in any position to tell us what we can and can't do," Milton said.

"But you *said*. You promised me you wouldn't release them. You *swore*."

"Will you look at that," Milton said. "Turns out I'm not to be trusted."

"I spoke to Hazel Lewsey about what happened to Roxanne," Ox said. "Roxanne's story is the thread that runs through the piece from start to finish. It's the human angle something like this needs."

"No," Huxley said. "You need to listen to me. You don't understand. The files on that drive are the only reason I'm still alive. I've had people out to the island whom you wouldn't want to upset." He gestured to Milton. "You saw Timofeyevich—you know how *powerful* he is? He can't go against me because he knows what'll happen if he does. But if I don't have these…"

Milton shrugged. "You should have thought of that before. It's too late now."

Huxley swung around so that he could look at Ox. "And you? Are you stupid enough to run something like this?"

"It's worth the risk. And the cat will be out of the bag. There's no point in going after me once it's all been made public. What would be the point?" Ox took out a digital recorder, switched it on and laid it on the table. "I want it to be fair to you, though. I want to give you the right to reply. I'm happy to give you a chance to answer a few of my questions."

"Are you out of your *mind*?"

"That's a no comment, then?"

Huxley was pale. "They'll arrest me."

Milton nodded. "That seems very likely."

Huxley looked as if he was ready to vomit. "I'll never get to trial. They'll kill me before that happens. They'll murder me and make it look like I killed myself. They know the damage I could do to them. They won't take the chance."

"That's not our problem," Milton said. "It seems to me you haven't been quite as clever as you thought."

"Last chance," Ox said, holding up the recorder.

"I'm not talking to you," he said.

"Fine."

Ox took out his phone and opened a saved browser window. He put the device on the table and turned it so that it was the right way up for Huxley to read. Ox had navigated to Buzzfeed News; the story he had chosen was topped by a boldface headline:

DIRTY MONEY

And beneath that:

HOW FINANCIER MADE BILLIONS WITH BLACKMAIL

Huxley got up a little unsteadily. "That's already online?"

"An hour ago. I finished the story on the night train."

"You have no idea what you've done."

Huxley left the table and walked to the door, pushing it open and disappearing into the street outside.

"Are you happy to let him leave?" Ox asked him.

"Where's he going to go?" Milton said. "As far as he knows, he's got Pakistani intelligence looking for him. If he's got any sense, he'll go to the nearest police station and beg them to protect him."

"And will they?"

"I don't care," Milton said.

"What about you?"

"What about me?"

"Will you be safe? *I'm* not worried—my byline is on the piece; there's no point in them coming after me. But you don't have that. What if the people he's been working for decide you might be dangerous?"

Milton glanced out of the window to the street outside. He saw a young mother with a pram, an old couple walking hand in hand, a young man with a dog at his feet. He knew that he would have to run again, but what was he really giving up? He didn't belong in their world. He had no ties. No one cared where he was. Running was what he did.

"I'll be fine," he said. "And Huxley needs to pay for what he's done."

Ox nodded. "What next? Where are you going to go?"

"There's someone I need to see," Milton said.

87

Hazel Lewsey had to switch off her phone in the end. Ox had said that would probably be necessary when the story about Huxley went live, and it had proven to be true. She had fielded calls from print journalists and those who worked on TV. The first had been from the United Kingdom, but it hadn't taken long before those who worked for American outlets called, too. Hazel might have been resentful at the intrusion, but she wasn't; she had tried to tell Roxanne's story for months, and it had never received any traction. There had been interest, but each time, without fail, the early enthusiasm had been replaced by excuses for why the story couldn't run, and then the journalists had ghosted her.

This felt very different. It had momentum.

There was a knock at the door. They hadn't been to visit her yet, but she knew that it was just a matter of time. Ox had suggested that she should arrange a press conference where she could read from a prepared statement rather than speak to hacks on the doorstep. She glanced out of the window, expecting to see someone that she didn't know, but, instead, she saw Hatti and Imogen. She had spoken to the survivors on a conference call before she had agreed to speak to Ox. They had agreed that she should, but none of them could have expected that the story would have grown so big as quickly as this.

She hurried into the hallway and opened the door.

"It's happening," Hatti said, her eyes bright with excitement.

Hazel ushered Hatti and Imogen inside and closed the door.

"Turn on the TV," Imogen urged.

Hazel led the way into the sitting room, found the remote control and switched on the TV. She clicked over to the twenty-four-hour news channel and saw a well-known reporter standing outside the familiar triangular sign of New Scotland Yard.

"Turn it up," Hatti said.

Hazel increased the volume.

"Financier Tristan Huxley has handed himself in to the Metropolitan Police in response to this morning's story in Buzzfeed News alleging that he was responsible for the abuse of young men and women at his property in Surrey and on an island he owns off the coast of Sri Lanka. Mr. Huxley, who denies the allegations, has reportedly stated that he fears for his life."

"It's happening," Hatti repeated.

There was another knock on the door.

"Probably journalists," Hazel said.

"Have you spoken to anyone?"

"Not yet."

She went to the door and opened it. There was no one there. She looked up and down the street, but, save for the postman, she couldn't see anyone. She looked down at her feet. A black canvas bag had been left on the doorstep with an envelope addressed to her atop it. She took the envelope and the bag and brought them inside.

"What is it?" Hatti asked her.

"I don't know."

Hazel slid a finger inside the envelope and tore it open. There was a greeting card inside that looked as if it might have been purchased from the garage at the end of the road. It had a sunflower on the front and was blank inside save for a single sentence that had been written in blue biro.

To do with as you see fit.

She handed the card to Imogen, knelt down next to the bag and pulled the zip. She opened the bag, reached in and brought out a thick wedge of banknotes. She held them up for the others to see. Imogen's mouth fell open. Hatti took the card and read it, and then her arm fell limply by her side. Hazel reached into the bag and took out another brick of banknotes, and then another and another.

Imogen gaped. "How much is in there?"

Hazel upended the bag and shook it; more and more money tumbled out and bounced across the rug.

Hatti knelt down and picked up one of the bricks. "These are fifties."

Hazel started to count the bundles, but stopped at thirty. There had to be ten times that many. How much money did that mean was scattered across her sitting room floor? And where had it come from?

"What does this mean?" Imogen said, proffering the card. "'To do with as you see fit.' Who's given this to you?"

Hazel realised that she knew.

"It's not for me," she corrected. "It's for us. He said he'd help, and he has."

EPILOGUE

Control turned off the road and found a space in the car park at the rear of the school. St Mary's was in Ascot, and her daughters had been coming here for the last three years. The twins had been moved around before that thanks to the postings that had taken Control around the world, and it had been something of a blessing to have found a boarding school that they both loved and where they could stay without the need to change. The school was equipped with fantastic sporting facilities, including the indoor pool that was hosting tonight's gala. She crossed the lawns, opened the door and went inside, and was immediately assailed by the smell of chlorine and humidity. She looked at her watch and saw that she had arrived in perfect time. She grabbed a programme from a table next to the stairs that led up to the spectating area and skimmed it as she ascended. The eldest twin, Flora, was swimming in the 200m breaststroke and one of the relays; her younger girl, Clementine, was competing in the 100m freestyle. Control took a seat at the end of the row and searched poolside for her children. She saw Flora and raised her hand in greeting. Her daughter noticed her and bashfully returned the gesture. Control allowed herself a smile; Flora was at an age now where parents were embarrassing, and public shows of affection were at a premium.

"Don't turn around."

Control froze. She recognised the voice.

"Milton."

"I know you won't want to do anything rash. Not here. You don't want to make a scene in front of all the parents or your children."

"I'm not a fool."

The threat was implicit and hardly necessary. She turned her head a little and caught a glimpse of him, leaning back slightly so that she could hear him even when he spoke quietly.

"You've been a hard man to find," she said.

"Have you been looking?"

"Group Three has made you a priority."

"I'm sure they have. But I didn't particularly want to be found."

"Coming here is a risk, then."

"One that was worth taking. I needed to speak to you. I need to decide what to do next."

Another threat. Control concentrated on poolside, where her daughters were stretching out in readiness for their first races.

"You want to ask me about Huxley," she said.

"How much did you know?"

"Nothing."

"He's been abusing young men and women for years."

"I know that now. I didn't before."

"And some of them wouldn't have been much older than your girls."

She could see now why he had chosen this place to confront her; he was making a point. "I knew he had vices, but nothing like that."

"Vices?" He laughed without humour. "Smoking is a vice. Drinking is a vice. *That*... no, that wasn't a vice."

"I don't know how many different ways I can say it—I didn't know."

"Would it have made any difference if you had?"

She allowed her anger to smoulder. "My girls are down there. I'm a mother. Of *course* it would have made a difference."

Clementine's freestyle was the evening's first race. The girls took their starting positions.

"I don't believe you."

"Maybe you'd give me a little more credit if I told you what's happened to me since you decided to take matters into your own hands. My performance has apparently been 'disappointing,' and I'm to be put on probation prior to a full review. My superior—a man who has been angling to replace me with one of his puppets for months—is now taking an active role in the day-to-day management of the Group." She chuckled bitterly. "It's mostly your fault, of course. Colombia was a black mark, but this... well, *this* has taken the biscuit. My judgement in allowing you to be involved has been questioned. Of course, we'd have to ignore the fact that Huxley wanted you and that I was *told* to include you by my superior, but it seems that a scapegoat is required, and it's obviously going to be me."

"I didn't know."

"Of course not. You don't work for the Group anymore."

The starter sounded the klaxon, and the water splashed as the eight girls dove in and started to stroke.

"What about Number One?"

"I know that he helped you, and I know that he did it because of his sister. I know my agents, and I know that Thorsson blames himself for what happened to her. He's been trying to make up for it ever since he joined the Group."

"What will happen to him?"

"Nothing. Six is the only other person who knew what the two of you were doing, and she won't be telling anyone now, will she? I don't blame Thorsson for what he did. He doesn't deserve to be punished for it." She paused as a mother and father shuffled between them and settled into seats in the middle of Milton's row. "You can believe me or not when I say that I didn't know about Huxley. It doesn't really make any difference either way, does it? But I'd like you to believe that I did agree with what you and Number One did. It might have made my life more complicated, but it doesn't change the fact that Huxley deserves what's happened to him and what's *going* to happen to him."

"I presume he won't get to trial?"

"They won't let it get that far," she said. "He'll commit suicide in his cell next week. I'm just waiting for the right agent to be available to make sure that happens." She watched the leading girl turn and kick away from the wall. "You could've saved me the bother, you know. You were alone with him for long enough."

"I don't kill in cold blood," Milton said.

She didn't believe that, but let it pass. "You should know that you are viewed in a very different light now. You were a problem before—an irritation. But not now. What you did has caused serious problems. I'm sure you can imagine. The deal he was working on is dead, but that's not the half of it. Some of the men in the footage you released are very powerful. You've made a lot of enemies."

She reached down to her bag.

"Hands in your lap where I can see them," he said at once.

"I have something for you. I knew I'd see you again, and I wanted to be prepared."

"Do it slowly."

She reached back down for the bag, unzipped it and took out a manila envelope. She handed it over her shoulder to Milton and waited while he opened it.

"A passport?"

"You know that the John Smith legend is burned?"

"It was blown before Scotland."

"Eric Blair's burned, too. But that passport is brand new, courtesy of Group Eight. You can go where you want."

The winner touched the side of the pool. Control looked down for Clementine and saw that she had come in third.

"Look inside," she said. "At the back."

Milton flipped through to the back of the document and found the address that she had left there. "Stellenbosch?"

"We know that Christiaan Cronje helped Huxley get away with what he was doing. And we know that he left the country last night—him and two of his men, first class to Durban on Ethiopian. That address is a ranch that he owns on the Western Cape. That'll be where he goes."

"Why are you giving it to me?"

"I don't have a file on him," she said. "I thought you might like to pay him a visit."

"I'm not your agent anymore."

"I know," she said. "I'm not telling you to go. I'm giving you the option."

Control looked down as her daughter pushed herself out of the pool.

"Why are you doing this?" Milton asked.

Clementine looked up into the seats, and Control gave her a thumbs up. "Why am I helping you? Because MI6 knew *exactly* what Huxley was doing, and, rather than acting on it, they used it to their advantage. What they did was disgusting."

Control heard the clatter as the seat of Milton's plastic chair snapped back. She heard the sound of his footsteps and a jovial "excuse me" and "thank you" as he stepped around the feet of two mothers who were down the row from him. She turned and watched his back as he reached the stairs and climbed up to the exit.

She flinched at the sudden crack of the starting pistol below.

When she turned back again, John Milton was gone.

ALSO BY MARK DAWSON

IN THE JOHN MILTON SERIES

The Cleaner

Sharon Warriner is a single mother in the East End of London, fearful that she's lost her young son to a life in the gangs. After John Milton saves her life, he promises to help. But the gang, and the charismatic rapper who leads it, is not about to cooperate with him.

Buy The Cleaner

Saint Death

John Milton has been off the grid for six months. He surfaces in Ciudad Juárez, Mexico, and immediately finds himself drawn into a vicious battle with the narco-gangs that control the borderlands.

Buy Saint Death

The Driver

When a girl he drives to a party goes missing, John Milton is worried. Especially when two dead bodies are discovered and the police start treating him as their prime suspect.

Buy The Driver

Ghosts

John Milton is blackmailed into finding his predecessor as Number One. But she's a ghost, too, and just as dangerous as him. He finds himself in deep trouble, playing the Russians against the British in a desperate attempt to save the life of his oldest friend.

Buy Ghosts

The Sword of God

On the run from his own demons, John Milton treks through the Michigan wilderness into the town of Truth. He's not looking for trouble, but trouble's looking for him. He finds himself up against a small-town cop who has no idea with whom he is dealing, and no idea how dangerous he is.

Buy The Sword of God

Salvation Row

Milton finds himself in New Orleans, returning a favour that saved his life during Katrina. When a lethal adversary from his past takes an interest in his business, there's going to be hell to pay.

Buy Salvation Row

Headhunters

Milton barely escaped from Avi Bachman with his life. But when the Mossad's most dangerous renegade agent breaks out of a maximum security prison, their second fight will be to the finish.

Buy Headhunters

The Ninth Step

Milton's attempted good deed becomes a quest to unveil corruption at the highest levels of government and murder at the dark heart of the criminal underworld. Milton is pulled back into the game, and that's going to have serious consequences for everyone who crosses his path.

Buy The Ninth Step

The Jungle

John Milton is no stranger to the world's seedy underbelly. But when the former British Secret Service agent comes up against a ruthless human trafficking ring, he'll have to fight harder than ever to conquer the evil in his path.

Buy The Jungle

Blackout

A message from Milton's past leads him to Manila and a

confrontation with an adversary he thought he would never meet again. Milton finds himself accused of murder and imprisoned inside a brutal Filipino jail - can he escape, uncover the truth and gain vengeance for his friend?

Buy Blackout

The Alamo

A young boy witnesses a murder in a New York subway restroom. Milton finds him, and protects him from corrupt cops and the ruthless boss of a local gang.

Buy The Alamo

Redeemer

Milton is in Brazil, helping out an old friend with a close protection business. When a young girl is kidnapped, he finds himself battling a local crime lord to get her back.

Buy Redeemer

Sleepers

A sleepy English town. A murdered Russian spy. Milton and Michael Pope find themselves chasing the assassins to Moscow.

Buy Sleepers

Twelve Days

Milton checks back in with Elijah Warriner, but finds himself caught up in a fight to save him from a jealous - and dangerous - former friend.

Buy Twelve Days

Bright Lights

All Milton wants to do is take his classic GTO on a coast-to-coast road trip. But he can't ignore the woman on the side of the road in need of help. The decision to get involved leads to a tussle with a murderous cartel that he thought he had put behind him.

Buy Bright Lights

The Man Who Never Was

John Milton is used to operating in the shadows, weaving his way through dangerous places behind a fake identity. Now, to avenge the death of a close friend, he must wear his mask of deception once more.

Buy The Man Who Never Was

Killa City

John Milton has a nose for trouble. He can smell it a mile away. And when he witnesses a suspicious altercation between a young man and two thugs in a car auction parking lot, he can't resist getting involved.

Buy Killa City

Ronin

Milton travels to Bali in search of a new identity. He meets a young woman who has been forced to work for the Yakuza in Japan, and finds himself drawn into danger in an attempt to keep her safe.

Buy Ronin

Never Let Me Down Again

Milton is in the Outer Hebrides in search of a missing man. When he stumbles across a conspiracy involving Chinese intelligence, he'll need all his resourcefulness - plus the help of an old friend - if he's to escape in one piece.

Buy Never Let Me Down Again

IN THE BEATRIX ROSE SERIES

In Cold Blood

Beatrix Rose was the most dangerous assassin in an off-the-books government kill squad until her former boss betrayed her. A decade later, she emerges from the Hong Kong underworld with payback on her mind. They gunned down her husband and kidnapped her daughter, and now the debt needs to be repaid. It's a blood feud she didn't start but she is going to finish.

Buy In Cold Blood

Blood Moon Rising

There were six names on Beatrix's Death List and now there are four. She's going to account for the others, one by one, even if it kills her. She has returned from Somalia with another target in her sights. Bryan Duffy is in Iraq, surrounded by mercenaries, with no easy way to get to him and no easy way to get out. And Beatrix has other issues that need to be addressed. Will Duffy prove to be one kill too far?

Buy Blood Moon Rising

Blood and Roses

Beatrix Rose has worked her way through her Kill List. Four are dead, just two are left. But now her foes know she has them in her sights and the hunter has become the hunted.

Buy Blood and Roses

The Dragon and the Ghost

Beatrix Rose flees to Hong Kong after the murder of her husband and the kidnapping of her child. She needs money. The local triads have it. What could possibly go wrong?

Buy The Dragon and the Ghost

Tempest

Two people adrift in a foreign land, Beatrix Rose and Danny Nakamura need all the help they can get. A storm is coming. Can they help each other survive it and find their children before time runs out for both of them?

Buy Tempest

Phoenix

She does Britain's dirty work, but this time she needs help. Beatrix Rose, meet John Milton...

Buy Phoenix

IN THE ISABELLA ROSE SERIES

The Angel

Isabella Rose is recruited by British intelligence after a terrorist attack on Westminster.

Buy The Angel

The Asset

Isabella Rose, the Angel, is used to surprises, but being abducted is an unwelcome novelty. She's relying on Michael Pope, the head of the top-secret Group Fifteen, to get her back.

Buy The Asset

The Agent

Isabella Rose is on the run, hunted by the very people she had been hired to work for. Trained killer Isabella and former handler Michael Pope are forced into hiding in India and, when a mysterious informer passes them clues on the whereabouts of Pope's family, the prey see an opportunity to become the predators.

Buy The Agent

The Assassin

Ciudad Juárez, Mexico, is the most dangerous city in the world. And when a mission to break the local cartel's grip goes wrong, Isabella Rose, the Angel, finds herself on the wrong side of prison bars. Fearing the worst, Isabella plays her only remaining card…

Buy The Assassin

IN THE ATTICUS PRIEST SERIES

The House in the Woods

Disgraced detective Atticus Priest investigates the murder of a family on Christmas Eve. He's been employed to demolish the police case against his client, but things get complicated when the officer responsible for the case is his former girlfriend.

Buy The House in the Woods

A Place to Bury Strangers

A dog walker finds a human bone on lonely Salisbury Plain. DCI Mackenzie Jones investigates the grisly discovery but cannot explain how it ended up there. She contacts Atticus Priest and the two of them trace the bone to a graveyard in the nearby village of Imber. But the village was abandoned after it was purchased by the Ministry of Defence to train the army, so why have bodies been buried in the graveyard since the church was closed?

Buy A Place to Bury Strangers

ABOUT MARK DAWSON

Mark Dawson is the author of the John Milton, Beatrix and Isabella Rose and Atticus Priest series.

For more information:
www.markjdawson.com
mark@markjdawson.com

AN UNPUTDOWNABLE ebook.
First published in Great Britain in 2021 by UNPUTDOWNABLE LIMITED
Copyright © UNPUTDOWNABLE LIMITED 2021

The moral right of Mark Dawson to be identified as the author of this work has been asserted by him in accordance with the Copyright, Designs and Patents Act 1988.

All the characters in this book are fictitious, and any resemblance to actual persons living or dead is purely coincidental.

All rights reserved. No part of this publication may be reproduced, stored in a retrieval system or transmitted in any form or by any means, without the prior permission in writing of the publisher, nor to be otherwise circulated in any form of binding or cover other than that in which it is published without a similar condition, including this condition, being imposed on the subsequent purchaser.

Printed in Great Britain
by Amazon